PRAISE FOR USA TODAY BESTSELLING AUTHOR

Seabreeze Inn and *Coral Cottage* series

"Jan Moran is the new queen of the epic romance." — Rebecca Forster, *USA Today* Bestselling Author

"The women are intelligent and strong. At the core is a strong, close-knit family." — Betty's Reviews

"The characters are wonderful, and the magic of the story draws you in." Goodreads Reviewer

The Chocolatier

"A delicious novel, makes you long for chocolate." – *Ciao Tutti*

"Smoothly written…full of intrigue, love, secrets, and romance." – *Lekker Lezen*

The Winemakers

"Readers will devour this page-turner as the mystery and passions spin out." – *Library Journal*

"As she did in *Scent of Triumph*, Moran weaves knowledge of wine and winemaking into this intense family drama." – *Booklist*

The Perfumer: Scent of Triumph

"Heartbreaking, evocative, and inspiring, this book is a powerful journey." – Allison Pataki, *New York Times* Bestselling Author of *The Accidental Empress*

"A sweeping saga of one woman's journey through World War II and her unwillingness to give up even when faced with the toughest challenges." — Anita Abriel, Author of *The Light After the War*

"A captivating tale of love, determination and reinvention." — Karen Marin, Givenchy Paris

"An epic journey with the most resilient of heroines as our guide. It is a book to savor, like the most beautiful of perfumes…riveting from start to finish." — Samantha Vérant, Author of *Seven Letters from Paris*

"A stylish, compelling story of a family. What sets this apart is the backdrop of perfumery that suffuses the story with the delicious aromas – a remarkable feat!" — Liz Trenow, *New York Times* Bestselling Author of *The Forgotten Seamstress*

"Courageous heroine, star-crossed lovers, splendid sense of time and place capturing the unease and turmoil of the 1940s; HEA." — *Heroes and Heartbreakers*

"A thoroughly engaging tale, rich in all five senses." — Michelle Gable, Author of *A Paris Apartment*

"Jan rivals Danielle Steel at her romantic best." — Allegra Jordan, Author of *The End of Innocence*

BOOKS BY JAN MORAN

Contemporary

Summer Beach: Coral Cottage Series

Coral Cottage

Coral Cafe

Summer Beach: Seabreeze Inn Series

Seabreeze Inn

Seabreeze Summer

Seabreeze Sunset

Seabreeze Christmas

Seabreeze Wedding

The Love, California Series

Flawless

Beauty Mark

Runway

Essence

Style

Sparkle

20th-Century Historical

Hepburn's Necklace

The Chocolatier

The Winemakers: A Novel of Wine and Secrets

The Perfumer: Scent of Triumph

Life is a Cabernet: A Wine Country Novella

Seabreeze Christmas

JAN MORAN

SEABREEZE CHRISTMAS

SUMMER BEACH, BOOK 4

JAN MORAN

SUNNY PALMS

PRESS

Library of Congress Cataloging-in-Publication Data

Moran, Jan.

/ by Jan Moran

ISBN 978-1-64778-023-4 (epub)

ISBN 978-1-64778-024-1 (softcover)

ISBN 978-1-64778-025-8 (hardcover)

ISBN 978-1-64778-026-5 (large print)

ISBN 978-1-64778-027-2 (audiobook)

Published by Sunny Palms Press. Cover design by Sleepy Fox Studios. Cover images copyright Deposit Photos

Sunny Palms Press

9663 Santa Monica Blvd STE 1158

Beverly Hills, CA, USA

www.sunnypalmspress.com

www.JanMoran.com

CHAPTER 1

*S*ummer Beach, California

"WHAT A GORGEOUS WREATH," IVY SAID AS SHE GREETED HER parents on the stone steps of the Seabreeze Inn. The delightful pop of holly red and pine green against the gray marine layer encroaching on the winter beach caught her artist's eye. She pulled her sweater closed against the swift chill breeze.

"It's to celebrate the beginning of your first holiday season here at the inn," Carlotta said, hugging her daughters—first Ivy, then Shelly. As she did, chunky turquoise bracelets clinked, and the swish of her long, rust-colored skirt reminded Ivy of Thanksgivings spent on the beach with her parents years ago. A bag of fresh-baked rosemary bread hung from her forearm.

Ivy was thankful that she lived close to them now. Not that they were frail or feeble—far from it. Active and in their early seventies, they planned to embark on a sail around the world on their boat this spring.

"Your mother just finished making it." Her father held up

the large wreath woven of natural pine boughs wrapped with a red velvet bow. Into the greenery, her mother had tucked silver ornaments—tiny bells and sleighs—that Ivy remembered from years ago.

"I can hang it on the front door for you unless you'd like it somewhere else," Sterling said, his deep voice booming with cheer. He glanced at the bare porch and window sills. "We thought Shelly would be in full decorating mode by now."

"We've had other priorities," Shelly said, casting a swift glance at Ivy.

Ivy put her arm around her father. "The front door is perfect for this magnificent wreath."

"I wish you would've let me help more with this huge feast," Carlotta said.

"Making the bread was enough, Mom," Ivy said, smiling. But preparing dinner for their large family wasn't why they hadn't decorated. "Since we've been back east for so many Thanksgivings, this weekend is our gift to the family."

Ivy breathed in the scent of fresh pine needles from the wreath. Nearby, the ocean crashed against the beach, and the crisp scent of the sea mingled with other aromas wafting through the house. Turkey with garlic mashed potatoes, spiced pumpkin pies, and homemade apple cider from the nearby mountain village of Julian. These were the scents of her childhood and celebrations by the sea.

"Your first holiday feast at the inn is special," Carlotta said, taking Ivy's hand. "The first of many to come, *mija*. I'm so proud of what you and Shelly and Poppy have managed to do here."

"We have a lot to be grateful for this year," Ivy said. She and Shelly had arrived in Summer Beach in the spring—Ivy from Boston and Shelly from New York. Between renovations, summer guests, and a few surprises at the old beach house, they'd hardly had time to think about the holiday. However, after the summer crowds left, their occupancy and income experienced a sharp drop.

"What a lovely dress you're wearing," Carlotta said. "Is that new?"

"New to me." Ivy picked at a thread on her forest-green, crushed velvet dress. "I found it at a thrift shop and thought it could work for both Thanksgiving and Christmas."

"That was a real find," Carlotta said, admiring her choice. "That green is beautiful with your eyes."

Behind their parents, their twin brothers Flint and Forrest and their families spilled from their cars. Forrest had a solid, stocky build and made his living in construction, while Flint was a marine mammalogist more comfortable on the sea than land. Between the two men, they had nine grown children in their twenties, finishing college or starting careers.

Cheerful cries of "Happy Thanksgiving" rang out, and everyone hugged each other. Only their oldest sister, Honey, was missing. She and her husband Gabe lived in Sydney, Australia. Ivy greeted their daughter Elena, who had just arrived from Los Angeles.

"Looks like the holiday season at the Seabreeze Inn is officially underway," Ivy said to Shelly over the happy chaos.

As everyone poured into the grand old house, their footsteps clattered across the polished oak floors. The sound filled the high-ceilinged rooms as they roamed past the foyer, through the old ballroom, and into the enormous kitchen designed for a large kitchen staff or caterers. These days, it was filled with guests of the inn, new friends, and extended family.

Ivy made her way to the long kitchen counter to resume her work. Here the décor, like that of the rest of the house, had changed little since the 1950s. The kitchen looked like a photo layout from an old *Better Homes and Gardens* magazine. With a pair of vintage O'Keefe & Merritt stoves and twin turquoise refrigerators they'd named Gert and Gertie—plus a large prep-island—there were plenty of work stations for helpers.

Their young niece Poppy called out, "Can someone toss me another potholder?"

"Here you go." Ivy lobbed a silicone mitt in Poppy's direction. Her niece was removing grilled vegetables that Shelly had grown on the back portion of the property from one of the ovens. Poppy's blond hair was pulled back into a ponytail, and her face was pink from the heat of the kitchen. The aroma of zucchini and yellow squash sprinkled with oregano filled the air, along with the scent of crispy, garlic-rubbed turkey and baked ham slathered with honey.

"If there's room in the oven, the bread would be delicious heated," Carlotta said.

"Plenty of room, Mom. Poppy's also been on pie duty," Ivy added, nodding toward an array of crusty pies oozing with apples, cherries, and pumpkin, which would no doubt add to the stubborn muffin-top around her middle. But this was hardly the day to worry about that.

After greeting her relatives, Poppy spoke up over the din. "Everyone wash up. We need help slicing tomatoes and other veggies for the salads."

Plump, red heirloom tomatoes rested beside a cutting board and three large bowls that were filled with a variety of lettuce and spinach. With her horticulture experience, Shelly was still coaxing late-season tomatoes, lettuce, and herbs in the old greenhouse, even though it needed weatherproofing before the weather became too cold. Yet, winters were generally mild at the beach in Southern California, except for the occasional cold snap.

Chatter echoed in the kitchen, and Ivy smiled at the welcome music of family laughter. After the summer rush, guest reservations had declined until it was only family and a few long-term guests at the inn. Ivy had suggested that anyone who wanted to stay over the weekend was welcome, and they'd make a family weekend of it. Judging from the lack of holiday reservations, it might be the last crowd they'd have for a while. Ivy bit her lip at the thought.

She shrugged off her worry. "Who'll help me set the dining room table?"

Her eldest daughter Misty, a theater actor just in from Boston, hooked arms with her cousin Elena, a jewelry designer to the stars in Los Angeles. "What do you need, Mom?"

"In the butler's pantry, you'll find a set of harvest dishes, courtesy of Amelia Erickson. They've all been washed." Amelia and Gustav Erickson, wealthy art collectors from San Francisco, had built this house as their second home. They christened it Las Brisas del Mar, which meant *ocean breezes* in Spanish.

Antique dishes were only a few of the treasures they'd discovered in the house that had been vacant for decades before her late husband purchased it. Ivy led the way toward the dining room meant for large feasts and showed the girls what to do.

Shelly had brought in autumn colors throughout the foyer and dining room with tall shoots of goldenrod paired with orange chrysanthemum and curly willow branches from the garden. She'd arranged vases on the long sideboard, where they usually set up breakfast for guests.

Imani, one of their long-term guests who'd lost her home in the Ridgetop fire last spring, had given them armfuls of sunflowers from Blossoms, her flower stand in the village, before leaving to spend the Thanksgiving holiday with her family in Los Angeles to the north. Overhead, a vintage chandelier cast a warm glow on the antique table they'd discovered under a blanket on the lower level.

"Elena, you can place the silverware," Ivy said. "Misty, you and Sunny can put out the china."

With the girls' help, the table was set. A little while later,

Ivy drafted more of the cousins to carry platters of food from the kitchen.

Shelly clanged an old silver bell. "Dinner is served," she said.

After everyone was seated and Sterling delivered the blessing, he and Bennett—the Summer Beach mayor who was one of their long-term guests—carved the turkeys. Ivy passed around vegetarian options for others. Everyone dug in, and dinner flew by amidst happy chatter and good-natured joking.

Ivy saw Sunny shoot Bennett a side-eyed look as he was talking. She was pushing her food around her plate. Fortunately, Bennett didn't notice—or if he did, he chose to ignore Sunny's sullen attitude.

However, others were noticing. Ivy sighed. With reluctance, she let go of Bennett's hand under the table. She twisted the modest ruby ring she wore—one that the slightly eccentric Amelia Erickson had hidden under a loose floorboard in the bedroom.

Ivy watched Sunny. Since her father's death two years ago, it appeared that despite her earlier approval, Sunny was still wrestling with the idea of another man interested in her mother. Or maybe she realized that dating might lead to a permanent situation.

Ivy cleared her throat. "Anything wrong, Sunny?"

Sunny gave an exaggerated shrug. "I was just thinking about how Dad used to carve the turkey on Thanksgiving. After that, he'd take us for a walk around Back Bay and look at the lights."

"Those are good times to remember," Ivy said softly. It was only natural that her daughter was grieving, but Ivy suspected Sunny's attitude had more to do with something—or someone—else.

Sunny twisted her lips and flicked her mashed potatoes. "I wish we could have stayed there. You didn't need to have a great big house to play queen."

The conversation around the table quieted.

"That choice was forced on me." Ivy pressed her lips together and ignored the caustic edge to Sunny's voice. Due to the debt Jeremy had left, Ivy had to sell their Boston flat. He'd drained their retirement to buy this beach house without her knowledge. With its historic designation and extensive need of repair, it hadn't sold in a year, so Ivy had little choice but to move in and rent rooms—or lose it to a tax sale. She tried to remember only the good times, but sometimes it wasn't easy.

Sunny threw another disparaging look at Bennett. A couple of months ago, Ivy thought Sunny had accepted him as a family friend—and someone suitable for her mother to date. Now her daughter was acting downright rude.

"Yeah, but my friends—"

Misty cut in. "Hey, we could walk around Summer Beach."

"Not the same." Sunny smashed peas with her fork. "Remember that year Dad bought us new bikes and couldn't wait until Christmas to give them to us?"

"That was a good year, and so is this one," Misty said, swiftly changing the subject again. "I'm having the best time. Thanks, Mom. Here's to you and Aunt Shelly and Poppy." As Misty raised her glass in a toast, Sunny pushed back from the table and left.

"Let her go," Carlotta said. "She'll cool off, and there will be plenty of leftovers."

As everyone went back to their conversation, Ivy sighed. She'd speak to Sunny later. Leaning toward Bennett, she whispered, "I'm sorry for Sunny's behavior."

"It's tough to lose a parent," Bennett said. "She'll come around. But thank you for including me in the family celebration."

"My parents think the world of you." Ivy squeezed his hand.

"And what does their daughter think?" Bennett's eyes crinkled into a smile.

Ivy appreciated his humor, and she loved the warmth of his affection. "Now you're just looking for compliments."

Though Ivy and Bennett had once had a disagreement surrounding the use of the historic home as an inn—in part thanks to her husband, whom the city had sued to keep him from razing the house and building a high-rise resort—she and the mayor had become close over the summer.

Ivy and Bennett were more than friends now, though Ivy was hesitant to take the next step, partly because of Sunny. At the end of the summer, Sunny arrived from a semester and summer abroad to start her last year at a university in San Diego. While the locals had grown accustomed to seeing their widowed mayor with the town's latest newcomer, Sunny could be critical.

Yet Bennett was never far away. The Ridgetop fire had also damaged his home, so he was renting the apartment above the garage.

Sterling sat back and patted his stomach. "You've all outdone yourselves this year. I can't eat another bite."

"I hope you left room for pie," Poppy said.

"Maybe we should wait a little while," Ivy suggested.

"In the meantime, who is on dish duty with me?" Shelly asked, interrupting the Bay family chatter and laughter in the dining room.

Ivy groaned at the thought of the mess they'd left in the kitchen, but she loved having her family here. The house had been designed for large gatherings. Today had been a good day of laughter, love, and giving thanks—except for a little attitude from Sunny.

"You wash, Shelly, and I'll dry." Ivy turned to Bennett. "Would you help us clear the table?"

He squeezed her hand. "You don't have to ask."

Ivy picked up her plate and began to rise from her chair.

Behind them, Ivy's brother Flint clapped a hand on her shoulder. "No, you don't. Put that plate down." He snapped his fingers at his grown children. "Your aunts cooked for you, now clear this table, and make us proud. Skyler, Blue, Jewel, Sierra—move it, kids. No excuses." He winked at Ivy. "That's the way we roll."

A collective, good-natured grumble rose from the other end of the table.

Elena stood and clinked her glass. "Come on, mates, quit your whining. I'll turn on some music. It will be fun." Having grown up in Australia, she still had a light accent that Ivy loved.

Grateful, Ivy sank back into her chair. "I would love the help. Thank you all."

"These overgrown kids need to take some responsibility," Flint said, chuckling.

Ivy relaxed and sipped a little wine. She and Shelly had been cooking for days and arguing about which one of them had the idea of inviting the entire Bay clan for Thanksgiving—and Christmas. The Seabreeze Inn had plenty of room for their extended family. Why not start a new tradition?

This year, Ivy and Shelly had a great deal to be thankful for—starting with the roof over their heads. It was their turn to relieve their mother and sisters-in-law of the annual celebration. Living in Boston, Ivy hadn't spent a Thanksgiving with her family in almost two decades. Travel from the east coast to California would have been too rushed during the short holiday, and Jeremy had often worked the day after Thanksgiving, leaving little time for long flights.

Ivy watched her parents chatting—their heads bent together as she'd seen them so many times over the years. This was the last holiday season they'd have their parents before the retired couple left on their sailing adventure. Ivy's father had plotted out a journey that would take three to four years, and she was already thinking about how much she would miss them.

While Elena was cajoling her cousins, Flint's twin brother, Forrest, rapped his knuckles on the table and gestured toward his children. "Why are you still sitting?"

"Aw, Dad, okay." Punching each other on the shoulder, Flint's sons Rocky and Reed led the way, while their sisters Summer and Coral gathered empty vegetable dishes. Their other sister Poppy stood and stretched.

"Poppy, you should stay here with us," Ivy said. "You worked just as hard as Shelly and I did."

Poppy's eyes flashed. "And turn that crew loose in the kitchen? No way." She tugged at Rocky's sleeve. "Hey, no one walks away empty-handed. Rocky, you take the turkey. Blue, get the ham, and Jewel, grab those salad bowls. No pie for anyone until the kitchen is clean, and I mean it. I didn't bake those pies for a bunch of messy moochers."

Even though Ivy had indulged herself with turkey and stuffing, she could hardly wait to sample Poppy's pies. Mitch Kline, the owner of the popular Java Beach coffee shop, had shared his best pie recipes with them—courtesy of Ginger Delavie, one of Summer Beach's most fascinating residents. She had lived in a coral cottage on the beach for decades. And those recipes had originated with Ginger's good friend in Boston—none other than Julia Child, a mentor to Ginger when she was younger. Perhaps the recipes had changed a little in the translation, like that old rumor game that went around a circle. Nevertheless, Ivy wanted to save a couple of slices for Ginger, who was visiting her granddaughter Marina, a news anchor in San Francisco, and her children.

Mitch, who was dating Shelly, promised he'd meet them later this evening. Every year he opened the doors of Java Beach to serve Thanksgiving dinner to the less fortunate of Summer Beach—as he had been when he'd arrived in the seaside village. Bennett had helped him prepare part of the meal yesterday after City Hall closed for the holiday.

Poppy clapped her hands. "I wasn't kidding, Rocky." She pointed at the table. "Turkey. Now."

When a look of surprise crossed Rocky's face, Ivy grinned. "Poppy's in charge. She's giving the orders, and if I were you, I wouldn't ignore her."

Ivy winked at Shelly across the table. Their niece was the most organized one of them all. Ivy taught the art classes at the Seabreeze Inn and tended to guest requests and decorating, while Shelly led morning yoga and managed the gardening and exterior grounds. But it was Poppy who'd set up the online reservation and marketing systems.

Flint and Forrest chuckled as they watched their children troop from the dining room.

"Hey, Dad," Rocky said. "Aren't you and Uncle Flint going to help?"

Forrest swatted his shoulder. "Who do you think did all the dishes when you were young?"

Misty slid back from the table. "You don't have to ask, Mom. I'll get Sunny." She pulled her sister from the chair next to her. Although Misty was the actor of the family, Sunny was the more dramatic of the two.

Bennett shook his head. "A dozen cousins in the kitchen? That must be some sort of record."

"Or the beginning of a bad joke," Flint said.

"Every year, my grandchildren complain as if they've never done this before," Carlotta said, folding her hands on the table. "But I think they have more fun in the kitchen than we do. They'll have a party going in no time. Just imagine what it will be like in a few years with spouses and babies," she finished with a trace of wistfulness in her voice.

Sterling put his arm around his wife and hugged her. Ivy thought they were the best grandparents the children could have ever wanted.

"They'll probably beat me to it," Shelly said, lowering her eyes.

Ivy's heart went out to Shelly, whose long-term boyfriend in New York hadn't worked out.

As for Bennett, Ivy was grateful that he and her parents got along well. Although they'd liked Jeremy, her mother had confided that they'd always been concerned about the time he spent away from the family. Jeremy had worked hard as a technology consultant, though in retrospect, his schedule had created opportunity—and Ivy had been blind to it.

But Ivy didn't want to think about Jeremy's indiscretions today. She had enough on her mind.

The autumn doldrums had set in, and guest reservations had slowed to a trickle. The inn had been booked solid during the high summer season. Fortunately, with the proceeds from rooms and the well-attended art fair they had hosted on the grounds of the Seabreeze Inn at the end of the summer, Ivy had paid off the overdue real estate tax bill that Jeremy had left. She'd managed to narrowly avoid a tax sale and pay Sunny's exorbitant American Express bill.

Sunny was working off her summer travel indulgence by helping around the inn. Most days, she didn't mind, though she still had her moments. Such as today.

Still, between the taxes, utilities, and general upkeep, the inn had to maintain a certain minimum occupancy level, and they were far short of that.

Ivy looked outside, where clouds over the Pacific Ocean were turning an exquisite, dusky rose in the waning light. "How about drinks and dessert by the pool? It's going to be a beautiful sunset."

Ivy fixed this moment in her mind. If reservations didn't pick up, she might be forced to close the inn before they could make it to the next season—though she would do everything in her power to avoid that.

CHAPTER 2

"*S*ounds like the kids are having a good time in the kitchen," Ivy said. Above the ocean's roar, music blasted from the kitchen, punctuated by intermittent laughter. Their holiday party playlist ranged from Mariah Carey to Nat King Cole.

"Great music," Bennett said, helping her with the light-weight sweater she drew around her shoulders.

Along with the older adults, they made their way outside to enjoy the fresh evening breezes and watch the sunset. Shelly and their sister-in-law Angela had gone inside to make Sea Breeze cocktails, a specialty of the inn.

Behind the grand house designed by early Californian architect Julia Morgan, terraced tiles led to a lavish, recently restored pool that was a smaller version of Morgan's Neptune Pool at the Hearst Castle she'd designed in San Simeon.

The family made themselves comfortable on the patio. Beyond the beach, clouds deepened into shades of lavender and coral. Ivy made a mental snapshot. She'd painted several sunsets over the ocean, but this one promised to be spectacular.

Shelly and Angela appeared carrying pitchers of juice cocktails. "Glad I had extra cranberry and pink grapefruit juice chilling in Gertie. Here's the healthy version," Shelly said, pouring the juice blends into cups. "And Angela has the vodka-spiked recipe." Everyone called out their choice.

"Here's to my girls," Carlotta began, raising her glass in a toast. "Ivy and Shelly, we're all happy that you've returned and found solid footing here in Summer Beach. Here's to the continued success of the Seabreeze Inn."

"And here's to family," Ivy said, clinking glasses with her parents and brothers and sisters-in-law. "What a year it has been. Thank you all for pitching in to help us, from the clean-up and painting of this old house to the attic disaster. I don't know how we would have made it without you."

"And may we get some Christmas reservations soon," Shelly added.

Carlotta frowned. "I thought you said only this week was slow, *mija.*"

Ivy hadn't wanted to concern her family. Her parents had brought up five children to be independent adults. After Jeremy's death, she'd had a couple of tough years, but she'd made it. She and Shelly had recast their lives here in Summer Beach, and they were determined.

"We'll have Poppy post a special offer online," Ivy said. They'd already done that, but they'd have to try a different approach. *Or something else.*

"Maybe it needs to be more festive looking," Angela said. "Your fall decorations are lovely, but if it were more Christmassy, maybe visitors would stop."

Shelly shot a look at Ivy. "I have a few poinsettias for the entryway reserved at the Hidden Garden that I'll pick up this weekend," Shelly said. "Beyond that, decorations aren't in our budget. We'll do what we can to bring some holiday magic indoors."

"Didn't we used to string popcorn, Mom?" Ivy grinned.

"Well, yes, but—"

Tabitha snapped her fingers. "I know. You could put up a

huge tree in the ballroom and throw a party. That would be fabulous."

Ivy knew Angela and Tabitha were trying to help, but her sisters-in-law didn't realize what a tight budget she and Shelly had to work with.

"Didn't you ship all your beautiful decorations from Boston?" Angela asked. "I remember how lovely your place was that time we visited. We can help you put them up."

Ivy shook her head. "When I shipped my boxes from Boston, my holiday decorations never made it." After downsizing from her Back Bay condo, she'd only kept those with sentimental value. The clothespin moose, the cotton-ball snowman—the ones her children had made. Now, those were gone, too. And Shelly had left everything at her boyfriend's apartment in New York.

Bennett tucked her hand into his. "I lost our decorations in the fire, but I hadn't used them in a long time. Maybe it's time we make new memories."

Ivy imagined that Bennett hadn't decorated his home for the holidays since his wife's death—ten years ago. She understood.

After Jeremy died, she'd moved into a professor's extra bedroom. Celebrating the holidays was the last thing on her mind. That last year in Boston, she'd taken her daughters out for a holiday dinner at a little restaurant in the neighborhood, and they'd exchanged gifts. Still, it wasn't the same as decorating a home, bustling around the kitchen, and relaxing by the fireplace while snow fell outside.

She missed that. And she didn't want to dwell on what they didn't have when they already had so much.

Brightening, Ivy said, "This year, we're fortunate to have a home that we can share with others."

Across the table, she saw Shelly's tight smile. Her sister and her niece understood how tenuous their situation was this season. They had to make it through the winter until guests returned with warmer weather.

"Yeah, if only they'd make a reservation," Shelly said, biting her lip. "Ivy might have avoided the auction block for the overdue property taxes, but she just got another bill."

"They come every year," their father said.

"I know, but this fall was slower than we expected," Shelly said.

Ivy turned to her father. "Summer Beach slows down at the end of summer, so the winter is shaping up to be pretty lean. Fortunately, Poppy has a couple of good marketing gigs in Los Angeles, so she's covered."

Ivy and Shelly would struggle through the winter—at best. Their main concern was to keep on the utilities. That was no small feat in a drafty old home.

"A lot of businesses are seasonal in Summer Beach," Forrest said. "Could you get a loan from the bank to see you through the winter months?"

Ivy swirled the ice cubes in her glass. "Already tried. The banker wanted to see two years of tax returns on the business, which we don't have. We don't even have a year. But we've made it this far. I'm sure we'll think of something."

"If you need help, we're here for you," Flint said.

"Yes, *mijita*," Carlotta said. "We're all here for you."

Ivy touched Flint's hand. "You have your kids' college educations, and as for you—" She turned to her parents. "Nothing will come in the way of your sailing adventure." At their age, it was probably the last chance they'd have while they were both still in good health. "We'll be fine," Ivy added emphatically.

She wished she were as confident as she sounded. If ever they needed a Christmas miracle, it was now.

As the sun slipped beneath the horizon, the kids spilled out of the kitchen. "Wait for it," Reed yelled, pointing toward the horizon.

"There's no such thing as a green flash," Rocky shot back, popping him with a dishtowel. He was met with a chorus of cheers and jeers.

"Here it comes!" Coral shouted. Among the cousins, a countdown erupted. "Five, four, three, two…one! There, you had to have seen that."

Ivy laughed at their antics, which reminded her of what she and her siblings used to do.

"Nope, didn't happen," Rocky said. "Pay up."

"You lost the bet," Reed said. "We all saw it, right?"

A round of cheers went up. "Dunk him, dunk him!"

All at once, the cousins hoisted Rocky on their shoulders and trotted toward the pool. Moments later, Rocky soared through the air and landed with a splash into the pool, bellowing as he hit the water.

Shelly cupped her hands around her mouth and yelled, "Woo-hoo! The party is on."

"That water must be freezing," Ivy said, frowning. Without any guests using the pool, she had turned off the pool heater. "I hope he's a good swimmer." She'd already rescued one person from the pool—none other than Rowan Zachary, a famous actor. And at his son's wedding, no less.

"Better stand guard," Shelly said, laughing and clapping. As the youngest of the siblings, she wasn't much older than the oldest of the cousins. "Hey, you guys need to help him out. That water is too cold."

Rocky swam to the edge and reached out a hand. Reed bent to pull him out, but Rocky yanked him in. "Got you!"

The rest of the cousins cheered them on.

Ivy shivered as she watched. She hoped she wouldn't have to put her lifeguard training to use tonight. "Poppy, could you get some towels? They're going to need them."

"Will do," Poppy said, dashing inside.

Soon, the two brothers lifted themselves out of the pool, and Poppy flung towels over them. The breeze from the water kicked up, sending Rocky and Reed racing inside for a change of clothes.

Misty stopped beside her mother. "The kitchen's clean, and we'll bring out the pies. Mind if we head down to the beach afterward? A lot of kids are getting together tonight for a bonfire."

When Ivy raised an eyebrow, Bennett said, "They have permission to have a fire. It's become an annual event. We could go, too, if you want. A lot of families and neighbors gather and share hot apple cider or hot mulled wine."

"Well, what are we waiting for?" Ivy clapped her hands. "Let's get those pies going." They might as well have fun tonight. Tomorrow would be another day of work, but tonight was still Thanksgiving.

Bennett kissed her cheek. "I want you to know this was the best Thanksgiving I've had in a long, long time. And if you need my help over the holidays, I'm here for you."

Ivy appreciated that, but she was determined to figure this out on her own. This wouldn't be the only year she would face this situation. She turned to her sister and linked arms. "Come on, Shells, let's have pie and go watch a bonfire."

Shelly grinned. "You're on, Ives."

AFTER DESSERT, IVY AND HER FAMILY WERE IN THE FOYER preparing to leave when a knock sounded at the door.

"Excuse me, that might be a new guest," Ivy said, her heart lifting. She opened the door.

A thin young woman with a pale face stood at the door. "Happy Thanksgiving," she said shyly.

"Paisley?" Ivy gaped at her. Of all the people she would've thought she'd see today, her late husband's former mistress had not been among them. Paisley's brassy blond hair was gone, as was her usually revealing dress. Now, her brown hair was pulled back from her face, and her plain dress grazed her knees.

The chatter in the foyer hushed, and Shelly and Poppy stepped beside Ivy, flanking her. The last time they'd seen Paisley, Imani had helped the younger woman escape from her abusive boyfriend, who was trying to gain control of the Seabreeze Inn through her by charging that Jeremy had bought it for Paisley. That had been a nightmare, but they'd come through it.

From the corner of her eye, Ivy saw Sunny and Misty standing beside their grandparents.

"I know I don't look like I used to," Paisley said. "At the women's shelter, I went through alcohol withdrawals, so I was admitted into an alcohol treatment program. I had a lot of things to work through."

Without hesitation, Ivy reached out to her. "Come in. We were just going to the bonfire on the beach, but I have time. We can talk in the library." Away from Sunny and Misty in particular.

Paisley shook her head. "This won't take long. I just wanted to tell you that I'm thankful for what you did for me this summer, even though I didn't deserve it. And..." Her voice trailed off.

Ivy stepped closer and put her arm around the young woman. Six months ago, that would have been unthinkable, but that was before Ivy had learned how damaged Paisley had been. "Do you need help?"

"No, but I want to return these to you." Paisley thrust out a shopping bag that held a lightweight, tan raincoat and a broad-brimmed sunhat that Ivy had given her that last summer evening. "I want to make amends and tell you how sorry I am."

"You already did," Ivy said as gently as she could. "You can keep those if you want."

"I can't keep them." Paisley paused. "Is Imani here? I want to thank her, too."

"She went to visit her sister, but I'll tell her for you." Ivy took the bag. "And I want you to know there's help for anything you're going through." She thought about their empty rooms, and how much she had to be thankful for. Reaching out to Paisley, she asked, "Do you need a place to stay?"

Beside her, Shelly coughed.

"No, I'm much better now. But that's kind of you." Paisley went on. "I met a woman that I admire very much. She's a social worker, and she helped me so much that I decided to become one, too."

"Are you sure?" Shelly cast a swift, doubtful glance at Ivy.

Paisley nodded. "I start college in January. That's been my dream."

"Why, that's wonderful," Ivy said, truly glad for her. Shelly started to speak, but Ivy nudged her.

"My mother thought college was a stupid waste," Paisley said. "She said they wouldn't take trash like me, so I didn't think I was good enough to be accepted. Ma told me I had to get out and do whatever it took to find a man to support me. But I know better now. And I'm ready."

Paisley lifted her chin and smiled, which gave her now cosmetic-free face a luminosity that Ivy had never imagined. "Ivy, I wanted you to know how much you—all of you— helped me. Even when I didn't deserve it."

"You were ready to help yourself." Ivy folded Paisley into her arms, smiling as she thought of what Jeremy would think if he could see them now. "I think it's good that you're following your heart. After all you've been through, you have a lot of wisdom you can use to help others."

Paisley reached out to hug Poppy and Shelly before turning to leave. With a final, "Happy Thanksgiving," and a shy wave, she got into a waiting car.

"Wow," Shelly said. "That blows my mind. Paisley, a social worker?"

Ivy leaned against the doorjamb and watched the car leave. "I think she's found her calling." She laughed softly.

Carlotta stepped forward and asked softly. "What's so funny, *mija?*"

Ivy grinned at her mother. "I was thinking about what Jeremy would have said if he could have seen us together." Six months ago, she couldn't have imagined saying that. She would always love the good times she'd had with her husband, but she'd learned that anger and regret were bitter desserts.

Ivy turned and clasped Bennett's hand, which felt warm and sure in hers. "Let's go watch a bonfire."

A dark expression crossed Sunny's face, and she stepped forward. "That was Dad's *girlfriend*, wasn't it?"

Ivy's heart sank. "Yes." What else could she say? Sunny had seen Paisley once before, but that was when the young woman had long, bleached-blond hair, heavy makeup, and a short skirt.

The edges of Sunny's mouth drew down. "So is this thing with Bennett just you trying to get back at Dad?"

"Hey, Sunny," Misty said, stepping in between Sunny and Ivy. "You don't mean that."

"Yeah. I do." Sunny motioned to her mother and Bennett. "This makes sense now."

Misty shrugged. "And so what? Bennett's a good guy. Come on. Let's go meet our friends." Casting an apologetic look back at Ivy, Misty pulled Sunny outside.

Ivy turned to Bennett and her family. "Just when I thought we'd get through this holiday without any fireworks. I'm so sorry about that."

Flint chuckled and threw his arm around Ivy. "Wouldn't be a family celebration unless something happens that we can all talk about next year."

Ivy poked her brother. "I'm concerned about Sunny."

"She'll come around," Carlotta said. "She reminds me of you when you were young. You had a mind of your own. Moved clear across the country for school, if you recall. Now, who's ready for a bonfire?"

Her mother had a point, Ivy thought. She took Bennett's hand and followed her mother and father out the door.

Sterling Bay was tall, trim, and as fit as men half his age. His face shone with love as he held out his hand for his wife.

Carlotta slid her hand into his. "*Gracias, mi amor.*"

Ivy loved to watch her parents together. They were so elegant, so old-school. Carlotta Reina Bay was an accomplished woman who had built a successful business alongside her husband. They sourced artwork and artisanal crafts from all over the world. Her mother's ancestors had been rooted in California when it was still part of Mexico—long before statehood and admission to the United States. One ancestor had been a Mexican ambassador to Spain, while a later one had been an American ambassador to Spain. Her father had become enamored with her mother in college.

Now that Ivy was older and understood the complexities of marriage, she was fascinated by her parents' relationship. They were respectful, honest, and accepting of each other. Even after all these years, they were still very much in love— and the best of friends. That sort of relationship was all that Ivy wanted.

Full trust, no secrets.

She'd thought she'd had it with Jeremy, but after his death, she'd learned otherwise. Though she'd let that go, casting those feelings of anger and disillusionment out to the sea, she couldn't deny that there was still a spot in her gut that churned at his mention, though it had diminished.

Would it always be that way? She sighed. Maybe, but she could rise above it.

She was mature enough to know the difference between endorphin-fueled young love and the type that developed like fine wine over time. Not that both couldn't be true in a long relationship, but sometimes the evolution didn't happen, and the sweet nectar turned sour.

As Ivy strolled across the sand toward flames that stretched into a darkening sky, she took Bennett's hand. Could they have the type of relationship her parents had? She loved him, but she was more guarded now. And her life was more complicated than it had been when she'd met Jeremy in college.

When they arrived at the bonfire, Ivy and Bennett greeted friends and gathered around the crackling fire. She gazed at familiar faces illuminated in the flickering light, thankful for their welcome and support over the past months. Maybe Summer Beach had been waiting for her all along.

As waves curled toward the shore and flames danced in the ocean breeze, Ivy shivered. Whether there was magic in the air or only an abundance of negative ions, the air seemed charged with fresh possibilities.

CHAPTER 3

*I*vy and Shelly burst into the kitchen, panting after a brisk beach walk. A chill laced the morning breeze, reminding Ivy of a New England autumn.

"Another coffee to warm up?" Ivy asked.

Shelly shivered and blew on her hands. "How about hot chocolate? It's the beginning of the Christmas season, after all."

"And we have to come up with a better plan for the winter." Ivy shrugged off her fleece jacket and hung it on a hook by the back door.

The house was quiet. Misty had boarded a plane to Boston, and the rest of the family had returned to their homes. The only guests remaining were Bennett, Gilda and Pixie, and Imani and Jamir. Barely enough cashflow to keep the lights on. And worse for Ivy and Shelly, Gilda's home would be ready soon, as would Imani's—though Ivy would be happy for them.

As Ivy measured milk and cream into a saucepan, she turned over ideas in her mind. What could she and Shelly do to bring in winter guests? Their usual social media posts were no longer working. While she considered this problem, she added broken chunks of chocolate to the liquid—along with a scoop of dark brown sugar, a splash of vanilla extract, and a pinch of ancho chili powder.

"Let's brainstorm," Shelly said, opening a junk drawer where they kept odds-and-ends. She pulled out a couple of small pads of paper.

Aside from the financial implications, Ivy also missed the activity of their guests. Gilda worked late into the night writing articles for magazines and slept until noon. Bennett and Imani worked all day, and Jamir was at school. Sunny was attending classes at the same university, which kept her occupied as well.

Too quiet. There were no vacationers asking for restaurant recommendations or inquiring about the history of the house. Ivy stirred the mixture and adjusted the flame under the saucepan.

"Shelly, would you turn on some music? This quiet is killing me."

"Jazz or holiday songs?"

"How about jazzy holiday tunes? We need to channel all things Christmas for inspiration."

While the milk and chocolate warmed on the stovetop, Ivy and Shelly pulled out stools and sat at the counter.

Ivy tapped her pencil on a pad. "We've got to think of something to get us through not only Christmas but the entire winter until spring. In Southern California, when the temperature plummets to light-jacket weather, everyone heads to Palm Springs and breaks out the swimsuits. What will bring them back here?"

"The art festival was a big success," Shelly replied. "Though it's too late for a holiday fair."

"Is it? We could contact all the artists who were here this summer to see if they're available." Ivy pushed back from the long serving bar to check the milk mixture.

Shelly brought out whipping cream from one of the

vintage refrigerators. "We can do that, but we don't have much tourist traffic to offer them."

"That's what we all need." Ivy cast an eye toward the refrigerator as she whisked the melted chocolate with the steamed milk and cream. "Gertie's been humming louder since Thanksgiving. Think we overworked her?"

"Maybe." Shelly frowned. "I hope she recovers."

"Refrigerator repairs aren't in the budget," Ivy said, pouring the hot chocolate into a pair of mugs. "It's time Gert picked up the slack."

Shelly shook out her wind-blown hair, twisted it into a messy bun, and jabbed a pencil through the topknot to secure it. "I heard an interesting perspective. When I was picking up poinsettias at the Hidden Garden, Leilani said she was surprised we were still open."

Ivy whipped the cream in a blender with a little powdered sugar and cinnamon. She plopped a scoop into each mug, added a sprinkle of nutmeg, and perched on a stool across from Shelly. "Why would Leilani say that?"

"Seems a lot of places here close for the winter," Shelly said. "She and Roy close the garden shop and visit her family in Hawaii in the winter. The high school garden club takes care of the plants until they return. That's kind of cool. Leilani and Roy help support that program at the school and give the kids jobs." Shelly cupped her hands around the warm mug and sipped her hot chocolate. "Mmm, that's delicious. As good as Mom's."

"It's her recipe," Ivy said, smiling. "Anything else that closes?"

"The other inn and some cafés by the beach," Shelly replied. "I don't think anyone expected us to stay open."

"That could explain why we haven't received any holiday party bookings. But now it's too late."

"Maybe not. We could offer a first-year discount." Shelly

snapped her fingers. "I'll put up a flyer at Java Beach. Word travels fast there."

"That might work. I was hoping to get some of the locals' guest overflow during Thanksgiving, though we might attract some at Christmas." Ivy brightened. "Maybe we could have a holiday music festival. Celia's students might like to put on a show here. This is a beautiful venue for their parents and family. They could dress up and take photographs in the ballroom."

"Write that down," Shelly said. "It's a shame we can't decorate much. I got four of the largest poinsettias, but they're practically lost in this big house. I saw some amazing Christmas trees, too."

Ivy sighed. "No budget, no decorations. Maybe next year."

"I understand." Shelly lowered her eyes.

"However..." A thought occurred to Ivy, and she drummed her fingers on the counter. "Remember the photos we saw of the parties that Amelia and Gustav Erickson held here? They used to decorate lavishly back then. Didn't we see some photos of Christmas parties?"

Shelly nodded. "I wonder what happened to all those decorations. We didn't find any on the lower level."

"Or the attic," Ivy said. "It's not as if she would have hidden those either. I mean, what value could they possibly have?"

Shelly laughed. "Strings of rubies and emeralds?"

"Just decorations, I'm sure."

Suddenly, a male voice rang out. "Anyone here? Oh, hello. The door was open. I was wondering if you have any vacancies."

Startled, Ivy swung around to face a slim young man clad in faded jeans and a denim jacket. A premature shock of white hair threaded through longish, dark hair brushed back from a pleasant, unlined face. Thirty-ish, Ivy guessed.

"Oh, yes," Ivy said. "Sorry, we didn't hear you come in." They had a bell at the front desk, but Shelly's music must have drowned out the bell. "How did you hear about us?"

"From Mitch at Java Beach. He said the Seabreeze Inn has a lot going on." The man glanced around. "Kind of quiet at the moment."

"Just a holiday lull," Shelly said, turning down the music. "We have a wine and tea event every evening in the library, yoga and beach walks in the morning, and Ivy can give you painting lessons if you like."

The man looked between the two of them and inclined his head. "You're sisters?"

"That's right," Ivy said. She and Shelly introduced themselves, and Ivy asked his name.

"People call me Nick Snow," he said.

"Because that's your name, I hope," Shelly said.

Ivy ignored Shelly and extended her hand. "Glad to meet you, Nick. Any friend of Mitch's is welcome here. How long would you like to stay?"

"Through Christmas," Nick replied. "If you have the room, of course."

"Not a problem," Ivy said. "You can park your car around back in the car court."

He glanced out the window. "That's very kind, but I don't have a car." He paused, inhaling. "Smells delicious in here, as if Christmas arrived early."

"That's our special Mexican hot chocolate," Ivy said. "Our mother's recipe with cinnamon and chili powder, though it's not too spicy, just warming. Would you like a cup?"

"I would be very grateful for that," Nick said politely.

His tone held a level of gratitude that Ivy hadn't expected. "Have you had breakfast? I can make something for you." This morning, she had cleared the breakfast spread in the dining room right after Bennett, Imani, and Jamir left. Gilda seldom ate breakfast, but if she did, she knew where every-thing was. Like family.

A smile spread across Nick's face. "I'd like that very much, thank you."

"We have eggs and bacon, yogurt, berries, bagels, and muffins," Ivy said. "What would you like?"

"That all sounds delicious," Nick said with a slight bow of his head. "But don't trouble yourself with bacon."

Shelly eased off the stool. "While Ivy is making breakfast, I can get you checked in and show you upstairs to your room."

"I'd be very grateful for that, thank you."

As Shelly walked to the kitchen door, she said, "I can also put your credit card on file."

"I don't have one on me," Nick said easily. "But I will make arrangements for payment."

Shelly shot a look at Ivy.

"That's fine," Ivy said after a moment of consideration. Mitch had referred Nick, and it wasn't as if they had other guests waiting for rooms. They had never been stiffed by a guest before. She wasn't worried.

"I can help you with your luggage," Shelly said.

"I have all I need right here," Nick said, hitching up a strap on his worn backpack. "And I wouldn't dream of asking a woman for help with luggage."

"We're pretty modern around here." Shelly grinned. "You're traveling kind of light for almost a month here."

Ivy laughed. "He's a guy, Shells. And students backpack for months." As she brought out eggs from Gertie, she glanced back at Nick. Even though it was chilly out this morning, he wore leather sandals. However, that wasn't surprising in a beach community, where people dressed casually every day. He had that natural, slightly scruffy beach look.

"Those are fine old refrigerators," Nick said, lifting his chin toward the pair. "But one of them is struggling."

"That would be Gertie," Ivy said, placing the eggs on the counter.

"Do you mind if I have a look?" Nick stepped closer. "Beautiful shade of turquoise, isn't she? A reflection of the sea." He glanced out the window. "A peaceful sleep is ever there, beneath the dark blue waves."

"Nathaniel Hawthorne wrote that." Ivy inclined her head, impressed at his grasp of poetry. One couldn't live in Boston as long as she had and not know the work of one of Massachusetts's foremost writers. She tapped a finger to her chin. Nick had an interesting way of expressing himself. She wondered if he was a writer or an English major, or maybe even a teacher.

"I was going to call someone to service the fridge," Ivy said. "But if you have any experience in refrigerator repair, have at it." What could it hurt?

"Perhaps." Nick approached Gertie, put his hands on the old refrigerator, and leaned in as if he were a physician listening to its heartbeat. "She has been working very hard this past week."

"She keeps things colder than her partner Gert there," Ivy said, motioning to the other unit.

"Hmm." Nick shifted his hands and closed his eyes for a few moments.

Shelly arched a brow and threw a look at Ivy.

Presently, Gertie's rumbling noise slowed, and the old refrigerator settled back to its usual low hum. A satisfied smile curved Nick's lips, and he patted the refrigerator case.

"What did you just do?" Shelly asked as her eyebrows shot up in an incredulous look. "It looked like you used some kind of energy healing on our fridge. Like Reiki for household appliances."

Nick modestly shrugged a shoulder. "I have a way with gadgets. Probably just a loose wire in there. Must have shifted back into place or something."

Ivy smiled. "Whatever you did, I'm grateful. You've certainly earned my best breakfast."

Nick gazed around the kitchen. "This kitchen looks like it's pretty original."

"We think the owner updated it in the 1950s or early 1960s."

Nick touched the old stove with reverence. "This must have served many hungry people. Do you know much about the people who built this place?"

"We've been researching Amelia and Gustav Erickson," Ivy said. "They have a fascinating history, but there's still a lot we don't know." Ivy turned to her sister. "Shelly, would you show Nick to his room?" She added the number of one of their best rooms.

Since Nick was going to stay awhile, Ivy wanted him to be comfortable. And if he was handy with appliances, even better. He'd just saved her a repair charge. After Shelly and Nick left, Ivy brought out ingredients and a clean skillet. She struck a match and lit a burner on the stovetop.

After Nick deposited his backpack in the room, he returned to the kitchen.

"Almost ready," Ivy said. She had prepared a large breakfast for the young man. He looked like he could use a good meal.

Ivy prepared a plate for him and filled a mug with hot chocolate with a generous scoop of whipped cream. "Would you like this in the dining room or your room?"

Nick glanced around, his gaze settling on the casual table and chairs where Ivy wrote grocery lists and Shelly trimmed plants. "Right here in the kitchen is fine. It's homey. I like that."

People often enjoyed hanging out in the kitchen. Ivy supposed it reminded them of home or a grandparent's kitchen. "Where are you from, Nick?"

"Up north," he said.

"On the coast or back east?"

"That's right," he said, tucking into the eggs she'd made.

Ivy started to ask which, and then she realized that technically, both could be correct. As she washed the skillet, she thought about that. In her few months as an innkeeper, she'd learned not to ask too many questions of people. They were paying guests and entitled to their privacy, especially during the holidays.

Some people had nowhere to go for a variety of reasons. The holidays could be lonely for single people without families. In Boston, after her daughters left her at a restaurant on Christmas Eve to return to their busy lives of friends and work, Ivy returned to her rented room and stared at the walls alone, wondering what had become of her former life. And now, here she was, running an inn and serving guests.

Guests. Holidays. She and Shelly had been talking about old photos and how the house was decorated in Amelia's day when Nick arrived. As she dried the skillet and put it away, a strange sensation tickled the back of Ivy's neck, and she suddenly had an overwhelming urge to look at the old photograph album. If for no other reason than curiosity, she wanted to see how Amelia Erickson had decorated the old house.

At the table, Nick was eating breakfast with gusto.

"If you'll excuse me," Ivy said. "Shall I leave the music on for you?" Shelly's Christmas jazz was still playing in the background.

"I'd like that very much," Nick replied.

Ivy made her way out of the kitchen. Shelly was at the front desk on the computer.

Peering over her sister's shoulder, she thumped Shelly on the shoulder. "You're not to do internet searches on our guests. Remember our talk about privacy?"

"I can't find a thing on him," Shelly said.

"Maybe Nick is short for Nicholas, or Nicolo. He said that people called him that. But you need to stop that right now."

Ivy tapped a key on the keyboard to close out the window. "Did Megan return the photo album?"

"I think she left it in the parlor." Shelly made a face and opened the browser window again.

"Get off the computer and come with me."

Shelly glanced over her shoulder. "Did you leave Nick alone in the kitchen?"

"What? Like he's going to steal the silverware? For Pete's sake, Shelly, he just fixed the refrigerator and saved us a lot of money."

"Did he? That's not what I saw. I saw some kind of weird magic, and coincidentally, the fridge stopped making a noise. So I don't know why you think he fixed it."

Ivy couldn't believe Shelly's attitude. "You're usually the one quick to believe in ghosts and alternate explanations."

"I know you've seen Amelia," Shelly said. "You just won't admit it."

"Geez, Shelly. I have to sleep in that room, remember?" Ivy wasn't sure what she'd seen, but she refused to believe a spirit was inhabiting her bedroom. Or had even paid a visit. She shuddered. "Then why don't you believe Nick fixed the fridge?"

"I've still got a lot of New York in me, Ives. People have to prove themselves."

Ivy rolled her eyes. "Let's go find the album. Megan probably left it on the bookshelf."

"Okay," Shelly said with reluctance.

Megan and Josh, who had been their first guests last spring, were working on a documentary film of Amelia and Gustav Erickson, the former owners. Although the Ericksons had been wealthy San Franciscans who hired Julia Morgan—the first female architect in California—to design a beach house, tracing their past in Europe had been difficult. The couple loved art and had sheltered many treasures during the Second World War in this house. During the war, Amelia

Erickson donated the use of the home for physical therapy for injured troops.

"And turn off that computer. Do you want our guest to see what you've been up to?" Ivy tapped her foot, waiting for Shelly to close the computer. She felt a sudden sense of urgency to inspect the old photographs.

After Amelia's death from Alzheimer's disease, the old beach house remained unoccupied for decades, suspended in her estate and rented out only for occasional charitable fundraisers before Jeremy acquired it.

This past spring and summer, Ivy and Shelly and Poppy had found treasures ranging from priceless European paintings to crown jewels, but they'd returned everything to the rightful owners. Although that had been the right thing to do, Ivy almost wished now that they'd had the chance to profit from those discoveries. Though maybe they had. Some guests had made reservations at the inn out of curiosity after reading a news article.

Ivy led the way into the parlor. She scanned the bookshelves that lined the walls.

"Here it is," Shelly said, taking out a leather-bound volume and placing it on an antique table.

Ivy sat at the table with Shelly and opened the old album. She turned delicate pages with care until she found the party scenes they'd recalled.

Ivy and Shelly leaned in, peering at the sepia-toned, black-and-white photographs.

"Look at this," Ivy said. "This looks like a beach party." People posing on the beach by the house wore old-fashioned bathing suits—bathing costumes, her grandmother would have called them.

"That looked like fun," Shelly said as she turned a page. "And this must be Christmas."

Ivy peered closer. In one photo, thick strands of what appeared to be freshly trimmed, natural garlands lined the doorway, windows, and edges of the patio's stone wall. Not too different than what Ivy would do if she had the resources. Maybe they could take a trip to the nearby mountains and find some natural foliage.

Ivy squinted at a photo. Lanterns lined the walkway to the house—others clustered around the entry. "With candles at night, that must have been beautiful."

In other photos, a Christmas tree towered in the ballroom, and fancy ornaments dripped from its boughs. Stockings hung across the fireplace, and a trio of carved reindeer with ribbons stood by the sofa. A mantle cover was draped above the fireplace with figurines nestled in the folds, and large bows anchored the corners.

Everyone wore eveningwear—tuxedos and long dresses with embellished capes, hats, and gloves. Stacks of gifts crowded a table next to the tree. In another photo, a group of singers stood by the tree, captured in mid-song.

Even in old black-and-white photos, the effect was magical.

"I wish we could do something like this," Ivy said wistfully. As she turned another page, she sucked in a breath. "This photo was taken in the garage."

"Those are the reindeer from that other photo." Shelly tapped the page. "That looks like a young Amelia with a housekeeper in a uniform. And a lot of ribbons and wooden crates."

"But why there?" Ivy leaned in. "There's something behind her."

"Maybe they kept the decorations in the garage. Or they'd just been delivered."

"There was nothing in the garage except for some old tools and paint." Ivy opened a drawer and retrieved a magnifying glass. Holding it over the photo, she said, "I'll bet that's where they stored everything." She tapped the image. "Look, that doorway is open, and there are boxes stacked inside. You can just see them."

"There's no door on the back wall in the garage."

"No," Ivy said slowly. "But there is a tall cabinet on that wall where the property manager's handyman kept supplies. I organized that cabinet not long ago." She stared at Shelly, trying to jog her memory.

Shelly's eyes grew wide. "Are you thinking what I'm thinking?"

"You bet," Ivy said. "Let's go."

The two sisters closed the album and headed toward the garage. As they walked through the kitchen, Ivy noticed that Nick had disappeared. His clean plate sat in the dishrack. Ivy didn't think she'd ever had a guest wash their dishes before. She made a note to have a chat with him. Not that she didn't appreciate it, but it wasn't necessary.

Ivy opened the old garage door and hurried past Amelia Erickson's vintage, cherry-red Chevrolet convertible that had come with the house. Bennett had restored it for her, and she loved cruising around the beach town in it.

"Help me move this," Ivy said. She stopped in front of the old wooden cabinet.

Shelly rubbed her arms and shivered. "Are you thinking what I'm thinking?"

Ivy nodded. "No telling what we're getting ourselves into this time."

She placed her hands against the cabinet. This magnificent old beach house had sheltered its occupants and their secrets for a century. Each discovery that she and Shelly made had illuminated part of Ivy's heart. The discovery of the paintings inspired Ivy to take up her art again. Finding the attic encouraged her to share new discoveries about the history of the inn. This Christmas might yield yet another treasure, but a strange feeling came over her. Would it bring her family together or deepen rifts?

Ivy shuddered. *What prompted that thought?* Surely they'd find nothing but moth-eaten decorations—if anything.

Shelly frowned at the tall cabinet. "Old Christmas orna-ments. That's all we're going to find, right?"

"Right." Ivy braced herself. "Ready on three. One, two, three." With Shelly beside her, they leaned into the solid wooden piece.

The old wooden piece creaked, but it didn't budge.

CHAPTER 4

*B*ennett pulled his SUV into his designated parking space at City Hall. Not that it had been his idea, but if he didn't park there, Nan would be disappointed. As the receptionist, Nan tended to details and welcomed everyone to Summer Beach.

The hand-painted sign sporting palm trees and a surf-board stood at a jaunty angle in front of the space Nan had chosen for him. It had been his birthday surprise, so he'd had little choice but to accept it, though he preferred a more egalitarian approach to parking. The lot was plenty large enough for everyone.

In Summer Beach, people were more concerned about the weather at the beach than finding a parking place at City Hall. He grinned and tucked his cotton polo shirt into his khaki pants and slipped on a windbreaker—his standard winter uniform. The December air was crisp and growing colder, thought the sun was still warm on his shoulders.

At least he'd talked Nan into putting the sign near the entry of the lot instead of by the door. "I run miles on the beach, so I think I can make it to the front door," he'd told her, good-naturedly. "Let's keep those spaces for visitors."

Bennett stepped out of his vehicle and strolled into the

airy, mid-century modern building perched on a cliff over-looking the beach and ocean beyond. At the welcome desk, a sign proclaimed, *Life is better in Summer Beach.*

"Good morning, Mr. Mayor," Nan said from atop a ladder, where she was hanging silver garlands beneath clerestory windows. Her red curls framed plump cheeks, and she had a bright smile on her face.

"Why don't you let me do that?" Bennett was concerned for her. Nan was energetic for her age, but he didn't want any broken bones on his watch.

"That's what Arthur always says, but I like to keep fit." She climbed down. "Just finished, but thanks."

Bennett was relieved. "Any calls this morning?"

"Darla phoned. She called to tell you about a vagrant next door at the Seabreeze Inn. She called Chief Clarkson, too."

Bennett furrowed his brow. "I didn't notice anyone like that this morning. I'll check in with Ivy."

Darla was their resident busybody. When Ivy had converted the old beach house to an inn, Darla was so incensed she filed a lawsuit against her. In the end, Ivy had eased her neighbor's concerns, but Darla was always on watch. Every morning Darla stopped by Java Beach to see Mitch. The coffee shop was a hotbed for local news, and Darla was usually at the center of it.

Bennett greeted Boz, the head of the Planning Depart-ment, on his way to his office. Even though his hair was silver, Boz had a fit, muscular physique—the result of a lifetime spent on the beach. "How are the plans for our Holiday Boat Parade?"

"Attendance will be pretty good this year," Boz said. "Tyler and Celia are underwriting the entire affair, so anyone who wants to participate can."

Tyler had retired at a young age, having sold his tech company in San Francisco before he turned forty. He and his wife Celia supported several local efforts, including the school music program.

"They beat out Carol Reston and her husband?" Bennett shook his head. That wouldn't go over with Carol, who was a Grammy-award winning singer. Carol liked the spotlight.

Boz shrugged. "They offered first."

"We're going to hear about that, but she can find another way to contribute. They already do so much for the children's center." Inside his office, Bennett shrugged off his jacket and picked up the phone to make that call. Ivy answered, sounding breathless.

"Everything okay there?"

"You must mean Darla."

He chuckled. "She called here, too."

"Clark just left to go calm her down."

"Was there a problem with a vagrant?"

Ivy blew out an exasperated breath. "That's just Nick, our new guest."

"Does he look like a vagrant?"

"This is the beach," Ivy said, sounding frustrated. "Nick didn't arrive in a suit and tie. He was minding his own business, meditating by the pool, and Shelly and I were in the garage. Next thing I knew, the Police Chief pulled into the car court. If Shelly and I hadn't been nearby, I hate to think what might have happened."

"Well, it's been pretty quiet at the inn lately. Guess Darla has gotten used to that."

"Don't rub it in," Ivy said. "You'll meet Nick later. He's a quiet, polite young man. So what if his hair is a little long? Mitch referred him, so once Darla hears that I'm sure she'll back off."

Bennett grinned. "Disaster averted once again. Want to grill some fish tacos on the beach tonight? Surely we can give Nick a warmer welcome."

"If it's not too cold."

"I'm a guy," Bennett said. "And it's not like it snows in Summer Beach."

Ivy laughed. "It's snowed in San Diego before. My parents still talk about it. Back in the sixties."

Bennett promised to pick up groceries on the way back to the inn after work. After hanging up the phone, he leaned back in his chair and laced his fingers. Even though he saw Ivy every day, he loved hearing her voice on the phone. Her laughter reminded him of the surfer girl with startling green eyes he'd seen on the beach all those years ago—before she started college in Boston. She'd stolen his heart then, even before he'd known real love.

His wife had been gone ten years now, though it didn't seem that long. They had been excited to start a family, but Jackie had developed severe medical complications during her pregnancy.

After her unexpected death, Bennett had thrown himself into his work as a real estate broker in Summer Beach and later took on the position of mayor. The love and care he might have put toward children shifted to his sister Kendra's son. Logan was now ten, and Bennett was also close to Dave, Kendra's husband. If Bennett was honest with himself—which he tried to be—the town's residents knew how much he'd suffered and had become a sort of surrogate family, too.

Even Darla. With royal-blue hair and glittery visors, she was like everyone's meddling aunt. But Darla had suffered trauma, too. She had lost a child who would be about Mitch's age now.

Bennett scrubbed his knuckles along his jawline. *And now there's Ivy.* She'd rolled into town determined to bend the rules to suit her, much like her late husband had, although her reasons were quite different. Jeremy had been planning on building a resort and replacing Ivy with a younger woman.

By the time Ivy discovered the house and arrived in Summer Beach, she'd been desperate to earn a living. She'd done the best job she could of restoring the old house on a budget and converting it to an inn. Though Bennett had been against that, when a fire ravaged the ridgetop homes above the village, Ivy housed many of the displaced residents—himself included. When his house was repaired, Bennett found that he didn't want to return to an empty house.

Yet it was more than that. When Ivy came into his life, he'd started having feelings he hadn't let in for years. He hadn't wanted to leave her, so he'd leased his house to a family, who now wanted to buy a larger home in Summer Beach. Soon, he'd have no reason to continue to stay at the Seabreeze Inn. The truth was that he'd been happier in the old chauffeur's apartment over the garage these last months than he'd been in his home for quite a while.

But was Ivy ready for the next step in their relationship? He loved being around her, holding her hand, walking on the beach after dinner. He got on well with Misty, though Sunny was a challenge. Just when he'd thought they were getting along fine, Sunny snubbed him at the Thanksgiving feast. She was still grieving for her father, of course. The adult in him knew that, but how long would he have to wait for Ivy?

Ivy knew how he felt about her, but she had difficulty saying those three little words back to him. He'd told her he loved her before they embarked on a last-minute trip to Catalina Island at the end of the summer. They'd had a blissful couple of days. He'd respected her, but it hadn't been for lack of desire. Still, when they returned to the mainland, they slipped back into their separate roles. Part of that was out of respect for Ivy's daughter, as Sunny was making the difficult transition of starting a new school.

At times, he wondered if he was merely convenient for Ivy. Would she be open to building another life with him? Maybe it was time to find out. However, if she broke his heart, seeing her around town in Summer Beach would be tough. Would he be better off biding his time to increase his odds?

He could do nothing and continue the warm, comfortable

friendship they had. An occasional romantic dance on the beach, holding hands in public, even an occasional kiss that sent fiery desire he'd long thought dead through him—but nothing more than that. It seemed neither of them wanted to risk getting hurt.

Nan appeared in the open doorway. "Looks like you have a lot on your mind, Mr. Mayor." In her hand, she held a red velvet Santa hat with a broad white, faux-fur trim. "Mind trying this on? It's for the annual gift giveaway at the children's club. We're all wearing them this year."

Bennett shook thoughts of Ivy from his head and took the Santa cap from Nan. After putting it over his cropped hair, he held out his hands. "What do you think?"

"Like a surfer Santa." Nan giggled. "Maybe I'll get a white beard for you."

"Might as well complete the look," Bennett said. He took off the hat. "I have to review the final budgets for the coming year this morning. Let me know if I'm needed for anything."

As he reviewed the financials, through his open office door he could see Nan adding to the holiday decorations and hear her humming to the music station that was now playing holiday music around the clock. December was the quietest time of the year for him, both in city government and real estate. Shops in the village were busy, though few people ventured onto the beach except for the walkers and runners and surfers. It was too chilly to play in the surf.

He gazed out over the ocean, picking out ships on the horizon and sailboats closer to Summer Beach's marina. Turning his attention back to his work, he focused on his task until he realized it was after lunchtime.

With his stomach reminding him, Bennett finished his review and pushed back from his desk. After the lunch crowd, Java Beach would be slower. He wanted to talk to Mitch.

As Bennett walked into the coffee shop, he ducked under an old fishing net by the door and nodded toward a younger man in a tie-dyed T-shirt and sandy, sun-bleached hair. Vintage Polynesian travel posters adorned the walls, and beach reggae music filled the air. A few lingering lunch guests were on the patio watching the waves under heat lamps, a handy staple in mild Southern California winters.

"Hey, Mr. Mayor," Mitch said, grinning. "Hungry?"

"What's good today?"

Mitch leaned across the counter. "I can whip up a Havarti and Muenster grilled cheese with basil pesto on my home-made bread. And I've got a killer soup made with fresh mush-rooms, thyme, parsley, and bay leaves. Ginger Delavie shared another one of her Julia recipes."

"You're getting pretty fancy," Bennett said. He remem-bered when Mitch had been a surfing drifter, sleeping in his car and selling coffee on the beach. Bennett had been impressed with the kid's skills and ambition, so he'd helped him rent the space for Java Beach. Mitch was almost thirty now, and Summer Beach had become his home.

Mitch grinned. "Man, I never thought I'd get so much joy from cooking, but hey, here we are. Want to join me in the kitchen?"

"Sure." Bennett followed him into the tiny kitchen and eased onto a stool.

"You're going to like this." Mitch cut two slices of bread speckled with crunchy sunflower seeds, swiped his homemade pesto over the bread, and tossed the slices onto the grill. He added slices of cheese and adjusted the heat.

Bennett enjoyed watching his friend cook, and the kitchen smelled wonderful. "Heard you sent a guy to the Seabreeze Inn."

"Yeah?" Mitch frowned and turned up the heat on a pot of soup. "Sorry, I don't know what you're talking about."

"A guy named Nick. Ivy told me you sent him."

"Oh, yeah. Slender guy, white streak in his hair. Nick was here for my Thanksgiving dinner."

"Helping you serve?"

"No, he came in looking for a meal. Word spreads, you know."

"So you didn't know him before last week?"

"Nope." Mitch flipped the sandwich, and the creamy cheese bubbled out, sizzling on the grill. "Look at that," he said, tapping the top with his spatula. "Perfectly golden." He rested his spatula. "The guy asked about the old house on the beach, so I told him it was the Seabreeze Inn. Nick seemed nice enough. Smart guy, I think. Just down on his luck, know what I mean?"

"Sure do." Bennett wondered what Nick was doing at the inn. Perhaps Darla had been right to be concerned.

Mitch ladled mushroom soup from the pot into a bowl, garnished it with a few grilled mushrooms, and handed it to Bennett. "Your first course," he said with a wink.

Bennett sipped the soup. "Wow, delicious. Perfect on a cool day. Did you surf this morning?" he asked, changing the subject.

"Every day I can. Got a new wetsuit for winter." Mitch eased the crispy sandwich from the grill onto a cutting board and let it cool a little before slicing through the crusty bread. Cheese oozed slightly from the sides. Mitch waved his knife. "What did I tell you? Perfection."

While Bennett enjoyed his lunch, Mitch kept an eye on the front counter and shared news and happenings in the village. Mitch overheard a lot at Java Beach, and what he didn't, Darla did.

Just as Bennett was thinking about Darla, he saw her royal-blue hair bobbing through the doorway. "You've got business, Mitch."

Mitch stepped from the kitchen. "Hey, Darla? How's my best sweetheart?"

"I need a latte, hon. Guess you're going to hear that I called Chief Clarkson to check on a guest at the inn. His name's Nick something-or-other." She paused, her rhinestone visor glittering. "Why, is that the mayor in the kitchen? I called you, too, Bennett."

"Hello, Darla," Bennett said, dabbing his mouth. "Sounds like the Chief took care of the situation."

Darla sniffed. "We single ladies have to look out for each other. I did the right thing. And I'm going to keep my eye on him."

Mitch suppressed a smile. "How about some whipped cream on that latte, Darla?"

"You're such a good boy," she said, struggling to maintain her ire.

Bennett decided he would have to judge this Nick character for himself. Then again, maybe he was too protective of Ivy—and he had no right to do that. She was a grown woman and was certainly capable of running the inn and deciding who was welcome.

Still, he couldn't help watching out for her—that was simply in his nature.

CHAPTER 5

*I*vy put her hands on her hips and stared up at the cabinet in the garage. "Now, where were we before our neighbor called the police on a guest?"

Shelly laughed. "Poor Nick, we should probably comp him a night. It's not often you almost get arrested for meditating. Guess we have to start making nice with Darla again."

"I have been," Ivy said. "I was so embarrassed for Nick. But Darla's not so bad; she's just bored." The past summer, she and Darla had forged a truce after Ivy called the paramedics for Darla when she collapsed on the beach. In turn, Darla canceled the lawsuit, and Ivy came to understand her better during the woman's recovery. However, old habits were hard to change.

Ivy stared up at the cabinet again, which was easily seven feet tall. She flattened her hands against the wooden planks and planted her feet. "Let's try this again."

Just then, Bennett pulled into the driveway and got out of his vehicle.

Shelly lifted her chin toward him and grinned. "Maybe we should just cut to the sledgehammer part right now."

Ivy laughed. She and Shelly had taken down a wall one night that led to the lower level and discovered a cache of stolen artwork. "Not a bad idea. I'm determined to find out what's behind this cabinet."

"Whoa, no more sledgehammers, ladies." Bennett held a hand up. "What do you need help with?"

Ivy leaned against the cabinet. "This thing won't budge."

"And why do you want to move it?"

"We saw an old photo album," Ivy said. "I think this cabinet is covering up a doorway to a storage room."

"Or maybe it's a secret passageway," Shelly said, her eyes glittering with excitement. "Like *The Lion, the Witch, and the Wardrobe*. I loved that book as a kid."

"Let's see what we can do to get you to Narnia then." Bennett shoved the cabinet, but to no avail. "Might be secured to the wall." He ran his hand around the edges. "I don't feel any brackets."

Shelly folded her arms. "Why would it be stuck to the wall?"

Bennett glanced behind him at the old red Chevrolet. "My guess is that if an earthquake toppled this, it would have damaged the car. Because the car hadn't been driven in years, the former property manager couldn't start it, so here it sat." He pointed to the other side of the garage. "The manager used to keep a riding lawn mower and his jet ski on that side."

He opened the cabinet and shoved aside car cleaning products. "Here's the problem." He stepped aside so Ivy and Shelly could peer inside. On the back of the cabinet, bolts had been driven through the rear wall of the cabinet. "I'll try to get them off."

"If you can't, I bet we can," Shelly said, nudging Ivy.

"We only want to move it, not destroy it." Ivy watched Bennett as he slipped off his jacket.

Bennett was as fit as men half his age, and he looked much the same as he had the first day she'd seen him on the beach. His hair had been longer then, though he still played the guitar—and her heart still quickened as it had when she was a teenager. She could see him in her mind's eye—sitting cross-legged in front of a flickering fire, strumming and singing as their young surfing friends swayed to the music.

Bennett brought out a cordless drill and changed the attachment. With a few swift spins, the bolts fell out into his hand. "A lot easier than brute force," he said with a grin.

Shelly shrugged with exaggeration. "Not nearly as exciting, though."

"Come on, let's do this," Ivy said, eager to see what was behind the cabinet. Taking the spot next to Bennett, she pressed her hands against the old wooden piece again.

With his help, the cabinet began to slide, sending up screeches of protest from years of complacency.

Shelly shrieked and waved her hands. "Eek, spider webs!"

"We were right," Ivy cried. She wedged her fingers into a grooved space on the door and slid it to one side. Years of nonuse had made the door jerky, so Bennett helped guide it along its track.

A shaft of sunlight from the open garage filtered into the storeroom, where dust particles danced in gusts of fresh air like tiny fairies.

Ivy tried the light switch, but the old bulb no longer worked. Bennett brought out a pair of flashlights from the cabinet and handed one to Ivy and one to Shelly. Sucking in a breath of excitement, Ivy flicked on the flashlight and shone it inside the storage room.

"Wow," Ivy said, expelling her breath. A row of shelves lined one side of the narrow storeroom that ran the width of the garage. To one side leaned old, wood-handled gardening tools—a hoe, a rake, a shovel. Assorted pots and hand-tools filled the shelves.

"Shelly, you'll want to look at the gardening supplies." Ivy swung the flashlight to the other side where neatly arranged wooden crates rested on the shelves. Faded labels marked the bins.

"These are old fruit boxes," Ivy said, reading the labels. "Look at this. Sunkist lemons from Orange County. Avenue oranges from the Victoria Avenue Citrus Association. Peerless oranges from San Diego Land and Town Company." She ran her fingers along the dusty labels, appreciating them. "The artwork is beautiful, and many are well preserved."

"Look at those," Bennett said, peering farther down the row of shelves Ivy illuminated. "Seven-Up Bottling Company in Los Angeles. Dad's Root Beer. And Beech-Nut Brand Chewing Gum."

Shelly shifted her flashlight. "Old Bushmills. Now we're talking."

"These are treasures, but what's inside?" Ivy slid out a short crate marked Coca-Cola in faded cursive red lettering. "Each item is so carefully wrapped." Some had been packed in newsprint, while thin, unbleached muslin fabric covered others.

Ivy ran her fingers over the wrapped objects. "I can just imagine the household staff packing these. These crates must have held old glass bottles of soda." She raised her flashlight. "Look, there's more. Nesbitt's, Squirt, Mission. Those are old brands."

"Let's see what we have here," Bennett said, picking up a Coca-Cola crate and carrying it into the light. "Looks like these held two dozen bottles. Six cubbies one way and four the other. Might be old teacups or glassware packed in here."

"That's not what we think," Shelly said. "Our bet is on Christmas decorations. We saw an old photograph in that album that we found in the attic."

"That would sure come in handy," Bennett said.

"I've seen these old wooden crates at antique shops," Ivy said, tapping her fingers on the old wood. "I've always liked them. Wouldn't they look great in our kitchen?"

Gingerly, Ivy lifted a dusty, muslin-wrapped object from a little cubby hole. After unwrapping it with care, she held a shimmering, rose-colored glass ornament in the shape of a bell up to a ray of winter sunlight. "I've never seen anything like this. It's lovely and certainly made by hand."

"Woo-hoo! I bet we found the mother lode of Christmas decorations." Shelly's eyes flashed with excitement. "All these crates are probably full of the same things. We're going to celebrate in style after all." She flung her arms around Ivy, nearly lifting her from her feet.

Laughing, Ivy reached for another packed item. She unfolded the soft cloth, which looked like the old flour bag cloth her grandmother had used. Inside lay a cut-crystal angel with intricately etched wings. "How exquisite," she said, examining the details.

Bennett smoothed his hand over Ivy's. "There's an awful lot here. Shall I take some of these boxes inside for you?"

His simple touch sent tingles through Ivy. "To the kitchen, thanks. We can clean and sort on the big table."

Shelly pulled out another crate. "People back then were the original recyclers, weren't they? Wooden crates, reusable glass soda bottles. That was kind of cool. Why did we ever stop? Now we have plastic bottles littering the ocean." She surveyed the wall of colorful crates. "I can't wait to make videos of all this to post on my channel." Shelly started toward the kitchen, humming *Jingle Bells*.

Ivy smiled. Shelly hadn't been this excited since summer. Though she and Mitch were spending a lot of time together, Ivy could tell that her sister missed the excitement of spending holidays in New York.

Happiness welled up inside Ivy. "It looks like we'll do some extra special decorating this year."

Bennett took a step toward her and tucked a strand of hair behind her ear. "If you don't mind, I'd like to help. It's been years since I put up any decorations."

Ivy didn't have to ask why. After Jeremy died, she hadn't had the heart to do much for Christmas and went through minimal motions only for her daughters. After she sold their condo, she didn't have to pretend to be interested. But now it was time for a change.

"I'd like that very much." Ivy caught Bennett's hand and turned her cheek into it. Though his hands were slightly rough from sanding and refinishing his boat, she enjoyed the warmth of his skin.

Bennett slid his arms around her. "Maybe it's time to create new holiday traditions." His voice dropped a notch. "For us."

Ivy gazed up into Bennett's hazel eyes that creased at the corners. Faint tan lines from his sunglasses gave him sort of a *GQ* look—as if he'd just stepped out of a yachting ad. His lips curved into a smile, capturing her heart again.

Her mouth felt dry, incapable of forming words, yet her heart beat in sync with his. She loved so many things about Bennett. He'd first told her that he loved her on his boat just before they continued to Catalina Island. Even then, with love in her heart, she couldn't bring herself to say the words she'd only ever uttered to just one man.

These last few months, waiting for her to answer, Bennett had stopped telling her what she actually needed to hear, even though he showed it with every look, every touch. By the end of the summer, Bennett had earned a spot on her What-Ivy-Bay-Wants list. So why couldn't she say those three little words to him?

Ivy pressed her cheek to his. Was she ready for such a step? She thought about Sunny's reluctance to engage with Bennett at Thanksgiving. While concerning, Ivy was a grown woman and didn't need to seek her daughter's approval for Bennett's presence during the holidays—or any other time.

Still, she had to respect Sunny's feelings, too. Her therapist in Boston might have told her that Sunny was being manipulative, but wasn't her daughter's grief also a concern?

Bennett kissed her reassuringly as if he was aware of the

torrent of emotions careening through her. "This will be a very special holiday season. Our first of many, I hope."

The rear kitchen door slammed, and Shelly called out. "Hey, are you two lovebirds going to give me a hand with these boxes? Geez, I can't leave you alone for a minute."

"Yeah, yeah," Ivy said, laughing. "Same with you and Mitch." She gave Bennett another quick peck on the cheek. His face looked flushed, though it was chilly outside. "I think you're blushing," she said.

"Not from what your sister said." A smile danced on his lips, and he ran a hand over his closely cropped hair. "I have a meeting at City Hall I need to get back to." He squeezed her hand. "I just wanted to check on you and make sure you were okay. Is Nick around? I'd like to meet him."

"He went out right after Chief Clarkson left. I felt bad for him," Ivy added, thinking how sweet it was that Bennett was concerned—even though Darla had sent up a false alarm.

"I won't feel quite as bad once he gives us a credit card," Shelly said.

"We don't talk about guests' accounts," Ivy shot back.

Bennett glanced between them. Ivy swiftly changed the subject, gesturing back at the wall of dusty boxes in the narrow storage room. "Sorting through all this is going to take some time. We don't have the staff that Amelia had."

Bennett grinned. "But you have an army of volunteers ready to spring into action at the merest mention of food or Sea Breeze cocktails."

Ivy inclined her head and put her hands on her hips. "I do, don't I?"

"And I know who's the perfect person to rally a few helpers," Shelly said. "I'll call Poppy."

"My sister, the master of delegation."

Shelly slung an arm over Ivy's shoulder. "You know she misses us up there in the cold north."

Ivy arched an eyebrow. "She's in Los Angeles."

"Exactly."

"Hey, I like L.A.," Ivy said. "Well, maybe not the traffic."

The two sisters each brought another crate into the kitchen. Despite the sealed storage room, somehow decades of dust had filtered in through the smallest of crevices. Shelly wiped down the containers while Ivy unwrapped each carefully stored object.

"Amelia must have had a set of these bells," Ivy said. "Look, here's a mint-green one, and another powder-blue one. I'll bet there are more." She set them aside. As she unwrapped another package, she exclaimed, "Oh, how sweet. A child with his ice skates." Turning over the hand-painted glass piece, she read, "Made in Austria."

Shelly paused. "I wonder if Amelia and Gustav brought those ornaments with them or if they bought them here in the States?"

"I wish we knew their story."

"How is Megan doing on her research for the documentary?"

"She says there are still a lot of missing pieces." Ivy unwrapped another ornament, each one a sweet salve to her artist's heart. "Megan located photos in San Francisco, where the Ericksons supported the opera, the art scene, and different charities. And, of course, after Gustav died, the local newspaper lauded Amelia for opening this home to troops for rehabilitation. And then there were her final days in Switzerland before she passed away." Ivy held a miniature antique sled up to the light. "But I feel there is more to her story."

Just then, the back door banged open, and Sunny sailed through, her backpack slung over one shoulder and her strawberry blond hair streaming around her shoulders. "What's all that junk?"

"Priceless vintage ornaments," Shelly shot back.

"We found them in the garage," Ivy said. "Stored away all

these years. So we'll be able to decorate after all this year. Won't that be fun?"

"I guess so," Sunny said.

Ivy gestured to the chair beside her. "Why don't you give us a hand?"

"No, I have to talk to a friend right now."

"Will you be home for dinner?"

"Don't count on it," Sunny said.

"Homework?"

"Yeah, that's right," Sunny said, darting her eyes to one side. "Got to go." She grabbed a bottle of juice from the fridge and a blueberry muffin before disappearing to her room in the old maid's quarters behind the main house.

Shelly arched an eyebrow. "Did you believe that story?"

Ivy let out a sigh. "Not really. I don't know what's happened to Sunny. She began the school year with enthusiasm, but she's turned into the old Sunny from Europe in the last couple of weeks. I wonder if she's met a new group of friends. If they're anything like the last bunch, that would explain a lot. But at least she'll graduate this year."

Shelly nodded. "And with any luck, plunge herself into the real world. Like taking a cold shower."

Ivy unwrapped a hand-painted glass candle, its flame and holder tipped with gold. "Imagine the artistry that went into these. They're all hand-painted and hand-blown. There's nothing cookie-cutter about these. These are the finest I've ever seen—no surprise, of course, given Amelia's budget. Very expensive then, and highly collectible now."

Shelly leaned on the table. "I'm the one usually thinking about the value of the treasures we find around here. Are you thinking of selling these?"

"I wish you hadn't said that," Ivy replied wistfully. "These ornaments might be worth a fortune to a collector. But I'd like to enjoy them for just one Christmas. And if we can figure out how to create a winter business, we won't have to start selling things."

"Then let's do that." Shelly's eyes flashed. "It's not like we haven't done it before."

Ivy rested her chin on her hand and gazed out to the ocean. Its movement was incessant, resting only for a moment as the foamy saltwater clung to the shore before racing back again into the deep.

Was she so different?

"I grow weary of barely surviving," Ivy said. "What we do this winter will determine the future of the inn. If we can't be viable year-round, then we'll have to charge more in the summer. While we offer a good value, I don't think we can do that."

"Then let's make it a season to remember," Shelly said, pumping her fist. "Come on, let's do this."

Ivy laughed. "You're on."

CHAPTER 6

*I*vy paused in front of the hardware store's window. Nailed It always had beautiful, interesting window dressings. The co-owner, Jen, had superb artistic sense and changed the windows weekly to showcase their new, seasonal merchandise.

This week, a miniature train chugged through a snowy village complete with streetlights. Music played through a speaker outside the window, and Ivy hummed along to Mariah Carey's *All I Want for Christmas Is You.* Ivy smiled to herself. That was probably Jen's choice, too.

Shivering in the crisp morning breeze off the ocean, Ivy pulled her silvery gray down vest—once used for skiing—around her white cotton turtleneck. She'd pulled on black denim jeans today and added a lightweight wool, red-and-green plaid scarf with silvery threads. Since finding the vintage ornaments yesterday, Ivy was finally feeling the Christmas mood.

"Good morning, Ivy," Jen said, climbing out of a pickup truck parked in front of the shop. She had a natural, fresh-scrubbed look and wore faded blue jeans with brown cowboy boots and a fringed leather jacket. Her hair swung to her shoulders. "How do you like the new window?"

"I love it," Ivy said with a sigh. "Makes me miss waking to fresh snow outside my frosty bedroom window in Boston. The first snowfall of the season was always magical—a quiet, reverent display of the wonder of nature."

Imagining that moment brought back memories, and Ivy went on. "I used to take Misty and Sunny to the park to build snow families when they were young. The snow mother, father, kids, and even snow dogs. Sometimes we had a lot of snow to work with."

"You won't find that around here," Jen said. "If you want snow, head to the mountains—Big Bear and Mammoth Lakes are my favorite places in California for snow, but then, I love to ski. You should go while it's quiet at the inn."

"Not this year, I'm afraid." A trip was hardly in the budget. "But we have plenty to celebrate. And you'll never believe what we found stored in the garage."

"Tell me," Jen cried with excitement. "More treasures?"

Ivy laughed. "Yes, but not the kind worth millions. We found crates of vintage Christmas ornaments and decorations. They're handmade and utterly exquisite. I think most of them are from Europe."

"I would love to see them," Jen said. "You're putting up a tree, right?"

"We hadn't planned on it because we didn't have any decorations. But now, it looks like we're going to have to. Where's a good place to find one?" *A small one.*

"Leilani and Roy have the best trees over at Hidden Garden. They buy from Southern California tree farmers who follow sustainable practices, so that's pretty cool." Jen paused to smile and nod to a local woman who came out of the shop. Turning back to Ivy, she asked, "Anything I can help you with today?"

"I need some strong wire hooks for the ornaments," Ivy said. "Some of the pieces are pretty heavy. Although many of the ornaments have ribbons for hanging attached, others have old hooks that are rusted and mangled. I don't need anything fancy, just those wire type that I can bend to secure to tree branches."

"Come in. I have just the thing. And George should have the hot cider going if you'd like a cup." She opened the door, and the scent of apple and cinnamon wafted out.

Jen's husband was wrapping a train set for a customer. "Hello, Ivy," George said, his face wreathed in a friendly smile. He wore an old T-shirt with a lumberjack flannel shirt and jeans.

Jen poured two cups of hot cider and handed one to Ivy. "Now, about those ornament hangers you need." She bustled through the narrow, crowded aisles of the small hardware store. Although it was compact, Jen made sure everything was neat and attractively merchandised.

Warming her hands on the cup of cider, Ivy followed her. Jen's parents had established the hardware store decades ago. Here, people passed businesses and homes through the generations. As Ivy had come to know many of the shop owners in the village of Summer Beach, she discovered that wasn't unusual. The fast-food and big-box stores hadn't invaded the town as they had the neighboring community, so Summer Beach still had a unique charm about it.

Even more so during the holiday season, Ivy noticed. Everyone brought out decorations, and many of them looked like they'd been in the family for years. A pair of tall, hand-painted wooden nutcrackers stood at the entry to Nan and Arthur's antique shop. A rough-hewn wagon with a family of Christmas bears at the helm sat outside the Starfish Café.

Summer Beach might not have snow, but it had all the good cheer and charm one could want.

One. That thought gave Ivy an idea.

"Here you are," Jen sang out. "How many boxes do you need?"

"A lot. As Shelly put it, we found the mother lode of Christmas ornaments."

They scooped up several boxes. As George was ringing up her purchase, he asked, "Are you going to have an open house for the holidays?"

"I think we should," Ivy said. "I want to share what we discovered in the storeroom. The newest decorations are from the 1950s, though most of them look much older."

Jen and George exchanged an interested glance. "We'd love to see that. I bet a lot of people would."

"We need to do something to boost occupancy. It's been so slow since the end of summer."

"Summer Beach is such a family place, so I guess most people stay home during the holidays," Jen said.

Ivy raised her brow. "I wonder what people who don't have families do?" She remembered how lonely the holidays were for her in Boston after Jeremy died. Even though Misty shared an apartment with a friend nearby, and Sunny lived in university housing, Ivy had felt very much alone in her rented room at the professor's townhouse.

Ivy thanked Jen and George and promised to invite them to the open house. After returning to the inn, she sought out Shelly, who was photographing the vintage ornaments for a video montage.

"I got the ornament hooks, and Jen said the best trees in town are at the Hidden Garden. Want to come with me?"

A smile brightened Shelly's face. "When I picked up the poinsettias there, I saw some gorgeous Monterey pine trees. Let's take the Jeep so we can haul one back." Shelly shoved her feet into a pair of faux fur snow boots sitting by the back door and grabbed a puffy red jacket to throw over her yoga wear.

Ten minutes later, Ivy and Shelly were strolling through a Christmas tree village set up on the beautiful grounds of the

Hidden Garden nursery. Leilani waved and made her way toward them.

"*Mele Kalikimaka*," Leilani said, wishing them a Merry Christmas in Hawaiian. The garden and nursery owner wore a bright red sweater with a green Christmas tree on the front. Her dark, shiny hair was woven into a thick braid with red ribbons. "Hi, Shelly. Back for a tree, after all?"

"We discovered a storeroom full of ornaments," Shelly said. "So now we have to have a tree to put them on."

"I'm glad you came back," Leilani said.

Shelly ran her hands over the long, slender pine needles of a tall tree. "Your Monterey pine trees are so fresh and fragrant. *Pinus Radiata.* So full and such a bright shade of green. They're fairly rare on the roster of Christmas trees. Mostly grown along the California coast, right?"

Leilani nodded. "Monterey pines are native to Central California—on the Monterey Peninsula, the Año Nuevo area of Santa Cruz County, and the Cambria area around San Luis Obispo." As she spoke, Leilani picked up a tree and shook out the full branches. "You'll also find them on Cedros Island and Guadalupe Island off the coast of Baja California in Mexico. But did you know they're also native to New Zealand? They grow these pines quite extensively for timber."

Shelly and Leilani talked about the fine points of different trees for a few minutes while Ivy looked around. Ivy zoned out when they began speaking about stenotopic coniferous and pyrophyte trees, though she recalled that had something to do with ecological conditions—Shelly once explained how fire was needed to open certain species' closed pine cones for reproduction.

Ivy smiled at the two women speaking so intensely about trees, but that's the way she was about art. As a horticulturist, Shelly was in heaven here at the Hidden Garden with Leilani and Roy.

Leilani motioned to one of the tallest trees on the lot.

"That gorgeous ballroom is just crying for one this size. We'd love to see it decorated in all its glory at the Seabreeze Inn."

"That's lovely, but a modest-sized tree will do," Ivy said with a sigh. "We don't have many guests, so we don't need much." She glanced at the prices marked on a chalkboard and did a quick mental budget calculation. "Something in the four-to-five-foot range. Jen and George suggested that we have an open house."

"Of course, we have to," Shelly said. "It's going to be magical. Just wait until I get through with it. You'll be amazed. We can put the tree on a draped table, so it looks taller."

Ivy tucked her hand into the crook of her sister's arm. In New York, Shelly had created extravagant floral arrangements for weddings and parties and holiday affairs. If anyone could make Christmas look spectacular on a budget, Shelly could.

Leilani nodded, taking all this in. "One moment."

Ivy and Shelly watched as Leilani made her way to her husband. After speaking briefly with Roy, Leilani returned. "Roy and I agreed. If you're going to have an open house, you must have one of our finest tall trees for the ballroom."

"Maybe next year," Ivy said quickly.

Leilani pressed a hand to her chest. "This is our gift, not only to you but to all of Summer Beach. This community has become our 'ohana, our extended family. Please accept this as part of our welcome to Summer Beach. We're so glad to have you all here."

While Shelly embraced Leilani, Ivy blinked away the sudden tears that sprang to her eyes over this kind woman's generosity. "That's so sweet of you," Ivy said, hugging Leilani.

"Shelly has sent us so much business," Leilani said, holding Ivy's hands. "Megan and Josh are renovating their entire yard at their new home. And the landscaping jobs from the Ridgetop Fire insurance settlements have been a financial bonus for us. So it gives us great joy to do this. Roy can deliver the tree and help you set it up. You're going to need help."

"Bennett can probably help this evening," Ivy offered. Maybe Nick would be there, too. Bennett wanted to meet him, but Nick had disappeared. He'd missed the grilled fish tacos Bennett had prepared.

Ivy suspected that Bennett was feeling overly protective of her, given that Darla had called the police on Nick. While Ivy had assured Bennett that Nick was a perfect guest, quiet and polite, Bennett still seemed nervous about him. She couldn't imagine why.

"I'll have Mitch come over," Shelly added. "We'll have to plan a tree-trimming party, too."

"Roy will appreciate the help. He'll see you later today." After another hug, Leilani excused herself to help another customer.

As they walked back to the old Jeep that Ivy and Shelly had both learned to drive in, Ivy slung her arm around Shelly.

"I can hardly believe how generous Leilani and Roy are about the tree," Ivy said. "What she said about 'ohana, the Hawaiian concept of family, makes a lot of sense. I have an idea."

"Here we go again," Shelly said.

Ivy laughed. "I'll tell you over lunch. Is mom still coming?"

"As far as I know."

Shelly opened the door to the Jeep, got in, and opened Ivy's door from the inside. The Jeep was old and didn't have electric anything—doors, windows, or power steering—but it got them where they needed to go. Shelly used it most of the time for gardening. The heater was slow to start, so Ivy stuffed her hands into her pockets to keep them warm. While the weather wasn't as cold as Boston this time of year, it was chilly by Southern California standards. Still, Ivy liked the fresh nip in the air.

Carlotta arrived at the inn at the same time they did. Knowing that their mother would appreciate the handcrafted ornaments, Ivy had called her to help them unpack the crates. Poppy promised to come in over the weekend and said she'd try to bring Elena, too, though Christmas was Elena's busiest time of year. Her tiny, jewel-box of a shop on Robertson Boulevard was doing very well. Poppy had told Shelly that Elena was eager to see what they'd discovered, too.

Outside, Ivy and Shelly greeted their mother against the roar of the ocean before hurrying inside.

"We should make a fire in that enormous fireplace," Carlotta said, rubbing her arms. "Isn't it chilly in here?"

"The ballroom is pretty drafty until the afternoon sun pours through the windows," Ivy said. "It knocks the chill off." However, it didn't make that much difference. In truth, she was trying to conserve on the gas heating bill. Fortunately, heat rose, so the upstairs rooms were warmer. She and Shelly had distributed stacks of blankets they'd found in the attic. "I can start a fire if you'd like, but we'll be in the kitchen until we start decorating. We could turn on the old gas oven and crack the door."

"A fire would be lovely," Carlotta said with a little shiver.

"You start the fire, Ivy. I'll turn on the heat." Shelly threw Ivy a look that said, *don't be cheap.*

But Shelly wasn't the one who had to balance the budget. However, Shelly was contributing to the gas bill with her earnings from her videos and blog.

While Ivy laid the fire and touched a match to it, Shelly told her mother about the tree that was coming soon.

Carlotta gazed around the room. "That's a lovely spot for the tree by the palladium windows."

"Exactly what I was thinking." Ivy rose from the hearth and dusted her knees.

As soon as they walked into the kitchen, Carlotta let out a gasp at the crates of ornaments. "Oh, *mija*, what treasures!"

"I still can't believe we found all this," Ivy said, picking up a crystal icicle that cast a rainbow of refracted light as it spun in her hand. "Just when we thought this old house couldn't possibly have any more hiding places."

Shelly prepared a teapot of hot peppermint tea and turned on José Feliciano's holiday songs that Carlotta loved. Soon they were all singing along with *Feliz Navidad* as they had as children. Shelly and Ivy and their mother sat around the large kitchen table, affixing hooks to ornaments and unwrapping more ornaments and decorations. One crate was full of gilded golden apples and painted gingerbread man ornaments.

"These decorative arts are to be cherished," Carlotta said as she unwrapped a star-shaped crystal ornament. "They are fine examples of early 20th-century European artistry—and they are highly collectible. These bring back memories of my childhood, too. My parents often bought similar ornaments when they visited Europe, and your father and I found more on our travels. Unfortunately, when Boots tried to climb the Christmas tree, we lost most of them."

Shelly laughed. "I remember that crazy cat. So many good Christmas memories."

Ivy was tempted to ask what her mother thought the ornaments were worth, but she didn't want to know. She thought about the idea she'd had earlier in the day. It might provide the way out of this predicament.

"Most of my holiday memories have been good ones," Ivy said. "Except for the last couple of years after Jeremy died."

Carlotta reached out and touched her hand. "You had a rough time of it, but I'm glad you're close to the rest of the family now."

"So am I, but I learned something from that experience." Ivy sipped her tea before going on. "Being alone during the holidays is a special category of loneliness, and one that I don't wish on anyone." She told her mother about what Leilani had said about *'ohana*. "Mom, remember when you used to go to the spa in Ojai? You formed friendships with women who became like sisters to you."

"We would meet there every year," Carlotta said, her eyes lighting with memories. "The first time I went, you girls were young, and we were on a budget. So I signed up to share a room with another woman. Although she was a stranger, we were good friends by the end of the week. It was like being in college again. And it was so affordable that way." Carlotta laughed. "We had such fun and became like family. You know, I saw Marilyn and Dolores just last week. What dear friends they are."

Ivy leaned forward. "That's what I'm talking about, Mom. There are a lot of people who have nowhere to go during the holidays. Maybe they go to the spa, maybe they take a cruise—or they could come here. We could do something similar for the holidays."

Shelly's eyes widened. "You mean, like Christmas for one?"

"That's brilliant," Ivy said. "Something like, come alone, leave as family. I'm sure Poppy can come up with a better tagline."

Carlotta leaned back in her chair and lifted her teacup to her lips, ruminating on the idea. "You might have something there. Many women are alone during the holidays, either through divorce or death of a partner—or because they are quite happy on their own. During the holidays, they might feel a little left out. Oh, they might spend Christmas Day with their grandchildren, but quite often their grown daughters and sons alternate family visits with spouses' families, which leaves them alone or with friends."

Ideas coursed through Ivy's mind. "I think we have a real opportunity—not only to fill the inn but also to provide a unique experience where we come together as a surrogate family."

"If that had been available in New York, I know people

who would have loved it," Shelly added with enthusiasm. "Let's do this."

"And if it works for Christmas, we can plan other similar events. Think of Valentine's Day. We could throw a Galentine's Day weekend." Ivy felt good about this track. "We could offer special rates and plan all sorts of activities. From yoga to beach walks, painting classes, cooking classes with local chefs, and chartered outings on Mitch's boat. I'm sure we can find all sorts of activities for people to share and meet each other. We could have couples events, too."

Carlotta reached out to hug Ivy and Shelly. "I have the most creative daughters. I always knew that you would do wonderful things here at the inn."

Ivy was growing excited as more ideas bubbled in her mind. This could mean more than merely filling rooms. They could touch people's hearts, maybe change lives.

"Amelia and Gustav Erickson built Las Brisas to bring people together and celebrate life," Ivy said, feeling the heat of anticipation rising in her cheeks. "Over the years, this house has sheltered many people. It's given hope to those who despaired of life. It's time we continue the tradition."

"That's a noble thought," Carlotta said, nodding.

Ivy spread her hands as she spoke. "Like those men and women who served in the Second World War and underwent rehabilitation here, breathing in the restorative salt air—a new generation could discover the magic of old Las Brisas del Mar. And not only during the summer. Once again, a visit here would be a time to relax, recharge, and make friends. The winter beach is perfect for such a respite."

Ivy couldn't wait to begin.

The three women worked until lunch when they stopped to make a salad and heat butternut squash soup that Ivy had made the day before. After lunch, they continued unpacking crates and moving furniture to create room for the tree. In more wooden bins, they found velvet ribbons rolled into balls, a richly embroidered tree skirt, and stacks of silk cloths they could use for the tabletops.

Through it all, ideas for the holiday season percolated in Ivy's mind, and she couldn't wait to talk to Poppy about a new marketing campaign. Besides simply filling rooms, she wanted this season to be one of making new friends that would become family. She was more determined than ever to put this new concept into action.

CHAPTER 7

"*A* little to the left," Ivy said, directing the tree placement.

"Again?" Bennett groaned while Roy only grinned. Still, Bennett knew better than to question Ivy's artistic eye. "Okay, whatever the lady wants."

Positioned on either side of the tall pine tree, Bennett and Roy shifted the tree again. Bennett loved seeing excitement in Ivy's face again. The ballroom—the entire house, for that matter—had erupted in happy chaos, and laughter rang out alongside the roar of the ocean in the background.

Crates and baskets of ornaments stood ready to adorn the tree. Shelly was busy winding red velvet ribbons around the smooth wooden railing of the staircase. In the ballroom, Carlotta was creating a vintage village scene on a tabletop with miniature houses and shops reminiscent of Currier and Ives, and a trio of wooden reindeer was stationed by a sofa.

"Stop right there," Ivy cried. "That's perfect."

Bennett and Roy crawled out from under the tree and stood, brushing long, soft pine needles from their shoulders.

"Roy, I can't tell you how much we appreciate this," Ivy said. "We're going to fill this house with Christmas magic and invite the entire town to visit."

"Leilani and I are happy to help you share the joy of the season with our community," Roy said, gazing around. "Everyone's pleased to see the old Las Brisas estate transformed into the Seabreeze Inn. They'll all want to see it."

Ivy looked around, her gaze resting on Shelly. "My sister will do an amazing job. She is so talented, and what we found in the storeroom is more than either of us could've imagined."

Bennett loved listening to Ivy talk, and he saw the pride in her eyes for her sister. That was the way he felt about his sister, Kendra. Her son Logan would be amazed at these decorations. His nephew had only known the Seabreeze Inn as the local haunted house.

Just then, a slender young man with longish dark hair pulled back into a ponytail appeared in the entryway. A streak of prematurely white hair ran from his forehead. Bennett nodded toward the front door. "You've got company."

Ivy turned around, and a smile lit her face. "Nick, come join us. I'd like to introduce you to the mayor of Summer Beach, Bennett Dylan. He's a guest here, too."

Nick ambled over, weaving his way through crates of decorations. He stopped in front of Bennett and Roy. "How do you do?" he asked, shaking their hands.

Roy greeted him and said, "Glad you like the tree, Ivy. I've got a couple more deliveries to make, so I'd better get going."

Nick bowed his head slightly. "It was a pleasure meeting you, Roy. I hope to see you again soon."

Bennett noticed how courteous and mild-mannered Nick seemed. Though the young man was also a little disheveled, so Bennett could see why Darla had been concerned.

While Ivy said a few more words to Roy, Bennett spoke with Nick. "How long will you be with us, Nick?"

"I'm staying through Christmas," Nick replied.

"That's a nice long holiday." From the corner of his vision, Bennett saw Shelly cast a glance in their direction. He couldn't help but wonder if Nick had rendered a form of payment for his room yet—though that was Ivy's business, of course. It made him feel a little snarky for even thinking about that. Ivy hadn't said much, but without many guests, she had to be concerned. "So, what do you do, Nick?"

Maintaining clear-eyed contact, Nick calmly replied, "I make life better for people."

"That's a noble cause," Bennett said, flexing his jaw. "How exactly do you go about that?"

"Sometimes it's complicated." Nick's gaze drifted off into the distance as if in contemplation.

"I'd sure like to hear more about that." Bennett folded his arms. This guy was evasive.

Nick shook his head. "I wouldn't want to bore you." He looked up at the tree. "Besides, it's the holidays. Seeing how different people celebrate is interesting, isn't it?"

Before Bennett could reply, Ivy turned back to them.

"We'll have a tree trimming tomorrow," Ivy said. "Poppy just finished a marketing job in Los Angeles, so she's returning. Some of the cousins will be here, and we'll have such fun. In the meantime, will you two help us with other decorations? We're finding so many beautiful items in these crates."

"Work shared is never a burden," Nick said.

"So true." Ivy pointed to a crate. "Nick, you can start with that crate. And Bennett, would you help me with something in the kitchen?"

Bennett followed Ivy into the kitchen. She shut the door and turned to him.

"Why were you scowling at Nick and interrogating him?"

"Has he made arrangements for the payment of his room?"

Ivy recoiled. "And since when is that any business of yours?"

Instantly, Bennett realized he'd overstepped her boundaries, but he couldn't help himself. "I'm the mayor. I'm interested in everyone's business in Summer Beach."

"And do you ask other business owners about their financial dealings with customers?"

"Look, maybe it's not my place to ask you, but I'm concerned about you. I don't want to see you taken advantage of."

"What makes you think he's taking advantage of me?"

"If he hasn't paid you—"

"That's none of your business, and I'm appalled that you would even bring this up. If you don't start treating my guests with courtesy, even if you are the mayor, then you need to think long and hard about staying here. My business is *my* business."

Bennett spread his hands in appeal. "Ivy, you're taking this the wrong way."

"Oh, now this is my fault?" Ivy's eyes blazed. "Think about what you just said. What if Gilda or Imani were to ask me such a thing? Or what if I were to begin asking questions about how you're running the city?"

"Well, as a citizen, that's well within your rights."

Ivy threw up her hands. "This is hardly the same thing."

"Okay, but why are you so intent on defending Nick?" Bennett asked.

"It's not Nick I'm defending," Ivy said, taking a step closer and raising her finger to him. "I don't like being second-guessed by you and Shelly on guest decisions. I trust what Nick told me, and that's the end of it. No one has ever stiffed me on a room before. And if Nick is the first one who does, well then, I guess I will have learned my lesson. Until that time, I'd like to exercise my good judgment without being criticized for it." She threw up her hands. "For Pete's sake, it's Christmas. Can't you find some trust in your heart for a fellow human being?"

"Ouch. Guess I deserved that." Bennett had never seen Ivy so angry at him. He reached for her hand.

Ivy drew back. "If you can't join in the festivities without a scowl on your face or interrogating our guests, then you can go back to your room."

From the doorway, a slow clap erupted. "That's what Mom tells me, too," Sunny said.

"That goes for you, too, Sunny," Ivy said. She picked up a crate and sailed through the door.

Bennett stared at Sunny. "How long have you been standing there?"

"Maybe that's none of your business, too."

How did this evening go sideways so quickly? "Sunny, I'm only concerned about your mother. I don't want to see her get hurt. But you and I need to talk, too. I thought we were getting along well."

Sunny shifted her backpack. "That's when I thought you and Mom were just going to date."

"We've barely even gotten to *that* stage." Bennett shook his head. Not by his choice, but due to his respect for Ivy and her process. He understood her need to prove herself. And she was. *Patience*, he told himself, though at times it was painful for him.

"Exactly my point," Sunny said, putting a hand on her hip. "So why are you suddenly taking over like you're my dad? Carving the turkey with Grandpa. Telling Mom who she can and can't rent rooms to, nosing around in her money."

Bennett held up his hands. "Whoa right there. I'm not interested in your mother's money, only her financial security."

"Kind of sounds like the same thing to me."

"It's definitely not."

"Anyway, Dad was like that." Sunny tossed her hair back in frustration. "Watching every penny in Mom's household account while he spent whatever he wanted. She drove the ratty car while Dad whizzed around in his new Mercedes. She said she didn't mind. Said they were saving for our college. Except she was the only one economizing—he wasn't. But then, neither was I. Still, it wasn't just about the stuff. I've learned that now. Mom cared for us and our home, while Dad just threw money at problems."

Bennett had suspected that. Sunny seemed to have had a complicated relationship with her father.

Sunny threw up her hands. "I loved my dad, but he could be super old school, and not in a good way. I used to think it was because he was from France, but now I know better. I see things differently now. And Mom doesn't deserve to be treated like this."

Bennett considered this. It helped to understand how Sunny thought. "I'm really not like that. Your mother is a force, and I respect her and everything she has done." As he said that, he realized he might have been in the wrong—but for the right reasons. "When my wife was living, we shared everything. Marriage should be a true partnership."

"Hold it right there," Sunny said, raising her voice. "No one said anything about getting married. You guys can date or whatever you call it at your age, but you're not replacing my father."

"No one can ever replace him in your heart," Bennett said gently. "And now, your mother is free to make choices for her happiness, even if those decisions don't include me. She's still a young woman."

Sunny expressed a puff of air. "Right. She's forty-five."

"If life were a football game, that's only half-time, kid. Your grandparents are taking off to sail around the world."

"I know. It's unbelievable. Though my friends think that's kind of cool." Sunny heaved a great sigh. "Can we talk about something else?"

"Sure, but I hope we'll come back to this conversation. I truly care for your mother, Sunny." Bennett turned toward the rear door. "I'm going to turn in early, so why don't you go back and give your mother a hand?"

"Oh, stop it." Sunny grabbed his sleeve. "If I go out there

alone, I'll get blamed for driving you away. Even if she did tell you to go to your room."

"I haven't heard that one in a long time," Bennett said, chuckling.

"This doesn't mean I'm giving you a pass." Sunny shook her finger at him. "You be careful around my mom."

"I will. Scout's honor."

Sunny frowned. "I have no idea what that means, but let's go."

When Bennett and Sunny returned to the ballroom, everyone was in high spirits. Shelly had put on Christmas music, Sterling had arrived and was helping his wife arrange another tabletop village, and Nick was unwrapping items. Gilda had come downstairs with her Chihuahua, and Pixie was zipping around sniffing the tree and crates.

Imani bustled through the front door, followed by her son Jamir, who was studying pre-med at the university. In her arms, Imani carried a bouquet of flowers and greenery.

"Wow, look at all this," Imani exclaimed. "I brought holly with red berries, bay laurel, and seeded eucalyptus, along with roses, crimson lilies, ranunculus, and dahlias. I love all these red hues. Thought they'd give the foyer a festive look."

"Why, these are lovely," Ivy said. "And smell delicious. Shelly, could you—"

"On it," Shelly said. "I know just the vase for those." She hurried toward the butler's pantry.

"Would you like to join us?" Bennett asked.

Ivy glanced over her shoulder, allowing him the faintest of smiles. One corner of her mouth twitched, and she turned back to Imani and Jamir.

That was a start, Bennett thought. But he had a long way to go to claw back into her heart. Maybe he had been too heavy-handed in his treatment of Nick.

While Ivy chatted with Imani, Bennett busied himself by bringing in more crates from the storeroom. As he did, he made mental notes of anything that Ivy might need. He'd call a buddy who supplied firewood and have some delivered. One crate held numerous candlestick holders. He could stop by Nailed It or Antique Times to get candles.

Another crate had a variety of what his sister called knick-knacks. Bennett swallowed his pride and helped Nick unwrap pieces—and he took care not to quiz the young man.

Nick gazed around the room. "Seeing everyone helping each other is inspiring. I appreciate being part of this."

Bennett bit his lip. "That's what Summer Beach is all about. Neighbors helping neighbors."

"That's what I've heard." Nick unwrapped a glittery oval piece, its red enamel shimmering under the lights of the chandelier. "What a beauty this is. Think this would look good on top of that bookshelf?"

"Sure," Bennett replied. Maybe the guy was okay after all, but he was still going to keep his eye on him. "I'll bring in more crates and boxes. There's still a lot out there."

Nick stared at the sparkly knick-knack, admiring it. "This beauty needs a place of honor." He placed it on top of a bookshelf where a chandelier shone on it, bringing it to life. "Need a hand with those crates?"

Bennett saw Ivy watching him from across the room. "I'd like that," he said, gesturing for Nick to follow him. He'd do whatever he had to do to get back in Ivy's good graces.

CHAPTER 8

"*C*an you stay until Christmas?" Ivy asked, as soon as she'd greeted Poppy. Their niece, who'd gone to the University of Southern California, had been handling a marketing job for an animal rescue organization in Los Angeles. She'd also been working on campaigns for her cousin Elena, and Elena's friend, Fianna, a fashion designer.

"I'm yours through the holidays until January." Poppy peeled off her ivory knit cap, triggering enough static electricity to make her silky blond hair fly up. She laughed and brushed it down. "I disseminated press releases and set up the holiday rescue advertising campaigns. I can monitor everything online from here."

"I thought I heard you arrive," Shelly said, racing down the stairs. "You look fabulous." She enveloped her niece in a big hug and twirled her around.

"Courtesy of my fashion client." Poppy wore a nubby, ivory Irish sweater that she'd paired with cream-colored denim jeans. "Fianna is from Ireland, and she imports these fabulous sweaters."

"Having you here will be like summer again," Ivy said.

"Yes, and Thanksgiving was amazing, too. But I couldn't

miss our first Christmas at the inn," Poppy said. "I'm looking forward to relaxing and doing yoga in the mornings."

Ivy turned to Shelly. "You didn't tell her, did you?"

"Not exactly," Shelly said. Sheepishly, she turned to Poppy. "Actually, we have a new campaign we need you to work on."

"Well, so much for catching up on my favorite authors' new books." Poppy laughed and parked her suitcase by the front door. "What do you need?"

"Come on back to the library," Ivy said.

"How about a Sea Breeze?" Shelly asked. "My new holiday edition has a splash of pomegranate juice. Virgin or fully loaded?"

"It was a long drive from L.A.," Poppy said. "But it sounds like we're working, so I'll save the lightly loaded version until later."

"You got it. One virgin juice cocktail coming up." Shelly hurried to the kitchen.

As they made their way to the library, Ivy told Poppy about their idea to attract holiday business.

Poppy tucked her hair behind her ear. "So, you want to appeal to people who have nowhere else to go for the holidays?"

"Exactly," Ivy said. "We want to start a new tradition for people so they won't have to be alone."

"Okay, so we can target singles. Do you have a preference for women or men or people of a certain age?"

"I don't think it matters—unless they're sharing a room."

"We can target those by gender." Poppy nodded. "I'll create ads by demographic group, and it would help if Shelly could write some blog posts or create a video."

"She's working on some, so let's ask her."

Poppy smiled. "I think this is a great idea."

Ivy turned on the computer, and she and Poppy began sharing ideas about ad text and target geographic areas. By the time Shelly returned, they had already created the first ad.

Shelly leaned over their shoulder and read. "Alone for the holidays? Be a part of Seabreeze Inn's holiday celebrations, where our family is your family." Shelly grinned and gave Poppy a tall, fresh drink. "How about my idea of Christmas for one?"

"That's a good headline." Poppy squeezed lime into her drink and took a sip. "How's this? 'Now through New Year's Day. Single rooms and suites. Ask about our affordable share-a-room holiday program.'"

Ivy raised her eyebrows. "Do you think people will respond to that idea?"

"We'll see," Poppy said. "Can't hurt, right?"

Ivy leaned toward the computer screen. "Let's add our activities. Yoga, beach walks, painting classes…"

"How about Christmas cookie baking?" Poppy asked. "Or a gingerbread workshop?"

"I vote for gingerbread," Shelly said. "And we need more holiday activities. How about Christmas carols in the library? I bet some of Celia's students would like to practice and pick up tips during the winter school break."

"Bennett said there's a holiday boat parade," Ivy said. "Owners decorate their boats with lights and cruise the coast. Guests can gather on the beach to watch."

"Or by the fire pit," Poppy said, typing as they spoke. "They could roast marshmallows, and we could serve Grandma's Mexican hot chocolate. Made with cinnamon and a little ancho chili powder."

Shelly snapped her fingers. "We can also serve our traditional *Ponche Navideño* for Christmas. Guests can help slice fruit for the hot punch."

"You just don't want to do that part," Ivy said, laughing. She loved sharing their mother's traditional Christmas recipes.

"Do we want to serve a Christmas feast?" Poppy asked.

Ivy and Shelly looked at each other. "I think we're going to have to feed our guests," Ivy said. "Restaurants in Summer Beach are probably closed for Christmas."

Shelly nodded. "I can ask Mitch to cater it. He could prepare dishes ahead of time, and we can serve it buffet-style. Turkey and all the trimmings. Mom always likes to make tamales—we can serve those, too."

"I'll take pie duty," Poppy said. "I've gotten pretty good at pies."

"You could sell those at the farmers market," Shelly said.

Poppy chuckled. "I think I'll be busy enough here."

Ivy ticked off points on her notepad. "Since we celebrate on Christmas Eve with family, let's plan a Christmas Day brunch. An open house for anyone from Summer Beach." She paused. "But I don't think we can serve the entire community. Much as I like Mitch, that would be too expensive."

"Guests would probably be stuffed by the time they get here," Shelly said. "Or, you could make it a potluck day, and residents could share their holiday specialties."

"Now, that would be fabulous," Ivy said, adding a note on her list.

The three women continued to work, putting together a plan of special events for the holiday season and determining what they would need.

"With all the food, supplies, and extra electricity, we might have to charge a little more per room," Poppy said.

Ivy tapped her pencil. "I'll add up all these supplies, but let's try to keep it reasonable."

"We need merch," Shelly said.

Ivy frowned. "What?"

"Merchandise," Shelly said. "You know, T-shirts, caps, and beach towels. We could create a little boutique in the parlor."

Poppy's eyes brightened. "How about hand-painted Christmas ornaments? Aunt Ivy, I bet you could do that. If you teach me how, I could help."

Ivy smiled. "Poppy, you're a genius. I can paint T-shirts and teach guests how to make keepsake ornaments, too."

"Kind of like summer camp," Shelly added. "Only it's Christmas camp."

"Poppy, could you pull up the calendar?" Ivy asked. "I want to see when Hanukkah is this year." Poppy did, and Ivy made a few more notes. "We'll make latkes and all the trimmings, too. Maybe Mitch can make jelly doughnuts." She smiled at the thought. "This is going to be great. Winter at the Seabreeze Inn—who knew it could be so much fun?"

"What could possibly go wrong?" Shelly said.

"Shh!" Ivy swatted Shelly's arm. "Remember Halloween? Don't jinx it."

Ivy recalled the Halloween sleepover they'd hosted for a local girl's club, complete with ghost stories, popcorn, and bobbing for apples. The girls had slept in the attic rooms, while Ivy insisted that the parents stay in guest rooms downstairs. She offered a pay-what-you-like option and welcomed parents who otherwise couldn't afford to stay. One brought fresh-baked bread, and another gave her one of the beautiful hand-poured candles they made and sold at the farmers market.

The girls had laughed and giggled and screamed. They were so excited that they couldn't settle down. In the middle of the night, Ivy and Shelly moved Gilda to an outdoor sunset suite because Pixie was barking and howling at the girls. They also relocated Imani and Jamir so they could get some rest, too. Still, it was a special event those girls would never forget, and everyone laughed about it the next morning. *Thank goodness.*

"I'll create some short video clips," Shelly said. "If I start now, I can have a couple ready for Poppy to post ads this afternoon before our tree trimming party. Who's dressing up for this?"

"Sounds like fun," Poppy said. "Fianna insisted I take a

couple of sample outfits from her new collection. Aunt Ivy, you should dress up, too. And there's another surprise—Elena is driving down for the night. She said she has a client in town that she's going to see tomorrow."

"I just love you guys," Ivy said, feeling relieved at how her ideas were coalescing into a solid plan. However, she'd feel better once a few reservations came in.

By the time the sun was low in the sky, Ivy had completed her cost estimates, and Poppy had turned on their ads and sent news to the bloggers and nearby media on her list.

Ivy hurried upstairs to change. She hadn't given a thought to what she would wear as Poppy and Shelly had, but for the first Christmas here, Ivy wanted to look festive, too. After a quick bath in the large claw-foot tub, she toweled off and pinned up her hair, leaving soft tendrils around her face.

In the adjoining dressing room with mirrored closet doors, Ivy chose a soft crimson blouse. The loose silk top skimmed her waist, camouflaging her muffin-top middle, which persisted even though she enjoyed walking and yoga. Staying healthy and building her business were her priorities now. She pulled on a pair of flowing black palazzo pants with an elastic waist that she'd bought on a trip to Paris years ago when she and Jeremy had visited his parents.

She slipped on black heels, Amelia's modest ruby ring, and dangly garnet earrings. Not bad, she thought, appraising her outfit in the mirror.

As she came downstairs, she saw Bennett in the foyer talking to Poppy. His gaze rose to meet her, and his expression was all the approval she needed—not that she needed any, she quickly reminded herself. Still, she felt good, and it was nice to know that he thought she looked good—even if she was still perturbed.

"You look gorgeous," Poppy said, who was wearing a slim, ice-blue cocktail dress that fell to mid-calf and showed off her lean figure.

"Thank you," Ivy said, hugging her niece.

"I'm afraid Poppy beat me to it," Bennett said. "But I couldn't help it. You took my breath away."

Ivy suppressed a smile, though she enjoyed hearing that. "You look nice, too," she allowed.

Actually, Bennett looked more than nice, though she didn't want to blow up his ego until he'd properly apologized. He wore perfectly-cut dark slacks and a white shirt with a fine, herringbone-patterned sport coat that fit perfectly. A burgundy silk pocket square was tucked into his breast pocket. She liked this unexpected, sophisticated look for the beach-town mayor.

Everyone they'd invited to the tree-trimming began to arrive. Their parents, as well as Flint and Forrest, and their families. Imani and Jamir were there, along with Gilda, who was clutching Pixie. The Chihuahua wore a jaunty red bow on his collar. Mitch stood by the tree talking to Nick, who had thrown a denim jacket over his blue jeans but still wore sandals, even though the temperature was dipping near-freezing tonight.

It's the beach, Ivy reminded herself.

Violin music was coming from the ballroom. Bennett held out his arm. "May I? Celia is here with one of her proteges."

Poppy's eyes lit at the gesture. With a small sigh, Ivy slipped her hand lightly into the crook of Bennett's arm, but not close enough to give him any ideas.

Through the crowd, Elena waved. Ivy wondered who her niece's client was.

"Excuse me, I'd like to speak to Elena," Ivy said to Bennett.

Bennett patted her hand. "I'll check in with Mitch and Nick."

Ivy watched him walk toward the other two men. Bennett had made an effort to get along with Nick last night. But was he only doing that to appease her? She turned toward Elena, who looked chic in a black sweater and long skirt. Her short dark hair framed bright blue eyes, and a discreet blue diamond nose stud sparkled with brilliant fire.

"Aunt Ivy," Elena said, greeting her with a hug.

"It's so wonderful to see you again, sweetheart," Ivy said. "I spoke with Honey earlier today, and she said that she and Gabe just bought their airline tickets. I'm so thrilled they're coming for the holidays." Ivy missed her eldest sister, who had been such a large influence on her life.

Elena smiled. "Usually, I fly to Sydney, but my business has been on fire, so Mom and Dad decided to come here. They also wanted to see Grandma and Grandpa before they sail away."

"I'm so glad you could make it tonight," Ivy said. "Poppy said you have an important client in Summer Beach. We're dying to know who it is."

"I would have thought you'd guessed. Her daughter got married here."

Ivy lowered her voice. "Carol Reston? Well done, you. I hope she's a good client for you." The world-class, Grammy-award winning singer had also performed at the Seabreeze Inn—once for her daughter's wedding and again at the art festival.

"She's very generous with her friends," Elena said. "I made several custom pieces for her." Elena gazed around the room. "The antique decorations you and Aunt Shelly discovered are gorgeous."

"With your appreciation for design, I thought you'd find them interesting. Maybe something here will inspire you."

Elena's gaze traveled up to the top of the bookshelf. "That red enameled piece is unusual."

Ivy followed Elena's gaze. "We found that in a crate along

with the other ornaments. Nick placed it there, and I rather like it."

Elena stared at it a moment longer. "This house has had some amazing gifts, hasn't it?"

"Indeed it has," Ivy said, lifting her gaze to the walls that sheltered them. "We've probably seen the end of Amelia's hidden treasures. I don't think there's any place on the property we haven't explored."

But that's what Ivy had thought before they'd discovered the narrow storage room disguised as a faux back wall of the garage. Ivy wondered if the entrance had been hidden during the Second World War or when Amelia closed the house a decade or so later. By the time the property manager or a worker had bolted the cabinet to the rear wall, the storeroom had probably been hidden for decades, its concealment long forgotten.

Elena turned, her attention drawn to the tabletop village that Carlotta and Sterling had arranged. "That's a lovely scene, too."

Ivy and Elena spoke a little longer, and then Mitch uncovered the appetizers he had brought, and everyone lined up in the dining room for the buffet. It was nothing fancy—turkey sliders, grilled potato wedges, and salad. Earlier that afternoon, Ivy and Shelly had also prepared two large pots of hearty vegetable stew with carrots, onions, potatoes, and peas —one vegetarian and one with chunks of beef. They still had pies from Thanksgiving for dessert.

Poppy and her cousins brought everything out from the kitchen. Tonight, instead of china from Amelia's collection in the butler's pantry, they used paper plates for easy clean-up. After everyone ate, they would trim the tree with the old ornaments. Bennett had borrowed a couple of tall ladders for the job.

Ivy's heart filled with gladness as she watched their family and guests move through the line. Snippets of conversation rose around the room. Misty asked Elena how she liked living in Los Angeles. Sunny was talking to Coral about how much she'd enjoyed her study in psychology, which Coral had majored in and was now practicing.

Mitch was still in deep conversation with Nick, telling him about his business. Mitch might have had a tough start in life, but he'd turned into a bona fide entrepreneur between Java Beach, which was open for breakfast and lunch, and his afternoon charter excursions for dolphin and whale watching. He was catering parties now, and Ivy wouldn't be surprised if he was working on another idea. Shelly stood beside him, just as focused on the conversation.

Nick asked a lot of questions, almost like a seasoned reporter, Ivy mused.

Bennett was beside her in line, though he was talking with Jamir about school. Ivy took the chance to catch up with her parents. After everyone scooped a plateful, the party filtered back into the ballroom.

Ivy and Shelly stood. "We want to thank you all for coming tonight," Shelly began. "This is the first time Ivy and I have had a chance to spend the holidays with our family in a very long time. Here's to our family," Shelly said, raising a glass of wine.

"And to our new friends," Ivy added. "Now, we'd like for our parents to hang the first ornaments."

Everyone cheered as Carlotta and Sterling rose and selected ornaments. Carlotta chose a silvery hand-painted bell, while Sterling chose a red sleigh. They stood next to the tree with the ornaments, and everyone took photos. With her parents looking so happy and animated, Ivy thought about what a lovely painting that would make.

Shelly turned up the music, and all the cousins and friends pitched in to help trim the tree. Ivy noticed that Nick hung back until Poppy handed him an ornament.

"With a family like this, you have to jump right in," Poppy said. "You must not come from a large family."

Nick shook his head. "A very small family," he replied with a trace of sadness in his voice.

At once, Ivy understood why Nick wanted to stay through Christmas. Most likely, he was alone. She wondered if his parents were living. Perhaps he'd share some details about his life. Or not. Though Ivy was curious about all their guests, she'd learned not to pry.

As the tree filled with ornaments, Ivy was in awe. The colors and array were astounding and represented years of collecting. She could just imagine Amelia and Gustav adding to their collection as they traveled. Perhaps they'd brought some cherished family pieces, or maybe they'd asked artists to create special commemorative ornaments.

Ivy felt a strange duty to look after what they'd found in those old crates. She might only bring these decorations out once a year, but it would be an annual connection and homage to the woman who'd taken great risks to save significant works of art and shelter people from danger. If only Alzheimer's hadn't robbed Amelia of her memories in her later years.

Even before residents of Summer Beach knew of the old house's hidden treasures, they held Amelia Erickson in high esteem for her generosity to the small community. She'd bought land and donated it to the city for parks and the children's center, among many other activities.

Ivy couldn't match Amelia's level of philanthropy, but she and Shelly could make the Seabreeze Inn a gathering place for the community. She couldn't wait to share the joy of the season.

Poppy was standing on a ladder, hanging a sweet little birdcage with a tiny red robin inside when her phone buzzed. As soon as she finished hanging the ornament, she descended the ladder and checked her phone.

Poppy let out a squeal. "The ads are working!"

Ivy rushed to her side and motioned for Shelly. "Did we get a query?"

"We got a reservation," Poppy cried. Her phone dinged again. "Make that two reservations!"

Carlotta beamed. "I knew you girls were onto a big idea. I predict that you'll soon have full occupancy."

"Just not tonight," Elena said, and everyone laughed.

Poppy opened the reservations. "One is for a private room, and one is for a shared room."

Ivy pressed her hand against her heart. "Thank goodness. My crazy idea might just work."

Shelly flung her arms around Ivy and Poppy. "What a team we are. Poppy, we've missed you."

Sunny stood and joined them. "As soon as school is out, I'll be here to help, too."

Ivy brought her youngest daughter into their group. "I'm always thrilled to have your help." Sunny had been helping out after Poppy left for Los Angeles, but there hadn't been much work. Instead, Ivy encouraged Sunny to focus on her last year of school.

Once the tree was decorated and most of the family had left, Ivy stood by the fireplace, watching how the fire danced and threw light across the glimmering ornaments. At the very top, Bennett had secured a beautiful crystal angel.

Sunny had gone to bed, Bennett had followed, and now only Shelly, Poppy, and Elena remained with her. They'd helped her put away the food and tidy the ballroom. Now, they'd all kicked off their shoes and were lounging on the sofas, transfixed by the majestic tree and sipping wine, unwinding after a long day of work.

An evening chill had crept into the house, and Ivy warmed her hands by the fireplace. "Thanks for picking up more wood, Shelly. I'd completely forgotten."

"I didn't get the firewood."

"Who did, then?" Ivy asked.

"While you were getting ready, I heard Bennett outside with a couple of guys. They were unloading a truck."

Ivy blinked. "There's more outside?"

"It's stacked in the back," Poppy said. "Looks like enough for the entire winter. I figured you knew about it."

Pressing her lips together in consternation, Ivy wondered how much that had cost. She sure wished Bennett had asked her first.

Swinging her legs up onto the sofa, Elena leaned back and gazed up toward the bookshelf. "That piece up there has such brilliance. Mind if I look at it?"

"Go ahead," Ivy said. "It's a pretty rhinestone piece."

Elena padded across the hardwood floors and reached for the piece, but she couldn't quite get it.

Shelly bounced off the other sofa. "I'm a little taller. I think I can reach it." She stretched her hand toward the oval knick-knack. "Almost." She scooted a nearby ottoman over and stood on it. Her fingertips just touched the sparkling piece.

Shelly barely managed to push the piece to the edge of the top shelf. "I can just get it now." Her ankles wobbled on the soft ottoman, and she cried, "Watch out!"

Elena flung out her hands to catch the falling piece, but she was too late. The piece hit the rug and bounced, splitting open.

"Oh, no," Elena cried. "I broke it."

As half the piece came to rest, a tiny bird rolled out.

Elena picked up another portion that had been dislodged and had fallen out of the piece. Kneeling on the rug, Elena passed a hand over her face, which had gone pale.

"Elena, are you okay?" Ivy asked.

Looking up, Elena cleared her throat. Her voice wavered as she spoke. "Aunt Ivy, Aunt Shelly. You need to see this right away."

CHAPTER 9

*I*vy knelt on the rug next to Elena, examining the sparkling, red enamel piece that her niece had given her. It just fit in her hand.

"It doesn't look broken," Ivy said, trying to comfort Elena, who seemed shaken. "That could've happened to anyone. I'm always climbing up on wobbly chairs to get something. It's a wonder I don't break my neck."

"No, look closer," Elena said. In her other hand, she held a tiny piece dislodged from the oval-shaped decorative item. A golden nest, exquisitely portrayed. A delicate bird with glittering red wings. She fixed her vivid blue eyes on Ivy. "Look at what you called rhinestones."

By the light of the flicking fire, Ivy peered closer. She turned over the oval-shaped piece, which had burst open on impact. "It's so ornate. The outside is beautiful, but what's surprising is the inside is just as finished." Her neck began tingling with a strange sensation. "These stones…"

"Are definitely not rhinestones," Elena finished. "Diamonds and rubies, I would say, and very fine enamel work. None of the stones are large, but the design is beautifully whimsical. An outstanding work of art. You don't see pieces like this very often. I'd like to look at this closer tomorrow."

"It must be valuable." Ivy sat back on her heels. "I wonder why it was packed away with the Christmas decorations?"

Shelly and Poppy knelt beside them, and Ivy passed the gemstone encrusted piece to Shelly.

"Think about it," Shelly said. "The house staff would have packed and stored the decorations. Because it's red, maybe a new member of the staff thought this was part of the Christmas things."

Poppy made a face. "Someone probably lost their job because of this."

"Unless Amelia wasn't well and didn't notice it," Ivy said.

"Someone on the staff surely would have." Poppy shook her head. "Unless they were planning to come back for it."

"I'm glad that didn't happen." Elena gave Poppy the piece that had fallen out.

"This would make a beautiful pendant," Poppy said, holding it up to her ivory sweater. "Like a gift within a gift."

Elena's lips parted. "A gift...this reminds me of Fabergé's imperial eggs. Part of their appeal was that each one held a surprise gift inside. People have called the eggs the most expensive gift wrapping in the world."

Ivy pressed a finger to her lips in thought. "The diamond tiara we found was by Fabergé—or rather, August Holmström, one of the jeweler's master workers. If there's an AH mark on this, then it was one his creations—or his son's, who used the same mark."

"Yes, but there were other master workers under Peter Carl Fabergé," Elena said. "Michael Perchin created many of the early eggs, as I recall."

Shelly ran her fingers over rows of gemstones. "If this is a Fabergé, then it has to be worth a lot." She handed it back to Elena.

"The value would be in its history and relation to the Russian imperial family," Elena said. "Some of the Fabergé eggs are still missing—half a dozen or so. But the company made similar eggs for others, including the Rothschild family, as well as a Russian industrialist. I'll have to do some research on this."

Elena opened the glittering oval container again. "First, you'll want to authenticate the materials and research any works that might be missing."

"I can help with that," Poppy said.

Shelly pursed her lips. "This is probably part of the stolen crown jewels collection we found."

"In that case, I'd better call Ari again." Ivy sighed. Ari Steinberg had handled all the identification, tracing, and collection of the crown jewels and the paintings they'd found.

Ivy knew they couldn't get too attached to this piece as the probability was high that it was on the FBI's stolen property list. The jewelry they'd found sewn into a large doll in the trunk of the old Chevrolet had been returned to the rightful owners, as had the masterpiece paintings they'd discovered on the sealed lower level.

"Aw, do we have to?" Shelly made a face. "I think we deserve a Christmas gift after all we've been through. Besides, old Humpty Dumpty there had a great fall."

Ivy couldn't help chuckling at that. "If it's someone else's property, we can't keep it."

"I'll inspect this in the morning," Elena said, holding up the decorative egg. "I have to meet Carol Reston to give her the necklaces she commissioned, and she insisted I stay for lunch. I'd planned on driving straight back to Los Angeles, but I can push some appointments and stay over another night." Elena's eyes sparkled. "I'd really like to see what this is all about."

"Could that egg-thingie be a copy?" Shelly asked.

Elena lifted a shoulder. "Anything is possible. That's why you'd need an expert to authenticate this piece. I can inquire —discreetly, of course."

"I wonder if there are any similar pieces packed away," Poppy said.

"We went through everything but the gardening supplies," Shelly said. "Those are next, but I wouldn't expect to find much on that side of the storeroom except old rakes and shovels."

Ivy's gaze traveled up the tree. "Did anyone notice ornaments that were particularly stunning? There could be other items."

Shelly swayed. "You're kidding, right? You want to go over that entire tree with a jeweler's loupe?"

"All I'm saying is that I think we should check everything more closely," Ivy said.

Elena laughed. "All the ornaments I saw were hand-painted on glass or made of other materials."

"I can check out the tree tomorrow," Poppy said.

"We have other priorities right now," Ivy said. "We need to concentrate on advertising, getting reservations, and finishing the holiday activity plan."

Ivy knew it was one thing to make a list, but quite another to execute it. She was relieved that Poppy had returned, but they had priorities. "I'll put in a call to Ari in the morning. If that piece is authentic, then we need to rule out stolen property first."

THE NEXT DAY, IVY GOT UP EARLY TO LAY OUT BREAKFAST IN the dining room for guests. With a stockpile of firewood now, she put a few logs in the dining room fireplace and started a fire to knock off the chill in the large room. While Poppy was in Los Angeles, she and Shelly had been alternating mornings. She hurried into the kitchen to put out the juice and yogurt, start the coffee, and arrange the cranberry muffins that Mitch had left last night for the morning.

When she returned to the kitchen, she saw Elena at the

kitchen table and greeted her. Her niece was having a cup of coffee and scrutinizing the oval-shaped decorative piece with her loupe.

"See anything else interesting?" Ivy asked.

"Take a look at this, Aunt Ivy." Elena handed her the small magnifying glass. "Hold it to your eye and then adjust the distance of the piece."

Ivy leaned over to inspect the piece. As she brought the glittery egg into focus, the red enamel work blazed in her field of vision. "The depth of this enamel is amazing."

Elena gulped her coffee. "I have to meet Carol soon, but check out the gemstones and look at the workmanship."

"This is incredible," Ivy said as the stones and settings leapt out at her. "How in the world do they execute such perfect details?"

"Whoever created this was dedicated to excellence. It's one of the finest pieces I've ever seen."

Ivy lowered the magnifier and handed it back to Elena. "Do you think it's the real deal?"

Elena quirked her lips to one side. "Oh, it's real, but we still have a lot to learn. I made notes of the hallmarks. Take some close-up photos to email to Ari. I'll do more research after I meet with Carol."

Ivy was pleased that her niece was having success. "I'm glad Carol is a good client."

"She is," Elena said. "I met her through Penelope, who wore my designs on the red carpet. Hollywood can be a pretty small town."

"I remember that incident. You got a lot of publicity over that. How are you and that good-looking insurance investigator getting along?"

"Jake and I are doing just fine," Elena said, breaking into a smile. "Speaking of insurance, I doubt your policy would cover an item such as this. I have a feeling this could be worth a lot more than we think. Make sure you put it in a safe place, Aunt Ivy."

"Safety deposit box at the bank?"

"Perfect." Elena drained her coffee and deposited the cup in the sink. She picked up her bag and hugged Ivy. "Get a lot of photos before you lock it up."

After Elena left, Ivy took out her phone and snapped a series of photographs from every angle. The artistry gleamed in the morning sun, looking even more stunning in the light. She ran her hand over the intricate work. "What's your story?" she murmured. It seemed that everything in this old house had a fascinating link to the past.

Ivy sat down and gazed at the piece with her artist's eye, appreciating the color, design, and creativity that had gone into it. Being in the presence of such craftsmanship was a joy. Not many people understood how such artistry stirred her. She touched it with reverence.

Finally, Ivy leaned back in her chair and blew out a breath. As much as she would love to keep this beauty, she had to do the right thing. She found Ari's email address at the FBI, tapped a quick note, attached photos, and sent it.

That's it. She scrubbed her hands over her face. A possible fortune sat before her on the kitchen table, yet she worried about the electricity bill. And they had to have sufficient reservations to make the planned holiday events worthwhile.

Ivy glanced at the clock. Bennett must be running late. He usually ran on the beach, showered, then stopped by for breakfast. She peered outside to see if she could get a glimpse of him.

Ivy was surprised to see him getting into his SUV. He hadn't even come inside for breakfast. Since summer, they'd seen each other every morning for breakfast, and she looked forward to it. She stood by the window, her fingers pressed against the cool pane, though he didn't even cast a look in her direction.

Then she remembered that she was mad at him for interfering in her business. With a huff, she slid her phone into her jeans pocket and pulled her sweater around her cotton turtleneck.

She had too much work to do to worry about Bennett Dylan.

After putting the gleaming, gemstone-encrusted egg into the pantry for temporary safekeeping, Ivy made her way into the dining room. She stopped to greet Imani and Jamir, who were the only guests there.

"What a lovely fire we have this morning," Imani said. "That scent always reminds me of Christmas."

"I'm glad you like it," Ivy said. Having a fire in the fireplace did make it feel cozy and welcoming. She moved the pine branches from the mantle to a sideboard—just in case.

As they were chatting, Nick sauntered in. He wore a T-shirt and hoodie with jeans and sandals, which seemed to be his standard uniform for the day.

"Good morning, Nick," Ivy said.

"Thank you for including me in the tree-trimming party last night," Nick said with a little nod as he greeted each one of them. White wisps of hair escaped his darker ponytail, and he tucked the strands behind his ear. "The event meant a lot to me. You have a large, impressive family, Ms. Bay."

"Ivy, please. And yes, I am indeed blessed."

"Would you like to join me for breakfast?" Nick pulled out a chair for her at the nearest table and gestured to it. "Please, have a seat. What would you like?"

Ivy laughed. "I'm usually the one serving others." She had a lot of work to do today, but she could spend a few minutes with him. That was part of the job, and she enjoyed it.

"I insist," he said.

"Those cranberry muffins are yummy. I'll have one, and I'll bring a pot of coffee."

Nick returned with a plate full of muffins, blueberry and

strawberry yogurt, a double heaping of granola, and a large orange juice. For Nick's size, he seemed to eat a lot, and then the thought crossed her mind that maybe he didn't have money for food.

It had been almost a week since Nick arrived, and he still hadn't rendered any form of payment for his room. She hated to admit that Bennett might have been right about him.

They spoke a little, and after Imani and Jamir left, Ivy picked at her muffin. "Nick, I want you to know how much we enjoy having you here, and I'm glad that you chose the Seabreeze Inn." She shifted uncomfortably. "I heard that you attended Mitch's Thanksgiving dinner."

Nick smiled pleasantly. "I believe I mentioned that."

Ivy felt flustered. She'd never had a deadbeat guest at the inn. Yet, with Nick's refined manners, he didn't fit the mold— not that she knew, of course. She had to address this situation.

"I was wondering if you're able to make payment arrangements for the room yet?"

"I'm working on it," Nick replied pleasantly. He picked up the coffee carafe and poured more coffee in her mug. "More cream?"

"Yes, please." Maybe she should tell him to leave now, but she couldn't bring herself to do that if he were really in need. After all, it was Christmas. If he didn't have any family and ended up on the street, she'd never forgive herself. It wasn't as if the inn was full, and what was one more person over the holidays?

"I want you to know that you're welcome here," she began. "If you're having any financial difficulties, we can make arrangements."

"That's very nice of you to do that for guests."

"Well, it's Christmas, isn't it?"

He glanced around the dining room. A hand-painted St. Nicolas and trimmings from the pine tree graced the mantle above the fireplace. "Sure looks like it."

"We've only been in business for a few months. Shelly and I didn't expect it to be this slow during the holidays. We have plenty of work around here, and we can always use an extra hand."

"I will be happy to help you with anything you like."

This conversation wasn't going as Ivy had hoped, but at least she knew where they stood. She laid her palms on the table, relieved at his agreement. "I appreciate that. Well, I suppose that's settled. What are your talents, Nick? You could help Poppy with ads or Shelly with gardening. I have some decorating to do."

"I always had a keen interest in science."

"Science...that would be Shelly's department." Her sister was going to kill her for this, but she could use the help. "She has some tree trimming and planting that she's planning."

"Is that trimming with decorations?"

"Maybe that, too, but I meant trimming as in pruning branches. The entire grounds and trees were a dreadful mess when we moved it." Ivy didn't mention that her husband had let the yard and gardens go while he had it. "Shelly's a horti-culturist, which she calls a blend of science and art."

"This is a unique opportunity, indeed," Nick said, steepling his hands.

As he did, Ivy noticed how smooth his hands were. His fingers were long and tapered—probably more suited to playing piano than sawing limbs and digging holes for trees. She'd be surprised if Nick had ever held a shovel. He was a different sort; he was well-spoken and calm, and this soothed Ivy, too.

Shelly had gone out on errands, so Ivy would tell her sister about her new helper when she returned. Ivy rose from the table. "I'll let Shelly know, and I'm sure she'll reach out to get started."

"One more thing, please," Nick said, rising as she did.

"Yes?"

"What I've heard about the history of this house is fascinating. You mentioned Amelia and Gustav Erickson. Do you have any photographs or written history about them or the house?"

Ivy had grown accustomed to people hearing about the house because of news reports on the discovery of the paintings and crown jewels.

"We have an old photo album in the front parlor, and there's a book from the Summer Beach Historical Society. I'll leave them on the table in the parlor for you to look at."

"Thank you," Nick said. As she walked away, she noticed he went back to the buffet for seconds.

She wondered if Nick would stick around now that she'd asked him to work in exchange for his room. Shelly might explode, but Ivy wasn't going to turn out a nice young man right before Christmas. She knew what it was like to lose your home. Besides, Amelia Erickson had a history of providing shelter to other. From wounded troops in the ballroom to refugees in the attic, her house had been a sanctuary for many.

Nick was staying, and that's all there was to it.

CHAPTER 10

*B*ennett strolled along the marina, enjoying the crisp breeze off the water. It was Saturday afternoon, and the sky was clear. Behind him, palm trees rustled in the wind. He enjoyed walking through the village and visiting shopkeepers and restaurateurs. He learned a great deal that way. Who was opening a new shop, who was getting married or having a baby, or who was struggling and might need a hand. As the mayor, he was there to serve his constituents.

Bennett stopped by the old sport fishing boat that Mitch had equipped with long benches and inside seating to accommodate charters.

"Permission to come aboard," Bennett called out.

Mitch climbed up from below deck wearing an old sweatshirt and jeans. His spiky blond hair stuck out at weird angles, and he brushed his hand over his head, ruffling his hair even more. "How's it going, Mr. Mayor?"

"Getting ready for the opening of the Christmas market in the village square tonight."

Bennett stepped onto the boat and greeted Mitch with a warm bro hug. Mitch was like the younger brother he'd never had. "Chief Paula is bringing the fire department's vintage truck to decorate, Axe Woodson is organizing the *a cappella* carolers, and Nan and Arthur are organizing the shopkeepers."

"Even without snow, Summer Beach is my favorite place to spend Christmas," Mitch said. He pulled a couple of guava juice drinks from a nearby cooler. "Want one?"

"Sure," Bennett said, and Mitch tossed him a can. "In the past, we've trucked in snow from the mountains for the kids. No snowfall yet, though."

The two men eased onto aft benches and opened their drinks. Bennett took a swig and lifted his face to the salty breeze. Though the wind was cool, the sun was warm on his skin. "This is the life, isn't it?"

"Best one I've ever known." Mitch grinned. "Even the whales head this way. Word is the gray whales are migrating now. They've been spotted up north. Thousands of those beauties making their way all the way from Alaska to Baja California. That's why I'm getting this old vessel cleaned up. I'm already getting calls for charters."

"You did well last year with that, didn't you?"

"It was a good year. This year should be, too, as long as that part I'm waiting on isn't back-ordered again. Can you use another hand on your boat for the parade?"

"It's more fun that way," Bennett said, grinning at his friend.

Mitch tipped his drink back. "Seems the inn has been pretty quiet. Bakery orders are way down."

"Maybe not for long," Bennett said. "Ivy and Shelly started a special winter deal. I saw a couple of new guests already." He hoped they'd be able to make it through the lean winter months.

"Good for them." Mitch paused. "How's Nick working out there? Shelly says he's helping her in the yard." He chuckled. "She wasn't too happy about it at first, but now I think she's glad for the help."

"Can't quite figure him out." Bennett shook his head. "But he seems harmless, and he's there to stay for a while."

Mitch inclined his head. "That's what I thought when I rolled into town, too. And now look at me." He fist-bumped Bennett. "Hey, we should invite Nick on the boat for the parade. He seems like a good guy, and I bet it would mean a lot to him."

Feeling a little put on the spot, Bennett shifted uncomfortably. And yet, Mitch was right. "Go ahead. Why don't you ask him?"

"Will do."

Bennett and Mitch chatted a little longer, and then Bennett moved on to the next boat owners. Most of the people there today were decorating their boats for the annual Christmas light parade. He stopped to speak to Tyler, who was rigging up an animated Santa display on his boat. After talking with Tyler, Bennett continued to his boat at the far end of the marina.

Satisfied that everything was in order, Bennett left the marina and started back through the village toward the inn. It was a healthy walk, but it felt good to be out. As he passed Blossoms, he saw Imani wave to him. A thought came to him, and he jogged across the street.

"What's the hurry?" Imani asked. She wore a holly-red sweater over a long tie-dyed skirt with low heeled boots.

"I need something extra special," he said, perusing the cut flowers Imani had displayed in aluminum watering cans and brightly-colored buckets.

"What's the occasion?"

Bennett winced. "Let's call it a *mea culpa* peace offering."

Imani shook her head. "Has to be for Ivy, am I right?"

"You got it."

"Hmm. What'd you go and do this time?"

Bennet's mouth dropped open. "*This* time?"

Imani gave a hearty laugh. "You're trying to tell me this is the first time you've made a fool of yourself?"

"Well, no, but you don't have to be so blunt about it." He enjoyed sparring with Imani, though her words sure hit the mark. He shifted uncomfortably on his feet.

With a wink, Imani said, "You're a man. I have to be blunt. And it's my legal training."

"Okay, then." Passing a hand over his eyes, he said, "I might have questioned her judgment on something that wasn't any of my business."

"Ah-ha." Imani crossed her arms. "Then I'm afraid that would call for my best red roses. It's going to cost you, but I'll bet you're already paying the price, aren't you?"

"I'd asked her to go to the Christmas Stroll tonight, but she's not taking my calls or replying to my texts. I know she's had new guests arrive, so she's probably busy, but…yeah, I made a fool of myself." *And then some.* "It's quite possible— probable—that I insulted her intelligence and judgment."

"That calls for an even larger bouquet." Imani narrowed her eyes. "You do know you could just go upstairs, knock on her door, and apologize."

"Sure, but I figure an armful of flowers can't hurt. If the conversation turns ugly, I can hide behind them. So you'd better make it a huge bouquet." He held out his arms. *Yes, I'm a giant idiot.*

"I know just the thing," she said, plucking roses from a container.

Bennett sure hoped so. He'd made the date with Ivy—at least, in his mind, it was a date—before Thanksgiving. But she'd been so upset that he hadn't had a real chance to talk to her. Maybe he'd avoided her, too.

Yes, he had. They usually had breakfast together, but he figured he should let her cool off.

A few minutes later, he paid Imani for the largest floral

bouquet he'd ever seen. And now he had to walk through town with it.

Nan's husband Arthur was trimming a tree next to a pair of life-sized nutcrackers. He wore a Santa hat over his shaved head.

"Quite an impressive bouquet you have," Arthur said in his clipped English accent. Lowering his voice, he peered over his glasses. "Hope that makes up for whatever you did."

"How did you—?" Bennett stopped and shook his head.

"I've been married for a few decades," Arthur said. "I recognize the look in a man's eyes."

Bennett hadn't realized his stroll through the village would be a walk of shame.

As Bennett approached the inn, he heard laughter coming from the direction of the fire pit. He was curious, but he didn't want to be seen with the flowers, especially if Ivy were there. He raced upstairs to his apartment and deposited them in the sink. He wanted to give them to Ivy alone, not as part of a group, because those roses would be incomplete without an apology.

From his balcony, he saw a small gathering of people seated beside the fire.

Poppy spied him and waved. "Hi, Bennett. Come on over and meet our new guests."

Bennett made his way downstairs to them, and Poppy introduced him as the town's mayor. The guests had cranberry and ruby red grapefruit juice Sea Breezes, and spirits were high.

"And Bennett, I'd like you to meet our guests, Ophelia, Molly Ann, Rosamie, and Kristy." Poppy turned to an older woman who had bright eyes and glistening silver hair. "Ophelia drove in from L.A. She's a retired teacher and started a new career as a movie extra and model."

Ophelia laughed. "Who knew I could be a senior model? I

sort of fell into it, but I'm having the time of my life. This trip is a little reward for me."

"No kidding?" Molly Ann asked. "I'm a makeup artist, and I've worked a lot of sets."

"Is that a Southern accent I hear?" Ophelia asked.

"Georgia peach, through and through." Molly Ann clinked her glass to Ophelia's.

Poppy gestured to another woman. "This is Rosamie from Phoenix. She's an ER nurse."

Rosamie nodded. "This is my first vacation in three years, and it's so much fun to be with others who aren't attached. Where I come from, in the Philippines, we start celebrating Christmas in September."

"And this is Kristy," Poppy said, introducing a thirtyish woman with dark auburn hair and a cute sprinkle of freckles. "She's a pastry chef from Phoenix."

"We heard about the Christmas Stroll tonight in the village," Kristy said. "I'm ready to shop. Christmas is my favorite time of year, but this year, my ex-husband has the children, so it's always a little sad for me. I loved to bake with them because that's what my mother did when I was young. She inspired me to become a pastry chef."

Ophelia clasped her hand. "It's difficult to be alone this time of year."

Molly Ann took Kristy's other hand. "I never really had a family because I grew up in foster homes. I still see one of my foster moms, and although she's dedicated to the kids, it's not quite the same as having a natural-born family." She brightened. "The Santa Sprint caught my attention. We should do that together."

Bennett enjoyed meeting the new guests. "I'm in charge of the sprint next weekend. Sprinters and walkers are welcome. So are Santa hats and holiday costumes. Are you staying the week?"

"The room was such a great deal that I'm staying until

New Years," Molly Ann replied. "With daily yoga and beach walks, I'm going to greet the new year in great shape. Happy and relaxed." She turned Ophelia. "You should stay, too. There's an extra bed in my room, and Ivy said I might be sharing with a roommate. This is like winter camp for adults."

"I might do that," the other woman said, smiling at the idea. "I feel at home already. But I'd have to buy a few more clothes."

"You'll find a lot of good shops in the village for that," Bennett said. "They're all open late on the weekends for the Christmas Stroll. Be sure to bundle up. Even though we're at the beach and the sun shines during the day, it can get pretty chilly at night."

Rosamie shivered. "I drove in from Phoenix. Does it dip below freezing?"

"Not usually," he said. "Though it's cooler this year. Sometimes we have to turn on the air conditioner and light the fireplace."

Everyone laughed at the idea, but Bennett knew a couple of neighbors who did that. They liked the atmosphere of a fire crackling in the fireplace.

"I'm delighted to meet you all, and I hope you enjoy your stay in Summer Beach." Bennett was impressed with the number of new guests. The Bay family women sure knew how to produce results.

Poppy smiled at their new guests. "If you need our mayor for anything, you'll see him around a lot."

Bennett gestured to the apartment above the garage. "After my home was damaged in the Ridgetop fire, I was fortunate enough to find a room at the inn. I know you'll all enjoy it here. And I'll see you soon at the afternoon wine and tea event."

"We have a special guest tonight," Poppy said.

"One of Celia's music students?" Bennett asked.

Poppy's eyes sparkled. "I can't say. I'm to keep it a secret until the event. But you'll want to attend."

"Then I will." He hesitated. "Have you seen Ivy around?"

Poppy raised an eyebrow. "She's painting. You should proceed with caution."

He drew a deep breath. "Right." Bennett excused himself and raced back upstairs to retrieve the roses. After he'd thought about what Ivy said—and Sunny—he felt like a complete jerk. The last thing he wanted was to be lumped in the same category as Jeremy. He'd never thought much of the man, who had flaunted himself around Summer Beach when he first arrived with an overly made-up Paisley on his arm.

Ivy was a woman who deserved to be cherished and respected.

How could he help her to see that he was the man who would do that?

Bennett changed his shirt, then went into the bathroom to splash water on his face and freshen his cologne. He wasn't one to be nervous about much, though facing Ivy's continued rejection had him rattled. He might have been joking with Imani, but that was only to cover up his sorrow.

Since Ivy had come into his life, he felt as if he'd found his partner. His life had taken on new meaning and purpose that revolved around her. He hadn't felt this level of connection since his wife Jackie died.

In the kitchen, he picked up the bouquet of roses. Its sweet aroma was magical, and he hoped it would help spur Ivy's forgiveness. Summoning his courage, he made his way to the main house.

With one remark, one misstep, he stood to lose it all. That's how a demise began. He'd seen friends falter in relationships, never managing to work themselves back to where they'd been, to the joy that had once filled their heart and brightened their world. Love could be the strongest, most durable force on earth. But as with Achilles, the smallest of arrows plunged into a tender spot could bring it down. It was too easy for love to crumple in the winds of misgivings.

He prayed that was not the case now.

Carrying the fragrant bundle of roses that gave physical form to his apology, he stepped through the door of the enclosed sun porch where Ivy painted and taught her art classes. She was seated on a stool, dabbing paint on a row of ornaments on the table. It looked like a production line, and then he recalled the new boutique in the parlor that Poppy had mentioned.

"Excuse me," he began.

Ivy didn't move.

Bennett cleared his throat and tried again. No response. She was ignoring him. Nervous perspiration gathered around his neck.

His choices were few. He could turn and disappear from her life. Or he could let her know he had tried. He stepped into her field of vision and laid the flowers on the edge of the table where she worked and began to back away.

Catching his movement, Ivy lurched up, shock etched on her face. She pulled an earbud from her ear and fumbled to turn off the music on her phone. "I didn't hear you come in." As her gaze fell on the roses, she formed a small O with her lips.

"I've been waiting for you," she said softly, resting her brush on the edge of a jar of water.

At that moment, Bennett's fear dissipated, and he stepped toward her—the first step back into her world. "I have some apologizing to do."

Ivy hesitated, then she rose and threw her arms around him. As she did, she swept against her supplies, and the paintbrush cartwheeled through the air. In an instant, droplets of paint and water splattered their cheeks.

Bennett didn't care. Ivy was in his arms again, her luminous eyes searching his—waiting for more.

"Please forgive me," he whispered against her lips. "I should never have questioned you about your guests."

A small sigh escaped her lips. "You were right to be alert. I'd forgotten what it felt like to have someone truly interested in my well-being."

"I know we're not at that point in our relationship, but if we ever get there, I promise you, Ivy, I'm really not a jerk. I value and respect you. Believe it or not, I understand the meaning of a true partnership." If he had his way, he'd speed up this process, but with Ivy, he had to be patient.

Ivy pressed a paint-smeared finger against his lips. "I know you do. I didn't have the perfect marriage—as you and everyone in Summer Beach knows. But I have always yearned for the type of relationship my parents have. They are best friends, lovers, and protectors." She touched her lips to his. "This time, I will accept nothing less."

A surge of warmth spread through Bennett, and he basked in the light of her forgiveness. Wrapping her tightly in his arms, he swayed with her. "You have no idea how worried I have been."

As she looked up at him, a smile brought radiance to her ivy-green eyes. "Those roses are a fairly good indication. I'll bet Imani appreciated that nice sale."

Bennett threaded his fingers through her silky hair. "Am I that transparent?"

"Call it women's intuition." She leaned back. "Although I think you've forgotten our date."

So it was a date. "I haven't, but I didn't know if you'd still want to go with me on the Christmas Stroll." He lifted a golden-brown strand of hair from her forehead. "This is the beginning of our first Summer Beach Christmas. There's so much I want to share with you." *Like the rest of my life,* he thought, though it was too soon to say that.

"I like the sound of that," Ivy said. Laughing, she swiped a finger of paint across his cheek. "But I think we ought to clean up first. And I'll put the roses in water. Meet you downstairs in the foyer before tonight's gathering in the music room?"

"I heard there's a surprise at the wine and tea event tonight."

Ivy looked crestfallen. "Poppy didn't tell you, did she?"

"Try as I might, I couldn't chisel the secret out of her." Bennett wondered what she had planned.

As Bennett made his way through the hallway, he noticed a shopping bag from a local men's store outside of Nick's room. The bag stood open, and he peered inside. It contained a box of shoes and a few pairs of socks with a note that read, *A Gift for Nick Snow.*

Chastising himself, he stepped back. He'd promised Ivy he wouldn't pursue the inquisition of Nick anymore. That would probably include nosing around in the guy's present.

But who is giving Nick such a gift?

Immediately, Bennett felt ashamed at this thought. What did it matter? The poor guy was wearing sandals on near-freezing nights.

Bennett drew a hand over his face. Surely he could find room in his heart to help out a guy, too.

CHAPTER 11

*a*fter scrubbing the paint from her hands and face, Ivy changed into a lightweight faux suede skirt she'd often worn in Boston in the early fall, though it was a good weight for winter at the beach. She added a burgundy-red cashmere sweater Shelly had given her one Christmas and folded a matching cape over her arm for later. It might be the beach, but the evenings were becoming quite cool. After a summer of flip-flops, she loved changing into boots and sweaters.

As a final accent for holiday spirit, Ivy put on a pair of green jade earrings and a necklace her mother had brought back from Hong Kong on a buying trip for their business.

When she came downstairs, Bennett was in the parlor looking through the large volume that Nan and Arthur had compiled on the house. Nan was the acting president of the historical society. Many antiques linked to Summer Beach history passed through Antique Times. Ivy was looking forward to visiting their shop on Main Street this evening.

But first, Ivy wanted to meet their new guests. She was glad that Poppy had handled their check-in so she could work on the new boutique pieces. Ivy had cleared an area in the parlor within sight of the reservation desk. She'd painted and hung a sign: *Seabreeze Inn Gift Shoppe.* That might have been a little grand for a corner, but it could grow.

Bennett's eyes brightened when he saw her. "You look amazing."

Poppy and Sunny were at the welcome desk, where Poppy was reviewing the latest guest reservations with Sunny. "We're expecting these two guests sometime this evening."

Sunny jotted a note on a pad. "I'll be on the lookout for them."

"Thank you for watching the inn while we go out," Ivy said. After she and Shelly returned, Poppy, Sunny, and Elena would go out.

Ivy knew the younger women preferred to go out later anyway, even in Summer Beach. Hanging out at the beach, chatting around the fire pits, or enjoying wine at Spirits & Vine on Main Street seemed to be their top choices. Since it was walking distance from the inn, no one had to drive, but there was always the rideshare option if it was too cold.

She laughed at herself. The temperature hadn't even reached freezing yet. She was already thinking like a local.

"Sounds like we have a new music student," Bennett said. From the library wafted an ethereal melody.

"Might be the surprise," Ivy said, teasing him.

Bennett raised his brow. "A flutist, if I'm not mistaken." He listened for a moment. "And quite accomplished."

Sunny chortled with derision. "Don't you mean flautist?"

"Smart-aleck," Bennett said, grinning.

"Actually, both terms are used," Celia said, coming around the corner. "Flutist comes from the French *flûtiste*, and flautist is from the Italian *flautista*." With her sleek, dark hair pulled into a bun and her slim, black jersey dress, she looked like the artistic benefactor that she was. She and Tyler had moved back into their home after the fire, but Ivy still welcomed her to the inn to swim a couple of times a week.

When she was heating the pool, that is. Celia had been

understanding, but Ivy would let her know once the heat was back on. Someday maybe she could work solar panels into the budget to have heat year-round.

"Celia has made a new musical discovery," Ivy said, trying to maintain the mystery.

Celia gestured toward the library. "The music is just beginning, and Mitch dropped off the most delicious looking appetizers."

"Whoever it is, they're quite talented," Bennett said, walking beside her. "That's a beautiful rendition of *Ode to Joy*. From Beethoven's Ninth, if I recall." He hummed along, clearly enjoying the music.

Ivy couldn't wait to see Bennett's reaction to the surprise. She took his hand. She'd missed seeing him and was glad they'd overcome their disagreement over Nick. Bennett had apologized, but whether he had learned from that remained to be seen.

As much as she cared for Bennett, since her husband died, she'd learned to care for herself, too. She had to be more careful the next time around. If there was a next time. She'd sworn off complicated geniuses like Jeremy.

Ivy had married her husband when she was young and inexperienced. She'd been infatuated with his good looks, French accent, and keen intelligence. He was a high earner, so she'd been privileged to stay at home with their children. Still, he'd often made her feel like a second-class citizen in their home. He left her behind while he traveled the world—and she changed diapers.

Even though she often voiced her desire for him to treat her as an equal partner, he'd only laughed and told her that he loved how cute and American she was. And then he packed his bags and left again. Once the babies came, she threw herself into them.

She'd been practical, understanding, and realistic, but now she thought she might have been partly at fault for not standing up more for herself. The mistakes of youth—that's all she could think of now. But it wouldn't happen again.

Now, Ivy was realistic. It took time to come to know someone. As it turned out, she hadn't known everything about her husband—until it was too late. And Bennett? Even though he'd been her summer crush in high school, she was still learning about him.

Yet, even with this latest argument, the thought of Bennett filled her heart.

Ivy bit her lip, thinking about their disagreement. Unfortunately, she wasn't always right, and as it turned out, she'd been wrong about Nick and his ability or intent to pay for his room. Still, the young man seemed like a kind soul. Ivy wondered what Bennett would say when he learned he'd been right about Nick.

She was about to find out.

They turned into the library, and Bennett's lips parted in surprise.

"Nick?" His eyebrows shot up. "He's clearly had training," he whispered to Ivy.

Nick continued playing, and a young pianist under Celia's tutelage slid onto the piano bench to accompany him. The girl couldn't have been more than twelve, but she was accomplished, too.

"When Celia told me, I was surprised, too," Ivy whispered to Bennett.

"How did she find out?"

"Celia said he was out for a walk and stopped by the children's center. Some of the kids were practicing, and he joined in. Guess he had a flute in that backpack."

While Nick and the young girl played, Ivy and Bennett circulated among the growing number of guests. Ivy stopped to chat with Ophelia and Molly Ann.

"The Christmas Stroll on Main Street begins this evening," Ivy said. "It continues every weekend until Christmas, and you'll find some lovely gifts at our local boutiques. Java Beach will be open for hot chocolate and pastries, or you can stop at Spirits & Vine for wine and appetizers. We're going to walk there after this."

"That sounds like fun," Ophelia said. "Poppy and Bennett told us about that, so we're planning on it."

Ivy greeted Kristy, who was dressed in a claret-red dress to match her hair, and Rosamie, who was excited about spending Christmas at the beach.

"This reminds me of home in the Philippines," Rosamie said wistfully.

"My parents have visited there many times on buying trips," Ivy said. "They love the friendliness—and the food. That's one of their planned stops on their upcoming sail around the world."

Ivy chatted with the guests a little more. After excusing herself, Ivy felt a tug on her top. Shelly deposited a glass of wine in Ivy's hand. "Celia brought a case of wine back for us from their trip to Napa. You're going to love this wine."

Ivy nodded at Celia and raised her glass in appreciation. "Make sure to serve guests wine if they want. Or tea or sparkling water."

"Already on it," Shelly said. She checked the antique clock on the fireplace mantle. "After this, I'm going to help Mitch serve at Java Beach during the Christmas Stroll."

"Doesn't he have an assistant?" Ivy asked.

"Not like me, he doesn't." Shelly grinned and arched an eyebrow. "I'm going to be Mrs. Claus."

Shelly sailed off to deliver another glass of wine to a guest.

The music room was becoming crowded with the new guests, the young musician's family, and a couple of people that Shelly had invited. Imani and Gilda were chatting in the corner, and Jamir swooped in for a few empanadas that Mitch had prepared. Celia had insisted that she start paying Mitch for appetizers as she liked to invite the young performers' parents and families. Ivy had resisted, but Celia prevailed, and Ivy had been relieved.

For many parents of children in the school music program, this was a chance to see their children perform before a live audience. The children were always excited to keep the tips they earned, too.

After a while, people began to filter out. At the end of the hour, Ivy saw Nick hand the tip jar to the girl. "It's yours," he said.

That was generous, Ivy thought, especially since she knew he needed the money. He was probably too proud or kind to accept them. She made her way toward him.

"You can share tips with the youngsters, Nick. You've earned your share."

Nick grinned and shook his head. "I can't do that."

"That's kind of you. I don't expect you to play here every evening, but everyone has enjoyed listening to you. You're quite talented."

Nick's cheeks colored at the compliment. "I usually play for myself, though I like bringing joy to people."

"You're welcome to play anytime you like," Ivy said. "Here, or anywhere on the grounds. Your music is lovely."

Nick gave a slight bow. "That would mean a lot to my grandfather. He taught me to play."

This was one of the few insights he'd offered into his background, Ivy realized. She glanced down. "Are those new shoes?" They were brown suede hiking-style boots, and they looked warm.

"I should thank someone, but I'm not sure who," Nick said, shifting from one foot to another. "These were left with an unsigned note outside my room. Since they were a gift, I have to honor their generosity."

"And they look quite warm. You'll be glad to have those tonight." She wondered who had left them by Nick's door.

Bennett? Mitch? Celia? Then again, it could've been anyone at Java Beach.

Nick lifted the leg of his jeans. "Socks, too. When I packed to leave, I didn't give much thought to the weather. This was an incredibly thoughtful gesture."

Ivy smiled and touched his shoulder. "I'm not surprised. People in Summer Beach are like that. They welcomed Shelly and me, too, even though we came with a load of baggage. Metaphorically speaking, that is."

AFTER LEAVING THE INN, IVY TOOK BENNETT'S HAND AS THEY walked toward the village. "I have something to confess," she said. She hated to mention it, but if she were asking for honesty and trust, she had to live up to that bar, too.

Bennett put his arm around her. "I can't imagine what, but go ahead."

"Nick is helping Shelly with work in the yard and the garden. Trimming trees, transplanting, that sort of work."

"That's nice of Nick to spend his holiday that way."

She hesitated. "I hope you won't say you told me so, but we came to that agreement because he hasn't given me a form of payment for the room. You called it, but please don't gloat about it. Not sure I should be telling you this anyway because of guest privacy."

Bennett said nothing at first. "Perhaps there are extenuating circumstances. He doesn't talk about himself much."

"I thought Shelly would be upset, but actually, she welcomed the help. It seems Nick has quickly grasped the science of horticulture, and he has an artist's eye. Shelly maintains that people deserve a shot, which surprised me to hear her say that now."

Bennett turned up a corner of his mouth. "Sounds like a Mitch-ism."

"It does. But didn't you give Mitch his first shot here?"
Now it dawned on Ivy why Bennett was more understanding.

"I saw Mitch's talent and determination, so I thought he
deserved a chance. I remember the first time a seller trusted
me with a real estate listing, even though I'd never represented
a piece of real estate before or sold anything more than a used
car."

Ivy thought about the truth in that statement. Everyone
started somewhere. Megan and Josh had been their first
guests, and they'd put up with a few mishaps during their stay.
"Nick is talented on many levels. He'll be okay once he finds
his way."

As they passed Java Beach, Ivy noticed the line out the
door. The sweet aroma of hot chocolate wafted through the
air. She waved at Shelly, who was wearing a Santa hat with a
short red dress, white snowflake-patterned hose, and black
boots. *Mrs. Claus* was rendered in glitter on her cap. Mitch was
dressed as a surfing Santa, with a Hawaiian shirt under a red
Santa jacket lined with white faux-fur and long-johns under
red shorts.

"Shelly and Mitch look like they're having a great time,"
Ivy said. "Love their outfits."

"Mitch loves Christmas, and he does this every year."
Bennett waved to them. "It makes him feel like he's part of a
family."

"The Summer Beach family," Ivy said thoughtfully. "Our
folks also think a lot of Mitch, especially his entrepreneurial
abilities." Mitch had overcome many trials and hardships in
his past, including a short stint in prison. He'd turned out to
be quite a guy. "Nick is starting to feel like one of us, too. I
wish he'd stay longer."

As Ivy and Bennett passed Nailed It, they waved at Jen
and George, who were passing out candy canes.

"Maybe he will," Bennett said. "People end up in Summer
Beach for all kinds of reasons. Sometimes they're running

away from something—or running toward a lifestyle they want. Other times, they simply drift here and remain because they felt welcome."

"Nick is leaving on Christmas."

Bennett grinned. "We'll see, won't we? I once had a client who was anxious to sell a huge old house on the beach, and she's still here."

Ivy squeezed his hand. "I don't think she's ever leaving."

"I sure hope not."

As they walked on, more people filled the street, which was closed to traffic. Axe Woodson, the tall, barrel-chested contractor who was rebuilding Imani's house on the ridge, was directing the *a cappella* carolers. He joined in as they strolled from shop to shop. His strong baritone voice filled the air, reverberating through the night like a fine instrument.

Ivy was delighted at the Christmas Stroll sights and how Summer Beach had transformed itself. There might not be snow, but there was all the small-town warmth and cheer she could want.

Everywhere they went, people stopped to chat with Bennett and tell Ivy how glad they were that she and her family had transformed the old Las Brisas del Mar into the new Seabreeze Inn. They told her the inn had become an essential part of the Summer Beach community. After hearing that, she was even more determined to get through the winter months.

The sound of sleigh bells jingled nearby, and Ivy turned. "Oh, look," she cried.

A horse-drawn hayride trotted by, carrying people to look at the sights. In the square on Main Street, Fire Chief Paula Stark presided over a vintage fire engine decorated with lights and garland. Children were climbing all over the truck as parents and grandparents snapped photos.

"I love that," Ivy said.

Bennett chuckled. "My parents used to take Kendra and

me to play on that fire truck, too. That old fire engine is one of Summer Beach's originals. The fire department keeps it running just for special appearances."

All around her, the sound of laughter lifted Ivy's spirit. The fresh smell of hay and sweet apple cider hung in the air, bringing to mind cherished memories of autumn in New England when her girls were young. "This reminds me of Quincy Market in Boston. We used to take the girls there."

"Do you miss it?" Bennett asked.

"A little. All of New England is magical at Christmas, especially when it snows. I'll miss the Boston Pops Christmas concert and the tree lighting in the Commons. We used to ice skate there, too, and I just loved it."

She paused and kissed his cheek. "But Summer Beach is where my heart is now. Life is like a series of acts in what we hope is a long-running play. We have to enjoy the moment—even when we have a lesson to learn."

Bennett nodded thoughtfully. "That's a good way of looking at it."

"I remember the holiday after I sold our Back Bay condo and rented a room," Ivy said, blinking in the crisp air. "I felt so alone. But that time taught me to cherish my family and friends over things."

"That's the best part of life," he said.

They walked on and stopped by several shops, where Ivy picked out a few small stocking-stuffer gifts for her daughters. After the theater closed for the holidays, Misty would return from Boston, this time for an extended holiday until January.

Ivy was making most of her gifts for her family and friends this year. She'd been painting family portraits for Honey, Flint, and Forrest, and keepsake ornaments for friends. Her parents didn't need much since they were renting their home and embarking on a boat, but she had an idea for something small they would treasure.

As they approached Antique Times, Ivy said, "I'd like to stop and see what Nan and Arthur might have."

They stepped inside, and the aroma of spicy mulled wine tickled Ivy's nose. "That smells heavenly," she said.

"Tastes even better," Arthur said with a wink as he began to prepare two cups for them. "The tradition began with the Romans." He ladled warm red wine with sliced oranges and lemons into cups and added a splash of brandy and a cinnamon stick.

Ivy sipped the warm, fragrant concoction. "This is delicious. How do you make this?"

"That's Nan's department." Arthur motioned to his wife, and Nan bustled over to them.

"So glad you like it," Nan said. "I use Arthur's mother's recipe from England—but with a little twist. I use a good Malbec, Syrah, or Zinfandel, not too pricey but rich enough to stand up to the spices and fruit. Then I add honey, cinnamon, clove, and star anise. And, of course, sliced oranges and lemons. Pears and apples are good in that, too."

"Mmm, I love the fruits and spices," Ivy said. "My mother makes something similar with fruits and spices called *Ponche Navideño*, which is a traditional Christmas punch. Instead of wine, we add brandy. I'll have to make it for our Christmas Day open house."

"We'll be there," Arthur said.

"We also have stollen, chocolate panettone, and mincemeat pie if you'd like a little nosh," Nan said.

"I could sure go for that." Bennett turned to Ivy. "Nan is a wonderful cook."

"Arthur holds his own in the kitchen, too," Nan said, her red curls framing her bright smile. "He made the mincemeat pie, I made the stollen, and the panettone comes from the Italian market down the street."

"We're having dessert first," Ivy said, laughing, though they'd already had appetizers at the wine and tea hour at the inn. "This stollen is excellent," she added as she ate bits of the candied fruit bread with powdered sugar.

"Next weekend, I'll bring pigs in blankets," Arthur said. "For you Yanks, that's sausages wrapped in bacon. I grew up on those and Yorkshire pudding at Christmas, along with turkey, roast potatoes, and Brussel sprouts. And figgy pudding, of course."

As they enjoyed the treats, Ivy perused the antiques and selected a crystal paperweight that she knew would be a perfect addition to her sister-in-law's collection. "I've been going through the book that you and Nan compiled on Las Brisas again. One of our guests is interested in the inn's history."

"That must be Nick," Arthur said. "What a fine young man. He was in here just the other day."

Ivy was dying to ask why, but after she'd talked so much about guest privacy, she couldn't ask. From the corner of her eye, she saw Bennett grinning at her. Arthur was a regular at Java Beach and known to keep up on the town gossip.

Bennett sipped his mulled wine. Nonchalantly, he asked, "Was he looking for anything special?"

"He was particularly interested in Las Brisas around the time of the Second World War. Most folks like to chat about the paintings or crown jewels found there. Afraid I couldn't help him much on that count, either."

After Ivy paid for the paperweight, they walked to Spirits & Vine, where they ordered two bowls of steaming lobster corn chowder. Ivy knew the owners of the wine shop, and though the atmosphere was lively, the clientele never got out of hand. In a rear room that opened to the beach, young people often gathered for poetry readings and jazz.

Ivy and Bennett sat at a table by the window, and as they looked out, they saw Nick strolling along Main Street, stopping to talk to shopkeepers.

Ivy rested her chin on her hand. "I think Nick is just lonely," she said, though she felt she was missing a piece of the story. Not that it was any of her business—except as it had to do with the inn.

Still, she couldn't help but wonder. And there was no harm in that, was there?

CHAPTER 12

"*T*hanks for calling me, Ari." Ivy tapped her phone to hang up and turned back to Shelly.

Ahead of them, their new guests were charging along the water's edge. Ophelia and Molly Ann, who were now sharing a room, were laughing and talking with Rosamie. Nick and Kristy were strolling behind them, their heads bent together, engrossed in conversation.

Even though the guests had just met, friendships were developing. Ivy guessed they ranged between the ages of thirty and seventy, but they'd quickly found common interests.

Shelly gestured ahead. "You called it. This is like winter camp for adults. We should start promoting Valentine's Day soon. Or a January break. I'll bet we can make this one hot winter at the inn." She zipped up her soft yoga jacket and bundled her scarf around her neck. "So, what did Ari have to say? Do we have more stolen property on our hands?"

"I'm not sure," Ivy replied. "He and his team confirmed what Elena said about that piece. It could be one of the missing Fabergé imperial eggs, or it might have been made for another client. Or it could be a copy. He's running a check on the FBI and Interpol databases to see if it's on any stolen property lists." Ivy paused. "I also called Chief Clarkson to report the found property."

"That was such a long time ago." Shelly kicked a toe in the sand. "When do we get to keep some of the loot we find around this place?"

"I don't know if we ever will. Seems like Amelia Erickson was safeguarding property here. The rest of their collection—which we saw on display in the house in those old photographs—was properly documented and sold as part of the estate that went to charity."

"Does that mean this would, too?"

Ivy let out a sigh. "I spoke to Imani about that, and she thought the egg could be called mislaid or abandoned property. She's researching that." Ivy shivered and brushed wayward strands of hair from her face. "Frankly, that piece probably belongs in a museum."

Shelly twisted her lips to one side. "Or in a billionaire's private collection."

"If it were to go to auction, I suppose that's possible. But I like to think that people in need would benefit from the sale."

"You make it sound like it's not ours to keep."

"I doubt if it is. It's one thing for owners to leave behind a valuable chandelier that's attached to the ceiling—that's obvious and covered in the sale documents. But a rare jewel hidden away—even if by accident?" Ivy shook her head. "I'm being realistic."

"Amazing that no one would miss it after all these years," Shelly said.

"They might not have been around to reclaim it. Many people didn't make it out of the Second World War alive," Ivy added quietly. "We should not celebrate their loss."

Shelly pressed a hand to her mouth. "Oh, my gosh, I hadn't thought of that. That makes me feel awful."

"If that were the case, I'd want funds from the sale of that to help others. Then that person's life would be honored. I think any profit should go to benefit the charities Amelia named in her will."

Shelly was quiet for a long moment. "I guess that would bring good karma, but the roof needs replacing, the heating could stand an upgrade, and the refrigerators are wheezing. And I'm driving an old clunker that dates from the last century. When do we get to benefit?"

Ivy slung her arm around Shelly's shoulder and nodded back at the house. "We already have. The rest is just cosmetic."

"But that was your retirement savings—yours and Jeremy's."

"Do I look like I'm ready to retire? We're figuring this out, Shelly. Every single day. You're my partner, and I kind of like that old clunker. For now, anyway." Ivy nodded toward the group of women, who were watching the shorebirds skittering around the sand. "All we have to do is put what we're good at out in the world. A week ago, we'd barely thought of this new idea. And now, look how much fun these women are having. They've made new friends, so we've enriched their lives. We're doing our job."

"I know, I know. And profit flows back to us through our efforts." Shelly quirked up a corner of her mouth. "You have an interesting way of looking at things. But I kind of like it. Still…"

"Ari will call back if he gets a hit on his search," Ivy said. "In the meantime, I need to tuck away that egg for safe-keeping."

After the walk, Ivy brought her laptop onto the sun-filled veranda. Though it was still chilly, the walk had invigorated her. Being outside and breathing in the cool ocean air cleared her mind. She was curious about the egg and wondered if she could find any history on it.

Once her computer was on, she typed the words, *lost Fabergé eggs* in the search field. Faces from history stared back at her. *Romanovs, 1917, revolution.* The story of lost eggs led to other headlines. *Bolsheviks Nationalize House of Fabergé.* Peter Carl Fabergé was a court jeweler to the Russian tsars. While he was away in 1918, his business was ransacked and his inventory crated for storage in the Kremlin Armoury, surrounded by guards.

More dates and names flashed on the screen. *1927, 1931. Stalin.* A cache of pre-revolutionary Russian art. Ivy read more. *Armand Hammer. Marjorie Merriweather Post.* Russia needed funds for economic expansion, and Hammer brokered the sale of some valuable Russian artifacts to prominent collectors, including Mrs. Post, around the world. During the Great Depression, some of the pieces, including imperial eggs, sold for merely a few hundred dollars.

Ivy sat back, wondering. Could their Christmas egg be linked to that history?

LATER THAT AFTERNOON, IVY SWUNG OPEN THE DOOR TO THE First Summer Beach Bank on Main Street. In the wood-paneled, mid-century bank, the staff had trimmed the old-fashioned grills at the two teller windows with holiday decorations.

"I'm here to access my safety deposit box," she said to the young teller who'd helped her before. Last summer, she had rented a box for the jewelry they'd found. It was empty now, except for a few papers she had left there. Her will, the house deed, birth certificates, and car titles. She'd meant to close it, but the bank rented the box by the year.

Ivy shifted her bag on her shoulder, and the young man led her through a locked gate to a small room with rows of metal boxes. He looked to be a couple of years older than Sunny, and even though it was winter, his hair was still sun-bleached. He reminded her of a younger version of Mitch.

Even surfers had to work day jobs unless they were professional surfers.

"I'm Ivy Bay," she said, making conversation. "What's your name?"

"Diego. And before you ask, that's because I was born in San Diego."

"Good name." Ivy brought out her key. "How's the surfing?" she asked as he sorted through the keys on his ring to open her box.

"Pretty gnarly," Diego replied. "Excellent waves but cold, so you have to wear a full wetsuit."

"I'll keep that in mind. The waves look great."

His eyes brightened. "Cool. My aunt still surfs, too, though she's not as old as you are."

"Uh, thanks," Ivy said, smothering a laugh. He'd clearly misunderstood her, but his aunt still sounded impressive. Anything over thirty probably seemed ancient to him. She remembered those days. Smiling, she slipped her key into the lock.

"There are still some older dudes out there," Diego said. "Even saw the mayor on a board last summer."

"Really?" Ivy couldn't resist. "How did he do?"

"Not bad for an old guy who usually sits behind a desk. The mayor should keep it up so he can catch some waves before his legs give out."

She smiled, thinking about Bennett's reaction if she shared this with him. On second thought, maybe she'd spare his ego and keep this to herself.

Diego found the right key and inserted it into the second lock on the box. After pulling out the box, he directed her to a small, private room. Once he'd closed the door, she brought the glittery egg from her shoulder bag. Placing it on the worn wooden table, she rested her chin on her hand and gazed at the piece.

The crimson-red enamel work was fine and smooth,

almost silky, with a wavy pattern and incredible brilliance. Staring at it, her heart quickened. The craftsmanship was superb, even if the actual carat weight of any one gemstone wasn't that impressive. At least, not for a piece of this artistry.

Hundreds, maybe thousands, of tiny chips made up swirled patterns that encased the exterior. Beneath that, translucent red enamel was expertly applied over *guilloché* metal, a technique she recalled from her art classes in college. Inside, a smaller egg held a tiny cardinal bird with ruby-red feathers worked into brilliant platinum. A harbinger of spring, perhaps. Surely this had been a gift.

She took out the little bird and cradled it in her hand. Its wings could actually flap. Beneath the bird, was a little nest with tiny, miniature eggs. She lifted out the golden nest, marveling at the craftsmanship. And on the bottom lay the image of a small child affixed to a gold pendant.

To create these nesting elements with their attention to detail must have taken a senior craftsperson a very long time. Ivy knew the value was in the artistry, not necessarily in the gemstone or gold content.

Had this been a unique gift for someone, perhaps for the child's mother? She turned over the tiny bird in her hand. "Who treasured you, little one? Who cooed over you in delight?"

This was more than a mere *objet d'art*; it was a work of rarified aesthetic, an *objet de vertu*.

With a sigh, she returned the beautiful objects into the sanctuary of the oval case and tucked the egg into a soft cloth bag.

It was likely the last time she would be alone with the precious treasure. As she sat in the quiet room, she could hear the low roar of the ocean beyond like a constant, soothing lullaby. She wondered who might have risked their life to bring such a piece here, so far away for safekeeping? Or who might have sold it, in desperate need for cash?

Finally, she tucked away the treasure with care, sliding it into the large safety deposit box. She snapped the lid and called for Diego.

As Ivy was leaving the bank, she spied Ginger Delavie, a tall, energetic woman with ginger-red hair who was a beloved resident of Summer Beach. Her cottage—painted a vivid shade of coral—had stood as a beacon on the beach for decades, Ivy understood. Ginger's husband had been a diplomat, and they had traveled the world, collecting experiences and stories that Ginger loved to share. An invitation to the Coral Cottage ensured an evening of laughter and intellectual conversation.

"Hold the door," Ginger said. She held a covered platter in her hands.

Ivy held the front door to the bank for her. "Hello, Ginger. Whatever that is, I'll bet it's delicious." Ginger was known to have some of the best recipes in town, and she loved to entertain.

"Oh, my darling girl, you can't leave just yet." Ginger sailed through the door calling out to Diego and the manager. "Something sweet for you and your customers. And Ivy, you simply must try these as well. My classic gingerbread person cookies."

Ivy laughed. "Gingerbread *person?*"

Her green eyes sparkling with mischief, Ginger pulled off the cover to reveal puffy gingerbread figures. "Well, it's not as if they're anatomically correct, now is it? And since they share my name, I think I have a bit of the say in it, don't you? Do try one." She held out a cookie.

Ivy broke off a soft leg of the cookie and tried it. "Mmm, you've used just the right amount of spice."

"Cinnamon, clove, and ginger, of course. This recipe was from my good friend, Julia, although I've changed it up a little here and there. We always argued about that, though I still think my recipe was superior to hers. However, she was the one with the best-selling cookbooks, so what did I know?"

Ginger cast her gaze heavenward and added petulantly, "Sorry, Julia. But I still think mine is better. Just a little, mind you." She picked up another cookie. "Diego, my dear. Don't be shy. I made extra for you this year."

"Thank you, Mrs. Delavie," Diego said, his eyes widening as he stuffed half a cookie into his mouth. "These are awesome."

"You gentlemen take such good care of me during the year. It's the least I can do." Ginger put the platter down on the teller's counter. "I'll leave this right here for your customers. Now I have a few more to deliver, so I must be off."

Ivy thought about the ideas that she and Shelly had discussed. "Excuse me, Ginger, but would you be open to joining us for a gingerbread bake-off at the Seabreeze Inn?"

"What a thrilling concept," Ginger exclaimed. "But I'd rather judge it. We have some excellent young cooks and bakers in Summer Beach who should receive the accolades now."

"That's a wonderful idea," Ivy said, excited.

"As long as it's not too close to Christmas," Ginger went on. "I'm flying to San Francisco to join my granddaughter Marina and her twins, who are on break from college. Duke University, the clever pair. Along with Marina's sister Kai, a young theater actress who shows tremendous promise. I do wish they'd spend Christmas at the Coral Cottage, but they're all so busy now."

"How about next weekend?" Ivy knew she could post a flyer at Java Beach, and the word would quickly spread through the community.

"That's perfect," Ginger said, pushing through the door. "Is there anything you need me to do?"

Ivy rushed to keep up with Ginger as the woman strode

along Main Street toward her car. "All you need to do is bring your taste buds."

"We should have two other judges as well, just to make it fair," Ginger said decisively. "I'll ask Cookie from the farmers market and Mayor Bennett to accompany me as judges. I hope you agree."

"Let's save the date," Ivy said quickly. "I'll call you with all the details."

Ginger stopped beside her car. "We'll need a lot of people to eat these gingerbread masterpieces as well. Why don't you reach out to the children's center?"

"That's perfect," Ivy exclaimed. "Bennett is their guest Santa, too. Perhaps we could hold the event at the inn this year."

"You might have just started a new tradition here in Summer Beach," Ginger said proudly. A moment later, her face clouded, and she held up a finger. "But I have to warn you. We have some very competitive cooks in the kitchen."

Ivy laughed. "I can't imagine a gingerbread throw-down getting out of hand."

Ginger pursed her lips. "We'll see about that."

CHAPTER 13

$\mathcal{T}$he evening wine and tea gathering had just ended, and guests went their separate ways. Bennett was surprised at the number of new guests. Ivy had asked if he would build a fire in the ballroom to chase the evening chill. Many guests were exploring the old house, fascinated by the architecture, or making themselves comfortable downstairs and chatting in small groups near the Christmas tree.

Bennett was laying the fire when Nick strolled in. "Did you have a chance to try on that jacket?"

"I'm much obliged to you," Nick said, bowing his head slightly. "It's much warmer than my denim jacket."

"Just thought you'd get more wear out of it than I do. It's more your style anyway." Bennett had bought the sheepskin-lined denim jacket at an end-of-season sale last spring. He hadn't worn it yet, but he figured Nick would enjoy it more. "Not too big on you?"

"Fits just right," Nick said with a smile. "Leaves me enough room to wear it over my thick hoodie."

"Maybe I have a few other things you could use."

"I appreciate the thought, but there's nothing more I need now." Nick gazed thoughtfully at the chandeliers. "I was looking through old photographs, and I saw that this room was used as a gymnasium for physical therapy. Ivy told me it was during the Second World War."

Bennett stood and brushed wood bits from his hands. "Imagine the people who've passed through here. Amelia Erickson was an important part of the Summer Beach community."

"It seems that many people were indebted to her," Nick said.

"I don't think she ever expected anything in return," Bennett said. "I was too young to know her, but some of our older residents remember her. They were just kids back then, but she was memorable."

"What was Mrs. Erickson like?" Nick asked softly.

"Kind and generous. It's said this home was always open to people." He paused. "During the war, patients recuperated in the bedrooms upstairs. But recently, Ivy and Shelly found more rooms upstairs, concealed in such a fashion that other people could shelter there, and it appears they did. Amelia was strongly committed to doing what she thought was fair and right by people."

Nick grew more thoughtful. "I'd like very much to see those rooms if I could."

"I'm sure Ivy, Shelly, or Poppy would be happy to show you. They're comfortable but were clearly constructed to provide for as many as possible. You'll see bunk beds against the wall where families could stay. Ivy found that Amelia was inspired to do that after a shipload of European refugees were turned away. Many perished later, and she was so devastated that she took action. If the government wouldn't accept refugees, she would. She vowed to protect anyone who needed help. As long as they managed to get here." Bennett struck a match and touched it to the newspaper he'd tucked under the logs.

Nick nodded thoughtfully. "She might have been arrested for that."

"Quite possibly. But Amelia was wealthy and well-connected, and it's said that her staff was devoted to her. They probably assisted her in humanitarian efforts, too."

Nick gazed outside. "How do you think they would have come here?"

"Once they got across the Pacific, I would imagine they might have come through Mexico. Maybe even by boat." He lifted his chin toward the ocean. "They could have come fairly close to the shore and rowed in under cover of a dark, starless night."

Inclining his head, Nick seemed to take this plausible idea under consideration.

Bennett turned his attention back to the fireplace. The newspaper burned quickly, but the kindling was slow to ignite. *Possibly too green.* He blew on the flickering fire, sending up embers like confetti, which fluttered and sizzled on the hearth.

Picking up a poker, Bennett adjusted a log and went on. "During the holidays, it's said that Amelia and Gustav Erickson would have an open house for the entire community. They were a special part of Summer Beach."

"Much like Ivy," Nick said.

Bennett smiled at the thought. "Maybe in her way, Ivy is carrying on Amelia's work." He quickly added, "You're doing a fine job around here, Nick, helping Shelly with the grounds. You have many talents we could use here in Summer Beach if you'd like to stay on. Look at what Mitch has accomplished."

Nick gazed at the fireplace as if mesmerized. "Well, now, that's an interesting thought."

Slightly frustrated, Bennett poked the logs again. He couldn't coax a blaze from them.

Nick put a hand on Bennett's shoulder. "May I try?"

Bennett shrugged. "Have a go." He straightened and sat back on his haunches, watching for a moment. He'd have to get more kindling to start this fire.

Nick squatted on the hearth. With a long, steady breath,

he blew gently toward the kindling, although Bennett couldn't see any promise of fire there. Nick held his hands over the logs as if in a trance.

Noticing Nick's breath control, Bennett thought of the flute that the young man had played with such expertise, passion, and heart. He needed to go out for kindling, but Nick's patient, determined actions were intriguing, so he waited.

Within a couple of minutes, a flicker of orange appeared, and Nick continued his steady ministrations.

Before long, Nick had coaxed the fire from its lethargy. Flames began to lick over the logs, igniting the bark and settling in.

"That was quite the trick," Bennett said, rubbing his hand across his chin. He prided himself on starting a good fire, but somehow Nick had brought forth flames from a seemingly cold fire. "Must have been a hot ember back there."

Nick turned a corner of his mouth. "Perhaps."

Just then, Bennett and Nick turned at the sound of heels tapping across the floor. Ivy and Shelly were walking toward them.

Bennett rose. "Ivy, Nick has a question for you."

Pausing, Ivy raised her hands to the fire. "What a lovely fire. What can I help you with, Nick?"

"Bennett tells me you have an attic with an intriguing history behind it," Nick replied. "I would be so grateful if you could show it to me." His voice held a distinct note of hope.

"It's truly fascinating," Ivy said. "I can show you tomorrow."

Shelly and Nick began talking about yoga, and the new guest, Kristy, meandered downstairs and joined them. Soon the conversation turned to the possibility of having relaxing evening yoga in the ballroom since more guests had signed up than they could fit in the room Shelly used as a yoga studio.

"Since you teach in the morning, I'd be happy to lead the evening session," Nick said.

"You're on," Shelly said. "Any problem with that, Ivy?"

Ivy quickly agreed. Bennett gazed around. Between the crackling fire, the glittering Christmas tree, and the soothing sound of the ocean just beyond the glass doors that opened onto the beach, the setting was ideal. "I might join you, too," Bennett said.

"Let's start tonight," Shelly said, and Nick and Kristy agreed.

"I'll tell Ophelia and Molly Ann and Rosamie," Kristy said, smiling at Nick. "Wait for us, will you?"

"Of course," Nick replied. He watched her hurry away.

As tempting as it was, Bennett had something else in mind for this evening. Ivy had mentioned that she missed ice skating in Boston. He touched Ivy's hand. "Want to go for a ride?"

"Let's take the old Chevy," she replied, her face lighting. "Where would you like to go?"

Bennett turned up a corner of his mouth. "Do you have a pair of thick socks and gloves?"

Ivy looked confused for a moment, and then she broke into a wide smile. "The ice rink?"

When he nodded, she pulled him by the hand. "I'll grab my gear and meet you by the garage."

Outside, Bennett rushed upstairs to his apartment over the garage to get his jacket. They'd talked about the outdoor skating rink at the historic Hotel del Coronado, a landmark on Coronado Island that locals referred to as The Del.

Soon, they were ensconced in the old Chevrolet Deluxe convertible—cherry red with a cream convertible top.

Ivy slid across the red leather bench set and rubbed her hands. "This is so exciting. I loved ice skating in Boston. I used to take Misty and Sunny to the Frog Pond at the Commons or Kendall Square. How do they get the ice to freeze here, I wonder?"

Bennett turned the key in the ignition and rested a hand on the large steering wheel. "The Del has a special system to create an ice rink on the beach, like an Arctic blast under the ice. Axe Woodson explained it once to me."

"I can hardly wait," Ivy said. "Let's put down the convertible top so we can watch the moonlight on the ocean as we drive."

"As the lady wishes," Bennett said, getting out to tuck down the top. "I remember cruising the Pacific Coast Highway in the winter with the top down and the heater on. This is winter, Southern California-style." He brought out a plaid lap blanket they'd discovered in the trunk for Ivy.

She looked up at him and kissed his cheek. "Can't you just imagine Amelia and Gustav on holiday from San Francisco doing exactly what we're doing?"

"That would've been in their old Duesenberg roadster probably, not this new baby from the 1950s." He tucked the blanket over her, rolled up the windows to reduce the draft, and shut her door.

With stars twinkling overhead, they cruised the coast highway, watching the waves breaking onto the sand. Ivy turned the dial on the old radio to a station playing holiday music, and on the way there, they sang *Jingle Bells* and *Rockin' Around the Christmas Tree*.

As they turned into the Hotel Del Coronado, an expansive wooden structure built in the late 19th-century, Ivy sighed happily. A vast display of lights outlined the Victorian rotunda at the entrance and stretched around the structure's perimeter. "All we're missing is the snow."

"I've found that if you squint your eyes, you can almost imagine that the sand dunes are mounds of snow." Grinning, Bennett pulled into the valet area, where the vintage car drew a lot of attention.

They wound their way through the gaily decorated grounds until they came to the ice-skating rink on the sand, where families and couples were spinning around the ice to holiday tunes.

Once they laced up their skates, Bennett glided onto the ice, holding Ivy's hand. Right away, he stumbled, and she held him up.

Bennett laughed at his clumsiness. "You're a much better skater than I am."

"I had a lot of practice back east," Ivy said, holding out her hand. "You're not too bad, just rusty. Come on. I'll go slow. Hold onto me."

Bennett did as she instructed, and they slowly made their way around the rink. With the moon rising, the waves crashing on the beach, and his arm around the most beautiful woman in his eyes, Bennett was in heaven.

Even if he did stumble from time to time.

Ivy had patience with him, just as he had to have patience with Ivy—and Sunny. He'd observed that each of her daughters had an aspect of Ivy's personality. Sunny could be just as determined as her mother, yet Misty had her mother's patience and compassion. Those traits could also be a function of age, he knew, as most people gained wisdom with age and experience—unless they became cynical and closed down.

Bennett never wanted to do that, especially to Ivy. He tightened his arm around her waist, enjoying their closeness. With every day that passed, he cared more deeply for Ivy. Now, there was no doubt in his mind that his feelings would continue to grow.

If only she felt the same for him.

Patience, he told himself. *Patience.*

"You're awfully quiet," she said, stroking and gliding with practiced ease.

"I'm thinking about what a wonderful evening this is."

She narrowed her eyes. "You have that look like you're about to get into trouble. Are you sure?"

"Cross my heart," Bennett said, but as he made the

motion with his arm, he lost control and bobbled his feet on the ice, wiping out and landing on his stomach with his legs and arms outstretched. "Oh, jeez," he cried as he slid to a stop. Fortunately, skaters parted quickly around him.

"I hope you're not hurt," Ivy said. "Do you need help?"

"Nope. I got this." He turned over and stared at the sky while he caught his breath. He prided himself on being athletic, but as with any sport, ice skating required practice. And he hadn't skated for a couple of years. *At least.*

"Hey," one kid shouted. "Isn't that Mayor Dylan?"

A group of teenagers skated swiftly past him, calling out, "Hi Mr. Mayor. How's it going?"

"Doing just great," he called back with a wave. "Never better. Great view from down here."

Bennett could hear Ivy smothering a laugh. If he was going to preserve any semblance of dignity, he had to get up. That much he remembered. He crawled onto all fours, then pulled a knee up and pressed his hands against his knee. As he rose, Ivy clapped and whistled.

"Hurrah," she said, cheering him on. "Look at you go."

"Yeah, yeah, I'm practically an Olympian." His face felt flushed, but he was having a great time. After having fallen once and gotten up, he was more relaxed, and he and Ivy circled the rink several more times.

After a while, they stopped to rest beside a fire pit that was blazing against the night sky. Bennett glanced at a menu card.

"Peppermint mocha hot chocolate sounds good," he said. "I hear it's good for bruised egos."

"Make that two," Ivy said, smiling.

After ordering, they huddled together, laughing and catching their breath, though every time they looked at each other, they cracked up again.

"I can't remember when I had so much fun," Ivy said, snuggling against him.

"You can always count on me to bring the comic relief," Bennett said wryly.

Ivy kissed his cheek. "I like to laugh and let loose with you." She leaned into him. "I've been worried about this winter, but I think we might manage to make it through the season."

As a breeze from the ocean teased the flames into a fitful dance, Bennett wrapped his arms around her. "I have faith in you, Ivy Bay."

Just then, a server in a puffy parka brought their fragrant hot chocolate, and Ivy cupped her hand around the steaming mug.

Bennett raised his cup. "To the best holiday season either of us has had in a long time.

"And may our future hold happiness—for us and those we love and cherish."

Staring into the most captivating green eyes he'd ever seen, Bennett brushed his hand along her cheek. "I won't say the words if it makes you uncomfortable, but you know how I feel about you, Ivy."

She lowered her lashes to cheeks pink from exertion. "I do. And you must know how I feel."

He didn't press her. Instead, he brushed his lips lightly across hers. Bennett couldn't deny his growing attachment to her, and yet, he wondered if she would ever be ready to return his deepest affection, or would he be the one to suffer a broken heart?

At this moment, he had to be patient. In reality, enjoying every moment afforded them was the only way to live. As he knew all too well, the future was merely a promise that could be too easily broken.

And yet, Bennett had hope now, and that hope infused him with a new resolve for living.

CHAPTER 14

*I*vy pulled her burgundy wool cape around her torso and breathed in the cool ocean air. The beach scene at The Del was enchanting tonight, and the ice skating had been exhilarating, even if she had taken it easy with Bennett. On one side, laughter rose from the skating rink, and on the other, the mesmerizing sound of a slumbering sea lulled away cares. With her worries momentarily diminished, she warmed her hands on a mug of hot chocolate and gazed up at Bennett.

"If I forget to tell you," Ivy began. "I've had a very merry Christmas."

Almost imperceptibly, Bennett's smile slipped. Perhaps he'd hoped she would say something else.

"Thanks for coming out with me tonight," he said, his deep voice sounding warm in the chilly evening air.

"Did you think I was going to say something else?"

Bennett's face flushed. "One can hope. You know how I feel."

For all the love Ivy held in her heart for Bennett, she wasn't quite ready for the next step with him. That would require more than a union between two people. "Our relationship will also affect my daughters," she said.

"I'm well aware of that," Bennett said. "Thanksgiving was interesting with Sunny giving me the evil eye. But I understood, and I know it's part of her grieving process to hold tight to memories. It's natural for Sunny to want life back the way it was, even though life has changed."

"She knows better, though."

"Intellectually, yes. But it can take a while for the heart to catch up. Been there, done that."

Ivy nodded, glad that he understood. "The family dynamics between the girls and me necessarily shifted when their father died. Overnight, I went from homemaker to breadwinner."

"Admirably, I might add."

"Not without incident," she said. "Misty has adjusted well, but Sunny still resents her father for dying, me for not dying, and the world for not continuing to spoil her as her father had." She shook her head. "It's complicated. Now we throw you into this mix, and explosions are bound to occur. Are you sure you're up for all that craziness?"

"We can take it one day at a time."

"I'd like that," Ivy said, feeling a measure of relief.

She clasped his hand. If she were to take the next step with Bennett, Ivy had to make a plan for her family. "Sunny is struggling with a new school, new friends, and a new home. And I know she's worried about finding work after graduation."

"I see that Poppy is training her."

"That's to work off her Amex bill, which is really about taking responsibility for her actions. But Sunny seems to like it, and she has hinted about working at the inn after school."

"Is that an option?"

Ivy shook her head. "I think it's better that Sunny try working for another boss. When I ask her to check a guestroom, I'm not asking as her mother. I'm directing her as the business owner. But she doesn't always take it that way."

"Spoken like a true boss."

Ivy grinned and bumped his shoulder. "No one has ever called me that before."

"That's what you are. I've watched you blossom into the role these last few months. Being a boss isn't only about delegating. It's looking ahead to create your future, holding to that vision, building your team, managing your finances, and being creative when you have to be."

Ivy threw her shoulders back and lifted her chin. "Then I'm your boss."

Bennett laughed. "One heck of a boss, in my book." He drained his hot cocoa and wrapped his arms around her.

Bennett made talking about tough subjects easier, and Ivy appreciated that. Plus, she couldn't remember when she'd had so much fun or laughed so hard. Seeing Bennett sprawled across the ice rink with teens from Summer Beach skating around him was priceless. Thankfully, he wasn't hurt, and he was a good sport about it all.

After returning their skates, they walked on the beach for a while, talking about the holiday events in Summer Beach and guests at the inn.

"I think we might have our first guest romance developing," Ivy said.

"I haven't noticed. Who?"

"Oh, come on." Ivy nudged him. "Haven't you seen how Nick and Kristy are often in deep discussions? The sky could be falling around them, and they wouldn't notice."

"Really? I'll have to watch for that." Bennett grinned. "The sky bit, too." He looked up and ducked.

"You're such a tease." But Ivy liked that about him. Bennett reminded her of how her father used to kid around with her and her siblings. Flint and Forrest were like that with their children, too. It might be silly, but it kept life fun.

As they drove back to the inn, Ivy slid next to Bennett on the bench seat. Fortunately, there was a seatbelt in the middle.

Sitting next to him with the blanket over her legs and the winter breeze in her hair reminded her of old film scenes. Although the trappings of day-to-day life had changed since the 1950s, the human heart still longed for the same closeness and connection.

When *White Christmas* came on the radio as they were driving past the Del Mar horse racing track, Ivy turned up the song. "My parents used to play Bing's Christmas album all the time. When my father was young, he worked for Bing Crosby and the group that developed Del Mar. They developed the racetrack in the 1930s, a little before Dad's time, of course, but Bing and his friends were still hanging out there in the sixties."

Bennett stretched his arm across her shoulders. "I used to strum this on the guitar for my folks."

He began to sing, and Ivy rested her head on his shoulder. His gravelly baritone reverberated in his chest and warmed her heart.

She could never have predicted this holiday season. Yet as they wound back to the inn on this wintry eve, she had a strange feeling that more surprises were still to come.

Ivy REACHED UP AND PULLED DOWN THE RETRACTABLE ATTIC staircase from the ceiling and locked it into place. "We haven't been up here much since we had a big Halloween party, so there might still be some stray popcorn around." Rocky and Reed had also slept here over the long Thanksgiving weekend. She gathered her soft denim skirt to start up the stairs.

"I appreciate your taking the time to show me the attic," Nick said, craning his neck to peer into the opening above. His eyes were bright with anticipation.

"We opened the attic during the art festival this past summer and led tours to share the history of the house." As she climbed the stairs, she told Nick about Amelia Erickson and how the house was used during the Second World War for recovering troops and to shelter people.

"Do you know who she was sheltering here?" Nick asked.

Ivy stepped into the attic room. "No one by name, no. In her journal, she wrote about how she was destroyed when a European refugee ship was turned back. Many of those passengers went on to perish in the war." Ivy paused to catch her breath.

"The *S.S. St. Louis*," Nick said.

"You know your history," Ivy replied. "Not many people these days are aware of that." She gave Nick a hand up the last steps. "History, science, music, inventions—you're a Renaissance man, Nick."

He blushed slightly. "My grandparents' influence, I suppose. I have a wide range of interests."

"And you've obviously had time to pursue them." She waved her hand. "This is an outer room, which was probably used for storage. We found some old boxes of tinware here."

Glancing around the small anteroom lined with shelves, Nick took in everything. "I grew up on a farm, so the period from planting to harvest was busy. However, during the winter, my family and I had to occupy ourselves."

"A farm?" Ivy was curious about Nick and his background, but she didn't want to probe. He would share when he was comfortable. She'd had portrait clients like that. At the commencement of the commission, they were quiet and concerned about their appearance, but as they relaxed, they'd let down their defenses. When their personality emerged, she was able to capture their unique character on canvas.

However, Nick didn't expound on his farm life.

"You're very intelligent," Ivy said reassuringly. "I'm sure you'll get the break you've been looking for someday soon."

Nick chuckled. "I've been trying to put the pieces together for a long time."

"You should think about staying in Summer Beach."

"I wouldn't want to impose on your hospitality too much."

"You wouldn't be. And Shelly is very pleased with your work. It's going to be fairly quiet around here until spring break and the summer season. We'll use that time to catch up on maintenance around the grounds and in the house. We're planning several special events right now, so we'll still have some busy periods." So far, she was encouraged by the reservations for the holiday season.

Nick raised his brow. "I'd planned to be on my way after Christmas, though I'll keep your kind offer in mind."

"Please do. Now, let's have a look at the rest of the rooms. They're small but functional." Ivy turned to go through a doorway. She flicked on the overhead lights that Flint had repaired for her.

"Pardon the dust," Ivy said. She bent down to pick up a few pieces of popcorn from the floor.

Nick stood in the middle of the small room, gazing around at the bunk beds built into the wall. In the center of the room sat a table and chairs. He seemed awestruck, taking in every detail.

"We found a receipt for materials dated just after the invasion of Pearl Harbor in 1941. Submarines had been spotted off the California coast, and we think that Amelia was preparing shelter for people who might need it. She lived through the first world war in Europe, so this was very real to her and must have been very frightening."

"She was a woman who took action for what she believed in," Nick said softly. He pressed his hand on a bunk bed with reverence. "I can just imagine the people who stayed here."

Ivy caught a note of emotion in Nick's voice. He didn't seem like the usual tourist curious about the past. *No*, she thought, *he has a special connection*. Perhaps an ancestor served in the war, but again, she didn't press him for details.

Nick followed her through the small rabbit-warren like rooms, noticing every detail. "Do you mind if I take photos?"

"Not at all." She sensed something that she couldn't quite put her finger on.

Nick paused in front of a charcoal sketch pinned to the wall. "This is...astonishing." He stepped back to take a photo. "Do you mind if I look at the back of this?"

"Go ahead, though that hasn't been moved in decades. No telling what you might find behind it."

Nick carefully lifted the sketch from the wall. It had been mounted on a piece of wood from an old orange crate. The label was still on the reverse side.

"I think that's a piece of history," Ivy said. "I wish I knew who the artist was. They had real talent."

"So talented," he said softly.

Though Nick was physically present, he seemed in a world of his own. Ivy stepped aside as he explored the rooms, stopping to touch an old blanket here or a notebook there.

As if talking to himself, Nick murmured, "Just as I imagined."

"Excuse me?" Ivy stepped forward.

Nick merely shook his head. "I know you have other things to do, but would you mind if I stayed here for a little while? It would be a nice place to meditate."

Ivy was surprised, but she couldn't think of any reason why he shouldn't. "Make yourself at home. I have to check on some new guests, but you're welcome to stay here as long as you like. You seem to have a keen interest in history."

"Yes," Nick said simply.

Ivy turned to leave and stepped through a low doorway. Remembering that she wanted to ask Nick to join them at the gingerbread bake-off later, she turned around to mention it. As she did, she saw Nick open a drawer to a small desk. He stared a moment before he picked up something and slipped it into his pocket.

Ivy was so shocked that she could hardly speak. She backed out of the doorway, feeling crushed by what she'd seen. She had trusted Nick, and it wasn't the value of the item, whatever it was, but that he had taken something that was not his. She tried to recall what was in the desk drawer, but all she could remember were some pencils and paper that were of no value.

No, that wasn't quite right. Wasn't there something else? She couldn't think what it was. Still, why would he risk taking anything that didn't belong to him?

Ivy descended the stairs and made her way toward the front desk to check on Poppy and Sunny. Although she smiled at the guests she passed, she couldn't shake the feeling that Nick was hiding something—and not only what he'd concealed in his pocket.

Why did people have to behave like that? Ivy had a sinking feeling in her stomach that she was being taken advantage of. Had Bennett been correct in his initial assessment? Just when she was beginning to relax and enjoy the holidays, now she dreaded having to ask Nick to leave.

LATER THAT AFTERNOON, IVY MADE HER WAY UPSTAIRS INTO the attic. She pulled her sweater close in the drafty room. Everything seemed to be as she'd left it.

She crossed to the small desk where she had seen Nick remove something. When she opened the desk drawer, she saw a few pencils, an old notebook, a pair of scissors, and not much more. She couldn't remember what else had been in the drawer, but it couldn't have been anything of much importance.

Unless it was something they had overlooked.

Or maybe he'd simply needed a pencil. She couldn't very well confront him over such a minor infraction. And hadn't he handled the jeweled egg? If he were a thief, he probably would have discerned its value right away.

Still, she had a strange feeling that she couldn't shake.

Ivy glanced from a small, high porthole window that looked out toward the ocean. Below, she could see Shelly and Nick in the yard. Nick was trimming branches and putting them in recycling cans for pickup in the morning. He'd been a huge help to her sister.

Shelly hadn't been a fan of Nick initially, but since he'd started working with her, she'd changed her assessment of the young man.

And unless Ivy wanted to risk another argument with Bennett, she couldn't discuss this incident with him. Or maybe they'd moved past that now. Either way, she hated to bring up the subject.

Ivy turned off the light and went downstairs.

It's only a pencil, she told herself. Wasn't it?

CHAPTER 15

"*L*isten up, everyone," Bennett said, pacing along the starting line he'd drawn in the sand. "The Santa Sprint is about to begin. From here," he turned and pointed down the beach, "to that lighthouse and back. The first one back wins bragging rights and free coffee for the next month at Java Beach." He tugged on his red Santa hat and grinned. "And the mayor's special reserved parking spot at City Hall through the end of January."

Hoots and hollers burst out in the cold morning air, sounding over the ocean's crashing waves and sending shore birds skittering. Bennett chuckled to himself. They'd soon find he'd taken the farthest spot from the front of the building.

Bennett glanced at Ivy, who was sitting by the marked starting line—a line of red chalk—cradling a cup of steaming coffee next to Ophelia. The two women had been collecting donations for the children's center and greeting everyone. Some had bought Santa Sprint sweatshirts that a local shop had provided. "Sure you don't want to join us?"

"Someone has to watch the finish line," Ivy said, shivering. "Just in case it's a close finish."

"And take photographs," Ophelia said. She raised her

camera, a fairly sophisticated instrument. "Smile and act sassy."

Snap, snap.

Bennett figured that Ivy was keeping Ophelia company. The older woman had twisted her ankle on the beach walk yesterday morning, and Ivy didn't want her to feel left out. These little acts of compassion and kindness endeared Ivy to him. Over the past months, he'd noticed it more and more.

Ophelia glanced between Bennett and Ivy. "Ivy, please don't feel like you have to stay with me. I'm bundled and warm against the breeze, but you look like you could use a brisk walk to get the blood going."

"Are you sure?" Ivy asked.

"Positive," Ophelia said. When Ivy rose to join Bennett, Ophelia gave Bennett a quick wink.

"I'll walk with you," Bennett said, nodding his appreciation to Ophelia.

"I thought you'd be running in the lead," Ivy said.

Bennett rubbed his thigh. "Not this time. I've got an issue with my quad muscle right now. Don't want to push it." He could, of course, but he'd won the Santa Sprint before, and he wanted to see others have a shot. Guessing who would win was half the fun.

When Ivy shivered again, Bennett picked up a red sweatshirt from a box and handed a few bills to Ophelia for the purchase. "You look like you need this," he said to Ivy.

"We'll match now," she said, laughing. She shrugged into the roomy sweatshirt, zipped it up to her chin, and pulled up the hoodie over her hair. "Much better, thank you."

"Woo-hoo, let's get the party started," Shelly yelled, jogging in place. Her hair was brushed into a high ponytail, and she wore bright red earmuffs. She and Mitch lined up next to each other.

"Ladies first," Mitch said, taking a step back.

Shelly tugged the sleeve of his old sweatshirt. "You get

back here. If I'm going to beat you, I don't want you to say you gave me any kind of advantage. Fair and square, got it?"

"You think you'll beat me?" Mitch bounced in place like a prizefighter. "You asked for it. Guess I should apologize in advance for kicking sand in your face."

"I don't think so," Shelly shot back. "You're the one who'll be eating my sand." She sank into a deep runner's stretch as if to taunt him with her limberness.

Mitch did a couple of air punches. "Okay, New York. I'll show you how it's done on this coast."

Wearing his university fleece jacket, Jamir lined up on the front line next to Jen and George, who were wearing matching *Got Nails?* sweatshirts and Santa hats. Contractor Axe Woodson was there with a Montana sweatshirt, looking amused at the costumes other runners wore. This year, they had plenty of Santas, a couple of elves, and a reindeer.

Inn guests Molly Ann, Kristy, and Rosamie, among others, were chatting in the middle of the group, while Arthur, Ginger, and Darla gathered with others who were walking in the rear.

Nan was passing out jingle bell necklaces to everyone. "Who needs a jingle necklace?" She shook the bells vigorously.

"Up here, Nan," Shelly said. "So I can make a lot of noise as I'm passing Mitch."

"Then I'd better take a couple, too," Mitch said.

"We're gladly accepting donations for these," Nan said as she looped strands over their heads.

"Winner pays," Mitch said, reaching into his pocket.

Shelly whipped out a bill and beat him to it. "Agreed."

Bennett stood before them, hands on his hips. "As many of you know, George is the one to beat this year. But I haven't seen him running on the beach as much these last few weeks. Just saying some of you might have a shot."

"Hey, don't jinx me," George said. "I've been running on my treadmill. Didn't want to scare anyone from coming out."

Good-natured jeers erupted from the crowd, and Bennett laughed. Regardless of who won or came in last, they'd all celebrate at Java Beach afterward.

Bennett blew the whistle around his neck and raised his hand in the air. "On your mark, get set, go!"

The crowd surged forward with Jamir, George, Mitch, and Axe in the lead. Shelly kept pace just behind Mitch. As they raced across the sand, the distance between the runners and walkers lengthened.

Bennett matched Ivy's long stride. "What do you think about our Santa Sprint?"

Ivy's laughter floated on the breeze, shimmering with lightness. "I think you're all a bit nutty, but I can't remember when I've had so much fun."

Bennett nodded ahead. "I didn't know Shelly would be so competitive. I don't think I've ever seen her running on the beach. I thought she was only interested in yoga."

"Shelly was on the track team in high school. With her long legs, she can cover some ground. And she's been running after yoga class—after you've left for the office."

"That makes sense," he said. "Maybe she's holding back."

"Shelly isn't known to hold back on much of anything."

Breathing deeply, Ivy set a brisk pace. Bennett enjoyed walking with her. Sometimes they strolled along the beach in the evening after dinner, sharing the events of their day. Those were times he treasured. He'd help wash the dinner dishes so they could take half an hour or so by themselves.

After dinner, Shelly and Mitch often lounged outside by the fire pit with blankets and a pot of tea or an occasional glass of wine. Sometimes Bennett and Ivy would return and join them, or Ivy might have guests or other business to handle.

Since the busy, crazy days of the summer, they had all

fallen into a different rhythm. Summer Beach was like that. Autumn and winter were the quietest seasons with few tourists, but Bennett enjoyed the tranquility.

As the leading edge of the runners reached the turn-around point at the lighthouse, Bennett checked his watch. "They're making good time. But now the fun begins. There's a lot of strategy going on now. Watch what happens when they merge through the other group."

As the runners neared the walkers, cheers and jingles rose in the air. Mitch and Shelly went wider into the soft, slower sand, while Axe and Jamir stayed on the harder sand, but they had to run back through the crowd, slowing and dodging them as they did.

Axe lost momentum while Jamir surged ahead, but when Mitch and Shelly pounded back onto the damp, hard-packed sand, Mitch took the lead, with Shelly in fourth place.

"Looks like Jamir might have the win this year," Bennett said. "Young legs have an advantage."

"We'll see how their strategies play out," Ivy said.

"A good plan is important, and that can change during a long race."

"I'll say," Ivy said.

"I take it you're not talking about the race."

"We had to pivot fast to fill rooms. And now look at our guests. They're all having a grand time." She glanced around. "Can we turn back? I don't care if I finish, but I want to watch Shelly."

"Sure, let's go."

Ivy turned and broke into a jog. Ahead they could see the top four runners, closing in on the finish line. Ophelia was filming, and a larger crowd of onlookers had gathered.

"Go, Shelly!" Ivy cried, picking up speed.

Suddenly, Shelly pulled around the men, her long legs pumping.

"Well, I'll be," Bennett said. "Look at her go."

"That's strategy," Ivy said. "I know my sister."

Shelly passed Axe, who seemed to be tiring and lagged in the crowd. Just before the finish line, she sailed past Mitch, and from where they were, it looked like she might have tied with Jamir.

Whoops of surprise burst from the crowd.

"Wow," Bennett cried. "Pretty impressive."

When they arrived at the finish line, both Shelly and Jamir were celebrating.

Ophelia was replaying her film. "Right there," she said, pointing to a slow-motion frame. "That's a tie."

Ivy raced to Shelly and gave her a huge hug. Shelly was panting hard and laughing, while Mitch looked dumbfounded.

"She actually did it," Mitch said. "I can't believe she beat me."

Bennett congratulated Jamir and gave Mitch a playful slap on the back. "These Bay family women are full of surprises. Does that mean you're training more next year?"

Mitch drained a bottle of water. "Looks like it."

"Hot chocolate is on me at Java Beach," Bennett said, and people began making their way toward the coffee shop.

CHAPTER 16

*W*hile Imani brought in bags of groceries from her car, Ivy brought out a set of sturdy ceramic mixing bowls from the butler's pantry. Imani and her son were baking gingerbread for the First Annual Gingerbread Bake-Off at the Seabreeze Inn.

"Let me know what else you might need," Ivy said as she placed the bowls on the kitchen counter.

"I think I have everything, thanks to you," Imani said. "My new house should be ready by summer, and I can't wait to have a kitchen and gadgets and a garden again." She quickly added, "Not that I haven't loved being here, but you know what I mean."

"I sure do," Ivy said, thinking about how much this home meant to her and Shelly. "Having a home of your own is special. But so is sharing a home with family or good friends."

Imani shook her head as she tied on an apron. "I never thought I would miss cooking, but it turns out I do. When Jamir was young, and I was in law school, we used to gather in the kitchen and bake for fun." She glanced up at the clock above the sink. "As soon as my son's last final exam is over, he'll be here. I know the rules. Both team members have to be present."

"Sunny has her last exam today, too," Ivy said, wiping down the counter for her. "It's been a tough semester for her, what with the new school and new friends. She's been nervous about her exams."

"Weren't we all," Imani said. "Sunny seems like a bright girl. She just needs to find the right path for her talents." Imani hummed as she removed flour, brown sugar, and ginger from a shopping bag.

Ivy was surprised at how many people had entered the gingerbread bake-off. Ginger Delavie had drafted Bennett and Cookie, the organizer of the Summer Beach farmers market, to serve as judges. Mitch had immediately announced his entry, and the Java Beach coffee group quickly spread the word. While no entry fee was required, Poppy was collecting donations for the children's center.

Ivy glanced at the clock. Shelly had just finished leading her yoga class, which met later on the weekend. Ivy could hear attendees chatting as they hurried to the dining room for a late breakfast.

Shelly sauntered into the kitchen in her yoga gear. "Good morning, Imani. Ready for the big contest?"

"You bet I am. I plan to sell my award-winning ginger-bread loaves at Blossoms."

Mitch opened the back door. "And I'm offering *my* award-winning gingerbread pancakes on the menu at Java Beach." He carried a basket of fresh cranberry and orange muffins that Poppy had ordered yesterday for breakfast.

"Ha, we'll see about that," Imani said. "I've been making gingerbread almost as long as you've been alive."

"Yeah? Well, I trained under the best."

Imani tilted her nose up and gave Mitch a smug look. "That doesn't mean you can execute. We'll let the judges decide, but I'm not worried. I know what I'm capable of."

Mitch grinned and gave her a high-five. "Game on, then."

After watching this exchange, Shelly twirled her work-out

towel and popped Mitch on his bottom with it. "You'd better take those muffins into the dining room before those women get a whiff of them and tear you to pieces."

Mitch leaned over and kissed Shelly on the cheek. "Yes, ma'am."

"Don't you *yes ma'am* me," Shelly said, narrowing her eyes. "And that better not be a dig at my age. I left you in the sand at the Santa Sprint."

Grinning, Mitch said, "I love dating a cougar." He swiftly dodged Shelly's towel again and raced from the kitchen, his box of muffins in hand.

While Ivy and Imani laughed, Shelly rolled her eyes. "Be honest. Do you think he's too young for me?"

Ivy slung her arm around her sister, who had always been the unpredictable one in the family. "Does it matter what anyone else thinks? Others' opinions have never bothered you before. Don't let them start now."

"Aw, I'm just kidding," Shelly said. She threw her towel around her neck and jerked her thumb toward the door. "Mitch is all right. More than all right, in fact."

Ivy heard a soft note in her sister's voice. "And exactly what does that mean?"

Shelly brushed back wisps of chestnut hair that escaped her messy bun. "We've just been talking…"

Ivy and Imani exchanged looks. "About what?" Ivy asked.

Shelly brought out a bottle of orange juice from Gertie and took a glass from a cabinet. "About the future." She poured juice and gazed out the window toward the sea as she sipped. "What we want for our lives."

"Oh, my, my," Imani said, smoothing a handwritten recipe on the counter. "Sounds like you two are getting serious."

Turning back, Shelly flushed. "Maybe. But don't let that get around."

"As if the entire town hadn't already figured that out," Ivy added.

Shelly had met Mitch the first day she and Ivy arrived in Summer Beach last spring. Shelly had just broken up with her long-time boyfriend in New York, Ezzra, who had been dodging the marriage question. Shelly wanted children and a family, so at thirty-seven, she was growing anxious.

Ivy understood that forlorn look of regret in Shelly's eyes. Her sister waited too many years for the wrong man. Ivy wondered if they would have an announcement to make by the end of the year. Although Ivy liked Mitch, she hoped he wouldn't waste Shelly's time.

Mitch stepped back into the kitchen, and Shelly brightened. "Why do I feel like you three have been talking about me while I've been gone?" He ran his hand over his spiky, sun-bleached hair like an overgrown kid.

Shelly shrugged into a hoodie and pulled gloves from the pockets. "Want to go with me to the Hidden Garden, sweetie? Leilani called yesterday, and she put aside a lot of trimmed branches that we can use in my wreath-making class for guests today. They can display them here until they leave, and I'll film a video for my channel."

"Sure," Mitch said. "My assistant can handle the late coffee crowd on her own."

"Wreath-making, huh? That was clever of you," Ivy said, thinking about how much time that would save them—and the inn would be beautifully decorated with the guests' unique contributions. "Think they'd be interested in my vacuuming class?"

"Nice try," Shelly said. "You have to get more creative. Like vacuum cleaner tango or something." She paused at the rear door. "I forgot to tell you, but I told one of our guests, Kristy, that she could use the kitchen for her gingerbread entry. I love how everyone is getting involved, even our guests."

"I'm sure they will all be happy to test, too." Ivy tapped her fingers on the counter, thinking about the awards. She had painted the winner's medallions by hand. "Perhaps we should add a popular vote category so everyone can choose their favorite."

Mitch and Imani traded competitive glances.

"That one's mine," Mitch said.

Imani shot back. "In your dreams, surfer boy,"

After a little good-natured jesting, Shelly and Mitch left through the back door and got into Shelly's old Jeep.

Imani raised an eyebrow. "As long as I've known Mitch, I've never seen him so serious about a woman. He's a good guy. Sure hope your family likes him."

"At least Shelly doesn't have to deal with daughters' opinions." Ivy folded her arms and leaned against the counter. "For having a tough start in life, Mitch has done well for himself. And Bennett thinks the world of him. Mitch is like the younger brother he'd never had."

"Shelly could do a lot worse." Running a finger down the recipe, Imani lined up the ingredients and measuring cups and spoons that she would need. "I don't think you need to worry about those two. Looks like you have issues of your own to resolve."

Ivy nodded with a sigh. After making sure that Imani had everything she needed, Ivy made her way toward the ballroom, where she found Poppy tidying the room. This afternoon, they would have close to a hundred people there, maybe more.

The directors at the children's center had been happy to move Santa's visit to the Seabreeze Inn. The children were excited to see the tall Christmas tree in the old beach house that they'd once thought was haunted.

Ginger Delavie would preside over the gingerbread judging, and Ivy figured they would have plenty of gingerbread for the children to enjoy. And that would give Bennett time to change into his Santa outfit. After the children had their fill of gingerbread, Santa and his elves would arrive with gifts that had been donated by community residents.

Poppy was busy moving art objects and holiday decorations to higher shelves. "We're going to have an army of young children here, so I thought I should secure the breakables."

"Good idea," Ivy said, picking up a blown-glass shell her mother had given them and moving it to a more secure location. "They're going to be so excited. I can't wait to see them all. Bennett said the children dress up, so let's clear a special area for them. Santa could sit right about there. Between the tree and the fireplace." She and Poppy moved furniture and shoved a large chair into position. Brushing her hands, Ivy stepped back to view the setting. "This will be a lovely photo op. I'm so excited."

"So am I. Oh, I forgot to tell you. Two last-minute VIP contestants confirmed by email this morning," Poppy said. "You'll never guess one of them."

"Carol Reston?"

"Bingo. And who else?"

"I have no idea."

"Rowan Zachary," Poppy said. "Carol thought it would be fun to enter a family recipe, and since Rowan is her house-guest for the holidays, he promised a special entry, too."

"Just keep him away from the pool," Ivy said. "I'd rather not have to go full lifeguard and dive in after his inebriated you-know-what again. Especially not in a dress and boots."

Rowan Zachary was a well-known Hollywood film actor, and last summer, his son and Carol's daughter married. When Carol's home was damaged in the Ridgetop fire, the wedding planned at her estate was quickly shifted to the Seabreeze Inn. Carol Reston sang her top hits, but an inebriated Rowan fell into the pool. As the only one there with lifeguard training, Ivy dove in to drag the distressed man to safety.

"I'll try to watch him," Poppy said as she relocated the

delicate ornaments on lower branches higher on the tree. "I used to do this to deter my old roommate's inquisitive cat, but that tabby was determined. She clawed down the entire tree on Christmas Eve."

"That happened with a family cat when we were kids, too." Ivy laughed. "At least we don't have to worry about that. And Gilda promised to keep Pixie away." Her phone buzzed in her pocket, and she pulled it out.

"It's Ari," Ivy said. "I'd better take this in the library." She answered the phone on her way through the house, then closed the door behind herself. In the course of dealing with the art discoveries she and Shelly had made in the old house, she'd grown rather fond of the FBI agent.

"Sorry to bother you on the weekend," Ari said. "I thought you should know about this. Are you sitting down?"

Ivy sank into a wingback chair. "I am now. So whose stolen or sheltered property have we found this time?"

Ari's laughter rolled across the telephone line. "We've run checks against every database we have. Is the egg in a secure place?"

"It's in the bank vault, the same place where you picked up the tiara and other crown jewels, so you know the way. Are you coming before or after the holidays?" She knew the process now.

Ari paused and cleared his throat. "It doesn't look like we'll be transferring the piece at this time."

"Oh, that's fine," Ivy said. "It can wait. I know you're busy."

"It's not that," Ari said. "An object of that value would certainly be listed in the stolen art database. We contacted our sources and shared the images you sent. Upon review, they identified this egg as one that Armand Hammer had for sale in the 1930s as a part of Russia's treasures-to-tractors program, a Soviet drive to generate foreign currency. From

1918 to 1938, Russia sold off many national treasures, as well as property stripped from homes of aristocrats."

"I read about that online," Ivy said.

"Then you know the history." Ari went on. "For this piece, the provenance on record includes Mrs. Gustav Erickson of San Francisco. While this is not an actual imperial egg, it did belong to a prominent industrialist whose property the Bolsheviks seized. Relatives have filed for restitution of some artwork and *objets d'art*, but in this case, it doesn't appear that there were any surviving heirs."

A prickly feeling gathered around Ivy's neck. "So, what do I do with it?"

"I suggest you contact an attorney, who will most likely contact the attorney who represented the estate on the property sale."

Imani had mentioned that. "Do you think this would be considered mislaid or abandoned property?"

"Couldn't say," Ari replied. "This happened a long time ago, but I'm not an attorney, which is why I suggest you engage one. If the egg is deemed yours, you can keep it or contact an auction house. Christie's or Sotheby's are good places to start for a piece with such high historical value. Should you wish to go that route, you'll probably realize an excellent price for it."

Ivy chewed her lip. This seemed so surreal. "I'm almost afraid to ask…"

Ari chuckled again. "A low to mid eight-figure value is my guesstimate, but again, I'm no expert. But please, keep it safe."

Ivy hesitated, calculating the zeros. As she gasped, the phone slipped from her hand and tumbled to the floor. With trembling fingers, she picked up the phone. She thanked Ari for his news and hung up.

Questions swirled in her head. She understood the historical significance of the piece. She wasn't sure what legal right she had to it. If any. After Amelia's death, the Erickson collection was auctioned to benefit charities.

Still, Shelly would argue that an eight-figure windfall was worth pursuing. Maybe she owed it to her sister. And to her children. What a difference that could make in their lives. Then she thought about lottery winners ill-equipped to handle sudden wealth, who suffered as a result.

However, establishing her right to the historical egg might take months. And years, perhaps, to go through the court system, as Imani had suggested. And who might she be challenging regarding ownership?

As she thought about this, Ivy groaned. If the provenance was clear, then the case would be between Ivy and the charities Amelia had named in her will. Torn, Ivy pressed her hands to her face and sighed.

CHAPTER 17

*B*y that afternoon, the aroma of ginger, cinnamon, and cloves filled the inn. All manner of delicious-looking delicacies were arriving cradled in the arms of the contestants. Imani and Jamir had just removed three ginger-bread loaves from the oven, and Kristy was decorating ginger-bread cookies.

"As soon as you're ready, bring your entries into the ball-room," Ivy said, glancing around the buzzy kitchen.

Ivy had changed into a deep-green sweater dress and matching short suede boots with furry tops. Just for fun, she added textured, snowflake-patterned tights. She was feeling festive and looking forward to kicking off this new event. She hoped it would become an annual affair.

Jamir was smoothing creamy frosting over the gingerbread loaves. "We'll be right there," he said. "You're not going to believe how good these are. My grandmother taught me how to make these."

"And my grandmother before her," Imani added with pride.

"Almost finished here," Kristy said. Her freckled cheeks were pink from the heat in the kitchen.

Nick was perched beside Kristy, watching her every move

with admiration.

Kristy had the kind of laugh that made Ivy think of tinkling bells. She peeked over the young woman's shoulder at a tray of gingerbread cookies that had painted faces with rosy cheeks and sweet smiles. "Wow, you're a true artist. You have an entire village of gingerbread people here. I don't think I've ever seen any so expertly produced."

Kristy beamed. "I trained as a pastry chef. For me, this is just for fun."

"To share food is to share joy," Nick said sagely between bites of a gingerbread man. "And when such love goes into preparation, it is even more delicious."

Leaving the cooks in the kitchen, Ivy continued into the ballroom where Poppy and Sunny had set up a space for the judges and other tables to display the entrants' gingerbread masterpieces.

"Everything ready to go?" Ivy asked. With so many people arriving, she was a little nervous about the event, but the guests were loving the happy commotion and chaos.

"Almost everyone is here," Poppy said. "Except for Rowan Zachary."

Ivy sighed. "Why does that not surprise me?"

"Maybe he wants to make a grand entrance." Poppy glanced toward the front door. "Look at all the people coming in. I'll greet them. Come on, Sunny." The two young women hurried away.

Shelly's wreath-making class had been a big hit with guests earlier today. As a result, beautiful fragrant wreaths graced the walls and tabletops, with a delightful variety of ribbons and ornaments and glitter. Ophelia had painted miniature red and gold apples that she affixed to her wreath, while her new friend Molly Ann's wreath featured a stunning array of shells and sea glass she'd collected on the beach. Gilda's wreath held a framed photo of her and Pixie, along with dog toys and treats.

Ivy strolled through the ballroom, greeting entrants and checking out entries. There were gingerbread cookies in every shape, gingerbread loaves, and gingerbread pudding. Ivy saw gingerbread eggnog, gingerbread cupcakes, and gingerbread houses decorated with candy. A gingerbread roll cake, gingerbread pancakes, and even gingerbread whoopie pies. She loved seeing the inventiveness of her neighbors.

Poppy crossed the room with Ginger Delavie, who wore a red sweater woven with silver threads and a green-and-red plaid skirt that fell to her calves.

Ivy greeted her with a smile. "We've had so many entrants. You're going to be quite busy sampling."

"I had a hearty hike to the ridge top this morning, so I'm ready," Ginger said, patting her toned torso. "I brought scorecards for us to keep track. Where are my fellow judges?"

Bennett stepped beside Ivy. Cookie, a portly gray-haired woman with a round face wreathed with a smile, joined the little group, too. They all knew each other, and Ginger began briefing them. "I've judged other events, so here's how we'll proceed."

"Ginger is in charge here," Ivy said, relieved that Ginger was so well organized. "I'm going to make sure all the participants have what they need."

Everything seemed to be running smoothly. Poppy and Sunny had given each entrant a number. Shelly was interviewing the amateur chefs and filming the vast array of wondrous creations. Her video channel had been getting a lot more traffic over the holidays.

On the other side of the room by the towering Christmas tree, a trio of Celia's young students was performing. The sweet string music of the violin, viola, and cello elevated the holiday mood. *Winter Wonderland, Jingle Bells, Frosty the Snowman,* and *Let It Snow* were a few of the songs Celia had promised for the afternoon.

In the foyer, children from the center with their parents were arriving. Ivy waved at the center directors. Everyone wore holiday clothes, and eyes grew wide at the sight of the tree with its vintage ornaments. Children squealed with delight. And Ivy could hardly wait to see Bennett as Santa Claus. She chuckled at the thought.

Ivy was thrilled that the event had come together so well. Shelly, Poppy, and even Sunny had been so helpful. Her parents and siblings were here, too, circulating in the growing crowd. Jamir and Imani whisked their creations to the assigned spot, and Kristy followed, carrying her platters of gingerbread people. Guests smiled and commented as the entrants passed through the crowd.

"Attention, everyone," Ivy said. "I'd like to introduce our esteemed judges for the First Annual Gingerbread Bake-Off. Ginger Delavie, Mayor Bennett Dylan, and Cookie O'Toole from the farmer's market."

A round of cheers and applause filled the room.

Ginger said a few words and explained how the judging would take place. "The judges will move down the line of entrants first, and then everyone is welcome to follow along. When we're finished, Ivy will tally the scores, and we'll present the winners."

Ginger led Bennett and Cookie to the first entrant. "First up is Mitch Kline," she announced. Reading the printed card beside his dish, she added, "Gingerbread pancakes with spiced syrup and whipped cream."

Mitch served three taster-sized plates of pancakes with a generous pour of syrup and a dollop of whipped cream speckled with cinnamon and ginger. He watched with pride as the judges tasted his creation.

Bennett and Cookie smacked their lips with approval, though Ginger held back her comments. She made a note on her scorecard and nodded toward Bennett and Cookie to do the same.

Shelly stepped beside Ivy. "Ginger's a tough judge," she whispered.

"Not tough, just high standards," Ivy said.

The threesome moved on to Leilani and Roy, who had created a gingerbread house, Hawaiian-style. "This is a *hale*," Leilani explained, gesturing to their colorful creation trimmed with a toasted-coconut thatched roof, tiny strings of candied lights, and Hawaiian flowers made of sculpted fruit. A gingerbread surfboard rested on a sandy beach made of crushed graham crackers. "This is a small replica of my grandparents' home, where our family gathers for celebrations." Leilani and Roy shared iced gingerbread slabs with the judges.

Next, Imani's loaves were lined up and ready to slice. "We use old-fashioned molasses and cream cheese frosting," she explained while Jamir distributed thick slices. "This recipe has been in my family for more than a century. You'll find nothing better." She shot a triumphant look toward Mitch.

"I think I should have run twice as far this morning," Bennett said.

"Pace yourself," Ginger said. "We have a long way to go."

Next, Jen and George had created a gingerbread roll, held together with fondant nails in a nod to their shop, Nailed It. Ginger nodded, clearly amused at the presentation.

Moving on, Nan and Arthur served old-fashioned gingerbread pudding topped with gingerbread ice cream. "We used an antique recipe from an old cookbook we have in the shop," Nan declared.

More Summer Beach residents stood with their offerings on the long table. Darla had whipped up crispy ginger snaps with frothy gingerbread eggnog, Police Chief Clarkson brought gingerbread whoopie pies, and Fire Chief Paula Stark presided over sweet gingerbread cupcakes topped with chocolate reindeer. Carol Reston scooped out a fluffy, layered gingerbread trifle with layers of cream cheese, gingerbread, and cranberry-orange sauce.

Ivy cut in behind Bennett and whispered to Carol, who was wearing strands of jingle bells around her neck and a Santa hat over her jazzy red, henna-colored hair. "Is Rowan coming?"

"I've been trying to reach him, too," Carol said. "He's so impertinent, but that's his charm, isn't it?" Just then, her phone in her pocket jangled. She pulled it out. "Speaking of that devilish charmer...he's in the kitchen, and he says he needs your help."

"Tell him I'll be right there."

Ivy tugged Bennett's sleeve. "Rowan just arrived. I'll help bring out whatever he brought."

Bennett raised his brow. "This should be interesting. Haven't seen him since he tried to buy your affection."

"And it didn't work, did it?" Ivy chuckled. "Relax, I know what he's all about." Last summer, Rowan had made a play for Ivy, professing his undying devotion, which turned out to be short-lived. He'd even had a new sports car delivered for her, but Ivy had firmly declined the car and Rowan. She hadn't been interested in fifteen minutes of fame or passion.

"Let me know if you need help," Bennett said, squeezing her hand.

Ivy appreciated that Bennett trusted her to handle Rowan, although she knew he'd have her back if needed. Ivy cut through the crowd. Rowan would be the last entrant, and she wanted to make sure he wasn't left out. Many of the parents were probably big fans.

When Ivy walked into the kitchen, Rowan looked up, his silver-screen eyes taking in every bit of her as before.

"If it isn't the loveliest woman in the world," Rowan said, crossing the kitchen to her with his arms outstretched. A lock of hair fell over his forehead like a silent film swashbuckler. "How have you been, my kitten?"

Ivy sidestepped Rowan and managed to catch his hand to shake it—and avert any potential fully-intended accidental touching. She did a quick waltz step—slide to the right, step back, slide to the left, step forward—which left him lunging into thin air.

Ivy suppressed a triumphant chuckle. "It's wonderful to see you again. Bennett and I have missed you."

Rowan's face fell with disappointment, but only for a moment. "My real woman, and one heck of a swimmer, thank heavens. I can think of no one I'd rather have guard my life than you."

"Is this your gingerbread entry?" Ivy asked, steering him back to the present. She eyed several bottles of alcohol on the counter with skepticism.

"Indeed," Rowan replied, his eyes flashing. "A well-kept secret in all the best circles is my specialty, The Flaming Gingerbread Martini."

Ivy narrowed her eyes. "As in spice or actual flames?"

"Don't worry, my dear. I'm well-versed in the art of pyrotechnics. Why, in one of my last films—"

Ivy interrupted. "You get the liquor, and I'll bring glasses. You're at the last spot on the table, and the judges are making their way toward you right now. You don't want to miss your opportunity to shine. And don't you dare give anyone under the legal drinking age a martini, or I'll have your hide."

"Spoken like a true western woman. Do you remember the film I did in Texas, called—"

Ivy snapped her fingers. "Rowan, your public awaits."

"Well, then, it's showtime, my lovely." Rowan waved a hand in a grand gesture.

Ivy groaned and hurried to the butler's pantry for martini glasses. Fortunately, Amelia Erickson had all sorts of barware. Ivy plucked four glasses and followed Rowan, who was making a grand entrance to applause.

Ivy positioned Rowan under large pine boughs arched into a wreath. Shelly had made this wreath and trimmed it with glittery painted burlap fashioned into a floppy bow. People would take photos, so Ivy had selected that spot especially for him. With Rowan's peppermint candy cane vest, it was a perfect photo op.

Ivy placed the martini glasses on the table and stepped back a few feet to make way for the judges.

Rowan began working deftly with the dexterity of a professional bartender. An accomplished showman, Rowan kept up the banter as he poured his ingredients for Ginger, Bennett, and Cookie—and one for him.

"This is of my holiday specialties," Rowan began, projecting his baritone voice to hold the audience in sway. "My world-famous Flaming Gingerbread Martini. I start with Irish cream liqueur, a generous pour of gingerbread vodka, and a splash of simple syrup made with brown sugar."

Ivy watched as Rowan held the audience in rapt attention.

Raising a hand to his mouth as if he had a secret for them, he lowered his voice in a conspiratorial manner. "And here's the trick. A drizzle of spiced rum, like so…" He tilted a bottle, gently pouring rum over the back of the spoon. "Rum is the most flammable spirit, so it must float delicately on top."

At the word flammable, Ivy's ears pricked up, and she held her breath. That meant high alcohol content. Not a favorable mix with Rowan Zachary.

"And now, for the flambé." From his candy cane vest, Rowan withdrew a long-nosed lighter similar to the one Ivy used to light the fireplace. Brandishing it with a flourish, he ignited the rum layer in the glasses.

Blue flames sprang to life, and the crowd applauded. Ivy let out a sigh of relief.

"*Voilà*," Rowan cried in triumph. He threw up his hands, holding the lighter above his head like a torch.

"No!" Ivy's lips parted in horror as the flame touched the burlap bow's long tail and raced up to the wreath.

In seconds, a circle of fire blazed above Rowan like a flaming halo, and gasps swept across the crowd.

CHAPTER 18

*I*vy stared in disbelief at the blazing wreath for a split second before Shelly's voice rang out from beside the fireplace.

"Hey, Ives! Catch!" Her sister heaved a small red fire extinguisher toward her as people ducked out of the way, and children screamed.

Ivy caught the extinguisher, jerked out the pin, and released the locking mechanism. Gritting her teeth, she aimed it straight above Rowan's head.

No time to think. Just act.

"Duck!" Ivy yelled.

While Bennett pushed Rowan to the floor, she unleashed a stream of flame retardant, sweeping it back and forth until the flames were out. In the corner of her eye, she saw Chief Paula racing toward the smoking wreath.

Shaking from the adrenaline rush, Ivy lowered the empty canister and caught her breath.

A cheer went up across the room, and above it all, Shelly called out, "Woo-hoo, Ivy! Way to go!"

The flambéed wreath was an official disaster. Or perhaps it was a disaster averted. With a house full of children and old timbered beams, Ivy couldn't imagine what might have happened if she and Shelly hadn't placed fire extinguishers around the house after the Ridgetop fire last spring.

Paula inspected the area and gave the official thumbs-up. "Quick thinking, Shelly. And good aim, Ivy. See folks, that's why it's good to have fire extinguishers in your home and business."

A wail went up from the floor, and Rowan stumbled to his feet. "My masterpieces," he cried, clenching his hands to his heart.

On the table under the wreath, the martini glasses dripped with the overspray of the flame retardant powder.

Smoke threaded through the air, and Ivy heard a few children cough. "Get the windows open," she said. Poppy and Sunny and Jamir sprang into action, flinging open the tall doors to let in the ocean's brisk winter breezes. Ivy shivered.

"It won't take long to clear the smoke with this wind," Chief Paula said. "Good cross ventilation here. And be sure to replace that fire extinguisher right away."

"We have extras. Do you think it's safe enough for the children to remain?"

Paula glanced over the crowd. "You should move the crowd to the terrace while we make sure. I'll have an engine come out to inspect the house, just to be certain no embers were sucked into a vent."

"I sure appreciate that. Everyone can bundle up, and we'll turn on the heat lamps on the terrace." Ivy had ordered some earlier in the season, and now she was glad they had them.

"Everyone outside to the terrace," Ivy said. "We're moving the party, so bring all the food." She glanced back at the beautiful setting for Santa Claus. Santa-by-the-pool would have to do. Fortunately, most of the parents and the children's center directors had already taken photos of the children by the tree.

Bennett stopped to hug her. "Pretty impressive reaction there. You and Shelly should join our volunteer fire brigade."

Her nerves still on edge, Ivy tried to laugh, but it came out as a strangled cough. "Sorry, the smoke is getting to me."

"Go on with the rest of the guests. I'll grab Flint and Forrest and their boys, and we'll move all these tables and food outdoors." He pressed his cheek against her and whispered in her ear. "I'm so proud of you, and I'm glad you're okay. You and Shelly, you saved us all, sweetheart. That could have been a catastrophe, but the Bay family women are incredible."

"Must have been my lifeguard training," Ivy said. "We were trained to act in seconds."

Still, after the adrenaline wore off, Ivy's muscles were trembling, though she managed to make it outside with the other guests. Her parents and siblings gathered around her and Shelly, telling them both how proud they were of their rapid actions.

"That's how major fires begin," Carlotta said. "Thank goodness you were both on top of it. I always said you two girls made the best team."

A fire engine from the Summer Beach fire department arrived, and Ivy could see Paula directing them. She slipped back into the house to see if they needed anything, but Paula waved her off. "All these young people are taking care of your things inside."

On her way out, Ivy picked up the hand-painted winners' medals she'd created for the bake-off.

"Way to go, Aunt Ivy," Rocky said. He and Reed hefted tables outside, while Poppy and her sister Coral carried food that had been far out of reach of the disaster.

The martinis, however, were a complete loss, as Rowan had left the bottles open. Which was just as well, Ivy decided. Children were here, after all.

Celia stationed her musicians near the warmth of a heat lamp—but not so close as to damage their instruments. Soon, music filled the air. The crashing waves provided stunning background accompaniment. Ivy thought she'd never heard a more beautiful rendition of *Jingle Bells.*

Once the tables and food were arranged on the terrace, and the heat lamps lit, people began to line up for gingerbread treats. It didn't take long for the party to resume.

"Time to tally the scores," Ginger said, waving to her judging team and carrying on with great aplomb despite the close calamity. While Ginger, Bennett, and Cookie gathered at a table, Ivy joined them to perform the official, unbiased tally.

At the table, Ivy added the numbers, and the final tally was closer than she would have thought. All the dishes were delicious.

A thought crossed her mind, and she motioned to her mother. When Carlotta joined her, she said, "Could you and Dad try to keep Rowan away from the pool? We've had enough disasters for one day." It might be just like Rowan to tumble in again so that Ivy could save him.

"I'll share that with Carol," Carlotta said with a firm nod of her head. "She and her husband should look after their guest. And maybe limit his alcohol, especially around children. Don't worry; I'll have a chat with them. I'm sure they're well aware of Rowan's behavior."

"Thanks," Ivy said. Over the years, her parents had supplied Carol and her husband with arts and crafts from all over the world for their Summer Beach home. They knew each other well.

Presently, Ginger clapped her hands. "All our entrants gather round. We have winners to announce." Everyone quickly crowded together.

"In the Traditional Category," Ginger began. "The First Place award goes to the mother-son team of Imani and Jamir Jones for their gingerbread with cream cheese. And a very close Second Place award to Nan and Arthur for their old-fashioned gingerbread pudding."

Cheers went up all around, and Ivy called them up to give

them their medals. She looped her painted medallion around Jamir's neck. "Pre-med, and you can bake. You're going to make someone very happy someday."

Beaming with appreciation, Jamir hugged Ivy and his mother.

Ginger continued. "The Best Cookie award goes to Seabreeze Inn guest Kristy Welch."

Kristy waved her hands. "No, I can't accept this."

Ginger peered over her glasses. "Why not? Your gingerbread people were exceptional."

"I'm a trained pastry chef, so please, give it to someone else." Kristy's face flushed. "I withdraw my entry. I only entered for the fun of baking."

Ivy saw Nick take Kristy's hand and rub it in approval. It was such a sweet gesture that Ivy blinked back tears. To see two young people falling in love was a lovely sight. If Ivy and Shelly and Poppy hadn't created the holiday special and run the ad, the two of them might have never met. It was funny how the world worked.

Ginger cleared her throat. "So noted and accepted, Kristy. Very kind of you." She announced the new First Place winner for Best Cookie and then moved on to the next one.

"First Place for Best Breakfast Fare goes to Mitch Kline for his gingerbread pancakes."

Mitch let out a whoop and high-fived the children standing near him before swinging Shelly around.

A smile played on Ginger's lips. "And our Blooper award goes to..." She strung out the last word until everyone chanted together, "Rowan Zachary!"

Laughter rippled across the yard, and Rowan took a bow.

After the award ceremony was over, the children happily finished off the gingerbread treats. While they were doing that, Bennett slipped away to his apartment unit. Ivy couldn't wait to see what he looked like as Santa Claus. As they waited, the director at the children's center addressed the parents and took photos with the children, who were so excited they couldn't keep still.

A little while later, Ivy spied Bennett creeping down the stairs in his cherry-red Santa suit. He had gone all-in with a faux white beard and a padded belly. As he approached the terrace area, one of the center directors, who was wearing an elf hat, gave him a bag full of gifts to carry. The elves also brought others.

"Ho, ho, ho," Bennett cried out.

Ivy waved at him and laughed. He made quite a convincing Santa, and he clearly enjoyed playing the part.

When the children spotted Santa Claus, they squealed with excitement, although one of two young preschoolers clutched their parents in apparent shyness. Parents helped their children line up to speak to Santa and have their photos taken with him. Kristy stepped up to help as well, no doubt thinking about her children.

Watching them, Ivy recalled taking her girls to see Santa. It seemed like yesterday, though now they were grown. When Misty and Sunny were young, the days were so busy and full—it seemed time would go on forever like that. Ivy remembered falling into bed, exhausted at the end of every day. And now, here she was. On her own for what might be many years to come.

As if reading her mind, Bennett glanced up at her and winked.

Ivy blew him a kiss. How could she not adore a man who dressed up as Santa and listened to every word those precious children had to say?

Glancing around, Ivy circulated to make sure their guests were having a good time and to see if anyone needed anything. The flaming martini fiasco seemed to have been forgotten, and everyone was enjoying themselves. Relieved, Ivy joined her family, but she couldn't keep her eyes off Bennett.

Watching Bennett, her heart felt so full of love. Here was a man so sure of himself and his place in the world that he happily donned a costume and made faces to turn children's tears into laughter. Every child would receive a framed photograph with Santa, courtesy of the high school photography club and the local camera shop. Each would also receive a gift that had been picked out especially for them, along with a gift certificate at a local children's shop.

Ivy had overheard Bennett speaking with Carol Reston, so she knew that Carol and her husband had supplied the gift cards. They made sure that these children had proper shoes and socks, and other gear for school. For the most part, their parents were hard-working, but some had fallen on hard times, while others held jobs that didn't pay very much.

No announcements were made to thank Carol and her husband, but as Ivy watched the couple, she realized that was the way they wanted it. The children's laughter and smiles were enough for them. Ivy saw the couple frequently wiping their eyes.

Near the edge of the terrace, Ivy spied Nick sitting alone, his hands clasped under his chin. He watched intently.

"Excuse me," Ivy said to her parents. "I need to check on a guest." She strolled toward Nick.

Making conversation, she said, "Bennett makes a pretty good Santa, don't you think?"

"He does."

"That's sweet of Kristy to help."

"She's a kind soul," Nick said thoughtfully. "Kristy wrapped the remaining gingerbread cookies she made, and she's giving them to parents to keep for their children. She misses her children, but more than that, I've noticed she truly enjoys helping others."

"She seems like a very caring person."

As Nick ran a hand over his scruffy chin, a philosophical look settled on his face. "I've found that when given the opportunity to be helpful, most people rise to the occasion. Like you."

Ivy shrugged off his comment. "I'm happy to help when I can." She wondered what he was getting at.

Nick laced his long, tapered fingers. "I suppose it's natural to want to share this human experience. For some people, goodness hovers closer to the surface than for others." He chuckled softly.

"How well I understand that." Ivy reflected on the people who'd come into her life to deliver challenges. Some were those she loved, while others seemed to have been dredged up from the muck, like Paisley's ex-fiancé, though he hardly deserved that title. Perhaps even he had a soft heart for puppies or something, as hard as it was to imagine.

Nick gazed at Kristy as he spoke. "Just look at all the people here, intent on giving and sharing happiness tonight. It's so beautiful. Yet, many people build fortresses around themselves."

"Maybe they're scared or want to show strength," Ivy said.

"Or hide their weakness," Nick added. "Some confuse kindness with weakness, so they perceive kindness as the opposite of strength. Yet, truly strong people are often the kindest. These are complementary concepts." He lifted his palms, shifting them up and down like a scale. "Like yin and yang. Or winter and summer."

"You're very observant," Ivy said, ruminating on his words. "Have you studied philosophy?"

"A little," Nick said. "What I've seen is that when people's hearts are touched and they give of themselves freely, they find strength, compassion, and love." He smiled. "During holidays, people often come together to lift up others, showing compassion and empathy toward their fellow human beings. Just look at everyone here. These are genuine smiles."

"If only we could be like that every day." She didn't often

engage in such philosophical discussions with guests, but Nick was different.

He clasped his hands, watching the children and Bennett with a smile of enchantment on his face. "When one person elevates another, it brings joy to both. When others help, the burden becomes lighter. That's what's happening here, isn't it?"

Ivy reached out and touched Nick's shoulder. "It takes a special person to see that. That's the magic of the season, a time of year when we open our hearts more fully to each other." She hesitated, thinking about that day in the attic. "Nick, I've been meaning to ask you something."

Nick turned to her with a peaceful smile. "Yes?"

She drew a breath to begin but found she couldn't ask the question. It wasn't the value of the item he took that concerned her that mattered—it was merely her curiosity. And that was no longer important. She waved a hand. "I'm sorry, it just slipped my mind."

Nick smiled. "When I set out a month ago, I had no idea where I was going. I asked that I be steered in the right direction, and here I am. You see, fate takes me where I'm supposed to be, lets me discover what's needed. It always has."

"And we're happy to have you. Things have a way of working out, don't they?"

"And they will for you, too." Nick placed his hand over hers for a moment. "Because you uplift others." Smiling, he turned his gaze back to Kristy.

Ivy glanced at the younger woman chatting with parents and taking photos for them with their children. She started to say more about Kristy, but the look on Nick's face as he watched her told Ivy everything she needed to know.

"She'll be back in a moment," Ivy said, rising. "It's been nice talking with you, Nick."

As Ivy made her way back to the crowd, she thought about what Bennett had once said about Nick. She didn't want it to be true, but she decided that whatever Nick's path was, at least she'd helped him along his journey this holiday season.

She smiled to herself, thinking about what he'd said about lifting up each other. Maybe that's what this unusual opportunity was all about.

Across the crowd, Bennett lifted the last child from his lap and waved at Ivy. She hurried toward him.

"Pretty impressive, Santa," she whispered so as not to destroy the illusion for the youngest children, whose eyes were wide with delight.

Bennett wrapped his arm around her and drew her to his knee. "What's your Christmas wish?"

After her deep discussion with Nick, any physical item she might've wanted seemed to pale in comparison. "Besides no more fires at the inn? I'd have to say that I wish every person here goes to sleep—and wakes—with a joyful heart this holiday season."

"That's a mighty fine wish." Bennett rummaged through the bag next to him and withdrew a small box. "I see that this has your name on it. It's Ivy, right?"

Laughing, she accepted the small red box. "Should I open it here?" It seemed so light. She couldn't imagine what it would be. Hesitating, she shook it lightly and listened.

"I promise it won't embarrass you," he whispered.

When Ivy opened the box, her heart leapt. "Yes, oh yes," she said, laughing again.

In her hand, she held a note that read: *Will you spend Christmas Eve with me after the children are tucked in their beds? I promise to get you home by midnight.*

CHAPTER 19

$\mathcal{T}$he Christmas Stroll was busier than usual, and Bennett made slow progress along Main Street, stopping to answer questions from locals and visitors. The decorations committee, headed by Nan and Arthur at Antique Times, had hired a couple of enterprising college students to wrap sparkling lights around palm tree trunks and to line the palm fronds. Against a starlit sky and the ocean's foamy tide, the palm trees swayed in a light breeze.

The effect was simply magical.

A young couple stopped him. "Hello, Mayor," they sang out. "How is your holiday shopping going?"

"Hello, Megan. Hi, Josh. A little slow this year. How's your work on the new house?" Bennett stopped to hear about the progress on the bungalow they were renovating that he had found for them as their real estate agent, as well as their work on the Amelia Erickson documentary. He always liked to make sure that new residents in Summer Beach were finding everything they needed.

They moved on, but a group of visitors stopped to say hello and ask for restaurant recommendations.

It had been Nan's idea to make him a button that said, *Say Hello to the Mayor.* At first, he'd thought that would be a nice touch, but virtually everyone he passed had stopped to talk to him. He'd only gone about twenty feet in the last hour.

Normally, he wouldn't have minded. But tonight, he was on a mission. After the last group moved on, he cut through a side alley and walked behind the shops until he came to the one he wanted. Skirting waste bins, wooden pallets, and a surfboard, he made his way to the rear door.

Arthur looked up from his rolltop desk, where he was writing an invoice. "Good heavens, Mayor Bennett," he exclaimed in his clipped British accent. "Why are you using the rear entrance?"

"It's been pretty busy out front on the street." Bennett motioned to the button. "Nan had me wearing this. I've been the official greeter out there for the last hour."

"My wife means well," Arthur said, grinning. "What can I help you with?"

Bennett slid a hand over his hair. "Something special for Ivy, but I have no idea where to start."

"Don't you, mate?" Arthur's eyes twinkled behind his glasses.

Bennett opened his mouth, but he couldn't come up with a good answer. He knew what Arthur was asking. Was he that obvious?

Arthur peered over the rim of his glasses. "For heaven's sake, don't look so gobsmacked. It's easy to see what's on your mind. Ivy is a fine lady."

Bennett rubbed his chin. "I don't think that's going to happen just yet."

Not that he wasn't considering asking Ivy the question closest to his heart. In fact, he had spoken to Ivy's father at the tree-trimming party, and Sterling made it clear that Bennett would be welcome in the family. That had been a little surprising, given how close Sterling was with his grandchildren— Sunny, in particular.

"Which one of you is afraid of taking the next step?"

"Good question. I know what I want." But did Ivy?

Arthur removed his glasses and rubbed a soft cloth over them. "There's hardly ever a perfect time. But the days roll past regardless. One day you might wake up to find that she's met another. Rowan Zachary certainly had his eye on her."

"Not a chance on her part."

"Don't be so sure. He can offer a lot of excitement, glamorous travel, the best restaurants, Hollywood parties."

"That's not Ivy."

Arthur held his glasses up to the light. "Many a man has worn down a woman's defenses. If not Rowan..." He shook his head. "Captivating woman, enormous house on the beach..."

"That's irrelevant to me," Bennett interjected. "Well, except for that first part." He drew a breath to quell his nerves. He was bumbling like a teenager. "It's barely been two years since her husband died. I'm giving her the time she needs."

"Is that what she said?"

"Not exactly."

Arthur put his glasses back on. "Perhaps she'd like to make that decision for herself."

Nan's voice rang out from the front of the store. "Is that invoice ready?"

"Coming, my dear." Arthur gestured for Bennett to follow. "Pay heed, young man. Now, let's see if we can find something unusual for Ivy."

After perusing the glass cabinets of vintage jewelry, Bennett spied a thin platinum chain with a cabochon emerald pendant that would accent her eyes. It was simple enough to wear every day, yet it would be beautiful with a dressy outfit, too. He thought the vintage piece would appeal to her.

"I'll take this one," Bennett said. "It reminds me of Ivy."

"Excellent choice," Arthur said.

Bennett clasped his hands and rocked on his feet. It had

been a long time since he'd bought jewelry for a woman, and he'd forgotten how much he enjoyed it.

While Nan wrapped it for him, Bennett perused the jewelry cases. Arthur had a point. Bennett didn't see anything that he thought might suit Ivy, but then, he'd never seen her previous ring. Knowing Jeremy's penchant for display, it had probably been significant.

Bennett tapped his knuckles on the glass counter. He was getting ahead of himself.

AFTER RETURNING TO THE INN, BENNETT TUCKED THE GIFT into a dresser drawer. Ivy's light was off, and the inn was quiet. Ivy and Shelly had organized a girl's night out at the Starfish Café. He decided to take a walk on the beach to think. He pulled on a fleece-lined jacket and started for the beach.

The waves were coming in rapid sets, breaking on the beach and sending a cool mist into the evening air. The moon shone high in the sky, illuminating the ocean's steely blue surface. Shoving his hands in his pockets, he set off.

As he walked, his warm breath formed puffs of clouds. In his mind, he turned over the events of the last year, starting with the day Ivy had arrived in Summer Beach. He'd never thought that the girl he'd dreamed about as a teenager would reappear in his life, though he hadn't recognized her at first.

The shy teenager with streaked blond hair half hiding behind a surfboard had grown into a confident, talented woman capable of handling the most adverse situations, from the death of her husband to confronting—and even accepting—his mistress. She'd renovated a white elephant of a house and created an income for herself and those she held dear—Shelly, Poppy, her daughters. As an innkeeper, Ivy took care of every detail, even though she'd never done anything like it before. She simply treated guests with genuine kindness and hospitality.

Not to mention the surprises she handled along the way—always with keen insights and wisdom.

This is the woman he loved.

As Arthur had asked, what was he waiting for?

Or, what was he afraid of?

If he told Ivy what was on his mind, he could almost picture her initial elation, and then her practical side would take over, and she would firmly, yet politely, decline his offer. He would be embarrassed, and they might never speak of it again.

Bennett blew out a puff of cold air. He would be devastated. Yet, he would have to continue to see her almost every day in Summer Beach. And that would break his heart.

For all the brave faces men put on, the fear of rejection from the women they cared for the most could be debilitating.

Jackie had been the love of his life, but that was ten long, lonely years ago. Rocking on his feet, he faced the ocean, conversing with Jackie in his thoughts, seeking her advice. Ivy and Jackie were of a similar temperament, though they were both utterly unique. However, the light in their eyes when they looked at him was the same.

Over the roar of the ocean, he seemed to hear Jackie's words as clearly as if she were standing there with him. *That's because she's in love with you.*

Was it too soon? On the other hand, if he waited, would he lose her?

For a man who prided himself on being decisive, he was having a hard time with these questions.

Once again, the words whispered over the ocean. *Let her decide.*

Bennett turned to walk back to his apartment over the garage. As he did, he heard a soft sob beside a lifeguard stand. Someone was obviously in distress. It was far too cold for a person to suffer alone out here. The tide was coming in, and the sea could rush over a person without warning.

The holidays could be hard on people who'd lost loved ones through death or divorce or breakups. This he knew all too well.

"Hello there," Bennett said. He put his head down against the chill wind, which stung his eyes and whipped tears into his hairline. The temperature was dropping; it was much colder than normal for this time of year. Yet this was California; the temperature might rise again next week. He shivered and turned up his collar.

This wasn't a night to be alone on the beach.

A slight figure huddled beneath a dark, hooded jacket sat forlornly beside the lifeguard stand. *Maybe a young runaway.* They'd had a few of those in Summer Beach over the years. The desperate parents had been relieved to find their child, and social workers spent time with the families to make sure disagreements were addressed and resolved.

"Are you okay?" Bennett circled in front of the person so as not to scare whoever it was. Kneeling on the cold, damp sand, he said softly, "I'm the mayor of Summer Beach, and whatever is troubling you, I can help."

Another sob broke forth from the person—a young woman, probably. Doubled over, she buried her face in her knees.

"It's going to get colder out here tonight."

"Go away," came the muffled reply.

"I'm sorry, but I can't leave you out here. The tide is coming in." Bennett pointed toward the inn. "See that house with the lights on up there? That's an inn, and the woman who runs it will have a place for you there. You'll be safe, and we can help you sort out whatever you need."

Shivering, the woman heaved a ragged sigh and lifted her head. In the moonlight, he could make out her tear-streaked face.

It was Sunny. Her lips were pale with cold.

Struggling to speak through numb lips, she said, "Y-you have no idea how h-hard this is."

Bennett unzipped his jacket and wrapped it around her slender shoulders. He sat cross-legged beside her with his arm around her, rubbing her back to warm her. The chill wind cut through the thin fabric of his cotton turtleneck.

"Maybe I do," he said softly.

Jutting out her chin in defiance, Sunny shrugged away but pulled the jacket around her torso.

"I have been right where you are. Totally broken."

She gulped a sob and seemed to be listening, so Bennett went on. He wasn't sure what was bothering her, but he had a pretty good idea.

"The holidays are the hardest," he said. "Everyone around you is happy, and you feel like you died inside. Hollow-like. Sometimes I come out here by myself, like tonight, and talk to the people I miss. My grandparents, my wife Jackie, my first dog Skipper. I like to think that out here, against that vast ocean, that somehow we can still communicate to them what's in our hearts."

"You talk to your dog?"

"I loved that dog. Broke my heart when he died."

A choked laugh gurgled in her throat. "That's not really the same." Sunny drew the sleeve of his jacket across her face, wiping her nose on it.

Bennett smiled at this. Sunny was still just a kid inside, missing her father. And on the outside, she was a young woman taking on the world. As volatile as she could be, he had a lot of respect for her. What she was going through mirrored her mother's experience, though Ivy was older and more experienced in handling the vagaries of life.

"Out here, you can tell your dad anything you want."

"I have. I asked him why he left us."

Bennett sighed. "I've asked that, too. It wasn't their choice, you know."

"That doesn't make it any easier."

"You can tell him how much you love him and miss him."

Unable to speak, Sunny nodded.

"If you're afraid of forgetting your dad, don't worry. You never will."

Sunny looked up with tear-rimmed eyes. "Never?"

"I can still hear their voices in my mind. I can still feel their love in my heart. And in the dark of the night, sometimes I imagine their hand on my face or their arms around me."

Sunny expressed a deep sigh. "I've felt that, too." She looked up at him through damp lashes. "I didn't think anyone else knew what it was like. How do you make it through the days?"

"It doesn't happen right away, but you remember them less with tears and more with a smile. Little things remind you of them. A silly song, the smell of their favorite food. In my mind, I say, 'hey, I'm thinking of you,' and send up a smile wrapped in love."

"I feel terrible for some of the things I said to my dad. I didn't mean them."

"And he probably knew that. I like to think that on the other side, they have the wisdom to know we didn't mean the things we said."

"I didn't think about that." Sunny's voice lifted a notch.

"It's okay to feel the way you do. And it's also okay to feel happy when you want. Your dad would want that for you."

"That's what my therapist said. Sometimes I feel guilty when I catch myself being happy."

"Above all, he would want you to be happy."

"I guess so." She smiled shyly.

"Want to go in? Get out this cold?"

"I'm pretty toasty now."

Bennett shook his shoulders. "Brrr. Speak for yourself, kid." He stood and stretched his hand to her.

Sunny gripped his hand and stood. "You're not so bad, you know. But dang, your hands are cold."

"Come on, you. Race you back to the house?"

Sunny took off, and Bennett jogged beside her. When they bounded into the kitchen, Sunny threw her arms around him. "Thanks," she said.

"Anytime."

She drew her sleeve over her nose again. "Want your jacket?"

The jacket was streaked with tears and mucus, but Sunny was okay. That's all that mattered. Bennett grinned. "Keep it. It's yours."

CHAPTER 20

*I*vy was grating potatoes in the kitchen, humming along with holiday songs on the radio. She was thinking about past holidays and how this year was so different. The scent of fresh russet potatoes and onions sizzling in oil on the stovetop filled the kitchen, spurring memories of breakfasts at a favorite neighborhood deli and Friday night suppers at a friend's house in Boston.

Cooking and baking for the holiday season were part of the traditions she wanted to share with her daughters. Misty would be flying in soon, and Sunny had been surprisingly calm this morning. She'd even offered to help grate potatoes, which Ivy appreciated.

Most of the guests were out shopping or having lunch, so the house was fairly quiet. Except for Pixie, who'd been yapping furiously at squirrels gathering nuts for the winter. Gilda had whisked her back upstairs to put a sweater on the Chihuahua's slender frame.

The back door banged, and Shelly stepped out of her gardening clogs beside the entry. "Nick and I finished weatherproofing the old greenhouse, so I should be able to start seedlings in there soon." She slipped her feet into a pair of woven leather slides, soft from wear. "Sure smells yummy in here."

Ivy put down the grater. "That's the latkes."

"Mmm, crunchy little potato pancakes. Are you serving them with applesauce and sour cream?"

"All the trimmings," Ivy replied. "I also picked up rugelach and brisket at the deli. I wanted to make this first night of Hanukkah special. And everyone is welcome, like Christmas."

"Cool. I finished the yardwork, so if you need a hand with dessert, I can make something."

"I just got off the phone with Mitch," Ivy said. "He promised to bring jelly-filled donuts and other treats. But you can slice off the Brussels sprouts from those stalks." She'd been to the farmers market after her beach walk this morning and had picked out the freshest produce for tonight.

"Sure." Shelly washed her hands and picked up a sharp chef's knife.

Ivy brushed the potato and onion scraps into a bag. "There's something I need to talk to you about as well. Imani will be here shortly to go over our options."

Shelly wrinkled her brow. "You sound serious. Is this about the Christmas egg?"

"Imani has more information for us." Ivy had already shared the egg's provenance with Shelly, and she'd asked Imani to look into the legal aspects. Though the thought of a financial bonanza was tempting, it might also come with a host of costly legal problems—and there was no guarantee she'd ever see any profit.

Shelly's eyes widened. "That egg must be worth a fortune. What would you do with that kind of money?"

As she considered this, Ivy turned the browning latkes in the skillet. Some of her old friends thought she'd struck it lucky with the beach house, but this place had been bought with money that she and Jeremy had saved and invested for twenty years. It wouldn't have been her first choice because the upkeep on the house was costly—and often unexpected. Still, Ivy was fortunate to have it. She realized that.

But to have tens of millions in sudden wealth? It was almost unfathomable.

Ivy patted more of the potato and onion mixture into little cakes and slipped them into the oil. They sizzled right away. "That much money wouldn't change what I already like to do," she said, resting the spatula. "Painting, walking on the beach, caring for my family and others. What about you?"

Grinning, Shelly said, "Take some outrageous trips, shop 'til I drop, party in New York."

"Really? And what about Mitch?"

Shelly frowned and brought her knife down with force. "Ouch! Dang it, I sliced through my fingernail." Blood pooled on her finger.

Ivy rushed to check on Shelly. "You nicked your nailbed, but it's not too bad. Wash it, and I'll get the first-aid kit." She shifted the skillet from the burner. *Enough accidents already.*

As Ivy pulled out the emergency kit from under the sink and tended to Shelly, she thought about how she and her sister usually agreed on things. However, this was a huge decision that could change their lives—for better, or quite possibly, for worse.

Ivy had weighed the consequences for herself and her children, as well as Shelly, though she was waiting to hear what Imani had determined. Technically, this was Ivy's decision. The house was in her name. Still, she'd committed to Shelly that they were sharing in the cashflow from the operation of the inn. As far as the ownership of the egg, it was better that Shelly hear the options from Imani.

While Ivy applied ointment and a bandage to Shelly's finger, her sister twisted her lips to one side.

"Actually, I lied," Shelly said with a sigh. "All that stuff—the partying and shopping—sounds great when you're young, but I've been happier here just hanging out with Mitch. I guess my priorities are shifting." She bit her lower lip. "I still wouldn't mind the money, though."

"I know what you mean."

As Ivy and Shelly were completing the prep work for the dinner, Imani bustled in carrying flowers.

"I just brought these in for Blossoms and thought they'd be perfect for tonight." Imani reached for the vase she often filled with flowers for the foyer. "White lilies and roses with blue hydrangeas and delphiniums."

Shelly leaned in to smell the bouquet. "Luscious. I have some curly willow with silvery glitter that will add a festive accent."

"That would be lovely," Imani said as she filled the vase and arranged the flowers. When she was through, the three women gathered around the kitchen table.

Imani drew a small notebook from her purse and opened it. "As you know, at the time of the Russian Revolution, the Bolsheviks confiscated the inventory of the House of Fabergé, the Romanov family, and other wealthy people. Some imperial eggs were thought to have been smuggled out of the country. I spoke with a contact at an auction house, and based on markings, they confirmed the provenance that Ari mentioned to Ivy."

Shelly clasped her hands and listened intently.

"A Rothschild egg sold for more than $18 million dollars several years ago, so Ari's guesstimate is correct."

Shelly shot her arms up the air. "Yes! We're rich!"

"Not so fast," Imani said, holding up a hand. "The egg should have been part of the estate, and it would have been had it not been misplaced. After Amelia Erickson entered a care facility in Switzerland, in all likelihood, she forgot about it."

Shelly's face fell. "But she didn't have any heirs. The estate went to charity."

"Exactly," Imani said. "Those charities may have a valid

legal claim on this piece. Now, if it were a dish or a chair—not one of great value, of course—then the benefit to them is negligible. Furnishings and household items left behind don't fall into this category. But an *objet d'art* worth eight-figures is unlikely to go unnoticed."

"So, ownership would be challenged," Ivy said.

"I'm afraid so." Imani looked at her notes. "All property found is classified as Abandoned, Mislaid, Lost, or Treasure Trove, which refers to antiquity, or much older property. Mislaid property is put somewhere with intent and forgotten. Most likely, the staff was directed to remove the decorations after the holidays, and the egg was stored away with other items, just as you two found it. Therefore, the object is the mislaid property of Amelia Erickson, so it is now the mislaid property of the beneficiaries of her will."

"Can't we argue that?" Shelly blew out a breath in exasperation. "Or are we just going to hand over the egg? The charities don't even know about it."

"No, but they would if we tried to sell it," Ivy said. "With the egg's history, news of it would reach the media for sure."

Imani nodded. "You're talking about a long, costly legal battle that you probably wouldn't win."

"I'm sure those charities could use the money," Ivy added.

"How about us?" Shelly flung out a hand. "At the rate we're going this winter, we might soon be classified as a charitable case."

"We're doing a lot better now," Ivy said. "Shelly, I don't want to be locked in a long legal battle that we have little chance of winning. Besides, Amelia wanted her collection to go to charity."

"But isn't our Christmas egg part of the house?" Shelly wailed.

"Imani went over that," Ivy said, reaching for her sister's hand. "This is the right thing to do. After the holidays, we'll turn it over."

"It will be put in safekeeping and probably auctioned," Imani said.

Shelly pushed back from the table. Drawing her hands over her face, she let out a yell. "Argh! I know it's what we need to do, but I wish we could've had some kind of benefit from this."

"And I wish I'd had better news for you," Imani said.

"I'd rather be realistic," Ivy said. The sooner she turned it over, the better. "Would you contact the attorney for the estate, Imani?"

Imani agreed, and after she left, Ivy reached out to hug Shelly. "I know how you feel. It's not just the money; it's the freedom from worry that money represents. But we're making our own money, Shells."

"It's okay, Ives." Shelly held up her bandaged finger. "Remember when you asked me about Mitch? I think I got my answer then. I've partied enough, and as for traveling, I'd have more fun with Mitch."

Ivy hugged her sister. "We'll always have the photo of our Christmas egg to hang on the wall. And a good holiday story for years to come."

That evening, as the sun set over the Pacific Ocean, new friends gathered in the dining room for a Festival of Lights feast. Ophelia officiated, and Nick, Kristy, Rosamie, and Molly Ann gathered around, along with other residents and visitors. Bennett sat by Ivy, and Mitch entered carrying a box of freshly made jelly donuts. Ivy was pleased that the latkes were a huge hit, and none were left over.

As they were eating, Rosamie remarked on the floral centerpiece. "I love all the flowers and decorations throughout the house. And Shelly's beautiful new wreath."

"Made from less-flammable material," Shelly said.

The conversation turned, and Nick asked, "So what's the latest on the egg we found among the decorations?"

"Imani just gave us legal advice on that today." Ivy

glanced at Shelly, who sighed and sipped her wine. "The egg is rightfully part of the original estate, so it will be put up for sale or auction to benefit the charities Amelia Erickson named in her will. I'm relinquishing rights to the egg, and the attorney who handled the estate will pick it up soon."

Nick turned up his palms. "I cradled that beautiful egg in my hands. It was a stunning work of art, but I had no idea of its true value. It should be in a museum for all to enjoy."

"That will be up to the new owners." Ivy glanced around the table. Sunny and Bennett were chatting amicably—thank goodness—and other guests had moved on to another subject.

Mitch raised his glass. "Here's to our hosts—and the upcoming Holiday Boat Parade on the water. Whether you're on a boat or on the shore, it's going to be awesome."

Ivy was looking forward to that. As the conversation shifted again, Ivy watched Bennett and Sunny. Something seemed to have evolved between them, though she wasn't sure why. At least for this evening, Sunny was behaving herself and treating Bennett with respect. Maybe Sunny was finally coming to terms with her father's death.

Ivy hoped that Sunny's new mood would last through the holidays.

CHAPTER 21

"*D*o we have everything we need?" Ivy asked, picking up her gloves from the table in the foyer. She and Shelly were on their way to the Holiday Boat Parade, a Christmas Eve tradition in Summer Beach. In the winter, the sun set before five in the evening. After the parade, they'd have plenty of time for a traditional Christmas Eve supper with their family at the inn.

"The Jeep is packed and ready to go," Shelly said. "Pre-party on the boat, here we come."

Most of the shops in Summer Beach closed before the annual water parade of brightly lit boats. Ivy was looking forward to the event; she hadn't seen it since she'd moved to Boston more than two decades ago.

Upstairs, the piercing scream of a small toddler sliced through the house. Shelly's eyes widened. "Do they always do that?"

"Just part of the scintillating soundtrack of childhood." Ivy hesitated a moment. A commotion erupted upstairs with the new young couple that had checked in.

Ivy caught the word *toilet* and placed her hand on Shelly's arm. "Maybe we'd better wait a minute."

Shelly rolled her eyes. "Industrial-strength plunger time?"

"Afraid so. You get it, and I'll check on the Jeffersons. Bennett and Mitch will have to wait."

"Can't wait too long, or that ship sails without us," Shelly said.

"Let's hurry, though we might have to watch from the shore."

Ivy climbed the stairs. "Hello, Mr. and Mrs. Jefferson?" She tapped the door. "It's Ivy. Is there anything I can help you with?"

A young mother threw open the door, her face masked with panic. Her hair was in disarray, and she had eyeshadow on just one eyelid. "I'm so glad you're here." The red-faced toddler on her hip screeched again. "Shh, calm down, Belle. Daddy's working on the toilet."

"We can look at that for you," Ivy said easily. "Old plumbing sometimes gets cranky."

"It's not that," the woman said. She bounced the child on her hip, desperately trying to calm her. "While I was putting on makeup, I only looked away for a few seconds, but it was long enough for Belle to send her pacifier swimming in the potty."

Belle erupted with another shrill scream. *Almost operatic,* Ivy thought, holding a hand to her ear. "Do you have another pacifier?"

"No, that's the problem," the young mother said, raising her voice above her daughter's screams. "She lost the last one, so we had to buy this one on the way here. It's special because it has a stuffed Christmas elf attached to the end of it. Like a WubbaNub."

"I've seen those," Ivy yelled back. She made a mental note. *Keep extra pacifiers on hand.*

Shelly appeared behind her at the door. "Someone call a plumber?"

"Oh, yes." Young Mrs. Jefferson looked surprised. "What

a nicely dressed plumber. Are you one of those smell-good plumbers I hear about on the radio in L.A.?"

"Of course," Shelly said, grinning at Ivy. "Today, I'm wearing Nuit de Noël, a company favorite for the holidays." Shelly waggled her eyebrows, hefted a bag of toilet tools and plungers, and headed toward the bathroom, leaving a lovely silage of rose, jasmine, amber, and sandalwood in her wake.

Ivy stifled a laugh.

"Impressive," the woman said. Little Belle shrieked, and her mother tried in vain to calm her. "She's teething. Must be terribly painful."

Ivy remembered those days, and she understood, but guests in the adjoining rooms would not. "I'll send our niece to pick up another pacifier right now."

"That's not really necessary," the women said. "We want Belle to learn to calm herself without a pacifier anyway." Yet, even as the woman spoke, she looked doubtful, especially when Belle let out another scream.

"Trust me, you'll rest better," Ivy said, patting her shoulder. *And so will everyone else*, she thought. She still remembered the anguished days it took to wean Sunny off her pacifier. "First child?"

Looking stressed, the woman nodded.

"Don't worry. We've got this. Maybe you'd like to watch the boat parade from the shore this evening. We'll have the fire pit going, and other guests are gathering there. You could bundle up Belle—she will probably be fascinated by the brightly colored lights on the boats. I heard there's going to be Santa and his elves on board."

The woman returned a grateful smile. "She might like that."

Ivy hurried down the staircase and met Poppy at the end of the stair. Gilda was standing beside her with a trembling Pixie.

"What's going on up there?" Poppy asked, alarmed.

"Young Belle flushed her pacifier." Ivy quickly explained the situation. "Take some petty cash and run to the children's shop in the village. We need pacifiers as fast as you can get them here. Buy several for us to have on hand, and if one has an elf or an animal attached, get that." Another wail ripped through the house. "Shelly is working on the toilet."

"I'll hurry back," Poppy said, grabbing her purse.

Ivy turned to Gilda. "I'm so sorry about this." Pixie's brown eyes were wide, and the Chihuahua was shrinking into her snowflake-dotted, red-knit doggie sweater in fear.

Gilda waved a hand. "It happens. But I'd better take Pixie for a walk until this is over. She's quite unsettled."

"Are you going to the boat parade?"

"Wouldn't miss it. And Pixie is all ready to go in her new sweater. After that, I'm joining old friends for a feast."

After Gilda left, Ivy palmed her face. *Of all days.* But that was the life of an innkeeper.

FORTUNATELY, SHELLY MANAGED TO RETRIEVE THE SOGGY ELF, which they immediately tossed into the trash. Poppy returned with a shopping bag full of pacifiers, including the one with the stuffed elf stitched to the end. Ivy figured that had to be the holiday gift-of-the-year among baby parents.

After assuring the Jeffersons that they were happy to help and not to worry at all, Ivy and Shelly raced to the old Jeep.

"I think we can just make it," Ivy said.

Shelly tossed her the keys. "You drive. You're better under pressure. Besides, I need to use those hand wipes in the glovebox. Yuk." She held out her hands as if they were contaminated.

Frowning, Ivy caught the keys and pushed through the back door. "Please tell me you washed your hands."

"Gotcha," Shelly said, grinning. "I just don't feel like driving."

Ivy shook her head. "Stop that." Yet, she couldn't help chuckling. "And Nuit de Noël—really?" They climbed into the vehicle.

"Actually, yes," Shelly said. "It's one of Mom's vintage Caron perfumes that I nabbed last week."

"You're incorrigible." Ivy sniffed the air. "But I like that scent."

"Why, thank you." Shelly bumped Ivy's shoulder.

Ivy cranked up the heat in the old Jeep that she and Shelly had each driven in high school and revved the engine. "Come on, at least get a little warm for us," she said, slapping her red-gloved hands together for warmth. She pulled her candy cane-striped knit hat lower over her ears.

The Holiday Boat Parade might start without them. "Would you text Mitch and let him know we're running late?"

"Will do. Geez, it's cold." Shelly rubbed her hands together. "Let's face it; we've gone soft, Ives. Remember when we were hardy New Englanders? Our blood has gotten thin living at the beach." She pulled out her phone and tapped a message.

"It's all relative," Ivy said. "I had a much better heater back then."

"Aw, this lovable heap is old. Give it a minute." Shelly threw her a look from the side of her eye. "Now, if we had a sudden windfall, like…oh, I don't know, maybe we won the lottery. Or found a jeweled-egg worth *squillions*. Then we could buy a new Jeep with a great heater."

Ivy drew her eyebrows together. "You are *not* going to throw that up at me forever. You heard Imani."

Shelly burst out laughing. "Got you again!"

Ivy slapped Shelly's shoulder. "You're a beast, you know that? And on Christmas Eve, too. You should be ashamed of yourself. Treating your older and smarter sister that way."

"Oh, really?" Shelly arched a brow beneath the floppy

Santa hat she'd just tugged on. "Well, I'll behave on Christmas. Just for one day, though."

"Yeah, you wouldn't want to spoil me." Ivy slid the gearshift. "We don't have a minute anymore. Bennett said the boats pull out into parade formation just after sundown."

As Ivy pulled out of the car court behind the house, the sun edged toward the horizon of the steely gray winter sea. As they drove past Main Street, shopkeepers were locking their doors and turning over their *Open* signs.

On the beach, families were already claiming spots and building fires on the sand. Christmas music floated above the happy chatter. Tyler and Celia had arranged for a sound system on the beach, along with refreshments.

Ivy lifted her hand from the steering wheel in a wave to people as they drove. "Looks like the whole town closes down for the Holiday Boat Parade."

"That's what Mitch said. Wonder how the guys are doing on the boat?"

"They should be ready to go." Ivy threw a worried glance at Shelly. "Did you grab the thermoses?"

"They're in the back seat. I'd already loaded them before Belle waylaid us. Hot chocolate for the drivers and hot buttered rum for the helpers."

"That's going to taste so good out on the ocean."

As they drove, Shelly turned to Ivy. "Can I talk to you?"

"Sure. What about?"

"Late last summer, when Mitch came to New York, we had some long talks about what each of us wanted in our lives. Despite our age difference, we're a lot alike."

"If that age difference were reversed, no one would even take notice."

"That's what I love about you." Shelly picked at a thread on her glove. "You know I don't always follow the rules, but I'm kind of old-fashioned in other ways. I mean, I want to have a baby, but…"

Ivy noticed how pale Shelly looked right now. As Ivy thought back over the last week or so, she couldn't recall Shelly eating much breakfast after yoga, not as she usually did. Was she having morning sickness? Ivy gripped the steering wheel. "Whatever is going on right now, I'm here for you."

Shelly drew a deep breath. "As soon as Christmas is over, I need to see a doctor. With the holidays, I've been pushing this out of my mind. I'm a little scared to do it, but I have to know for sure."

"You're not alone." Ivy understood what her sister was going through. "I'm so happy for you. Don't you think Mitch would be elated, too?"

Shelly chewed her lip. "On one hand, I hope so. On the other hand, I'm thirty-seven. And I do want a family. I don't think I'll tell him. I'll just do it."

Ivy was confused. "But if the baby is his…?"

"What?"

"You're pregnant!"

Shelly's eyes flew open. "Not that I know of! I just want to get checked out to make sure I can have a child. Otherwise, we could adopt. Or do both. But I should know for sure before…you know."

"Oh? It sounds like this is getting serious." Ivy was trying hard to follow Shelly's conversation, but she was trying to drive, too.

"Once I know where I stand, I'm thinking about proposing."

"What?" Ivy stared at Shelly. As she did, the Jeep bounced against the curb, and Ivy jerked the wheel back. "Hang on."

"Watch it," Shelly cried, grabbing the dashboard for balance. "Realistically, how long can I wait around? He has more time than I do, but I don't see any reason why I can't do the asking. At least I'll know, right?"

Ivy glanced at Shelly with fresh admiration. For all her sister's wacky ways, she was as determined as Ivy in what she wanted in her life. "You're pretty gutsy, Shells. Go for it. Mitch would be a fool to pass up an opportunity with you."

"That's what I'm thinking." Shelly grinned. "Keep your eyes on the road. Parking is ahead."

As Ivy turned into the lot for the marina, Shelly pointed ahead toward a vacant spot. "Pull into that one on your right."

"Got it." Ivy glanced over her shoulder. Only a sliver of sun remained. "Don't know if we can make it."

"They'll wait." Just then, Shelly's phone dinged with a message, and she made a face when she looked at it. "Or maybe not. Let's go." She tapped a quick reply. *We're here!*

Ivy and Shelly grabbed the thermoses from the rear seat and jogged toward the marina. When they hit the dock, their deck shoes slapped against the weathered wood.

As they raced past other boats, people called to them.

"Merry Christmas," Jen and George sang out. Their boat was a vision of twinkling lights and large glowing balls in every color. George was adjusting a spotlight on a stuffed Santa Claus.

"Better hurry," Tyler said as he started the engine on his sleek craft.

His wife waved from the middle of a group of animated elves in Santa's workroom. "We'll wait for you," Celia said.

Multi-colored lights surrounded them on the marina, and the scents of hot chocolate, pumpkin spice, peppermint, and cinnamon blended with the briny smell of the sea. Ivy felt like she was in the middle of an old-fashioned Christmas movie.

"Why does Bennett have to have the last boat slip?" Shelly said, jogging beside Ivy.

Ivy managed a laugh. "Says the woman who tied with Jamir for first place at the Santa Sprint—and he's almost half your age. Hey, at least we're getting warm." She tugged Shelly's arm. "Almost there, come on."

CHAPTER 22

*I*vy nodded ahead toward Bennett's boat with relief. "Looks like the guys waited." She slowed to a stop beside the brightly decorated craft.

Multi-colored strands of jewel-toned lights lined the boat, illuminating everyone on board and casting a kaleidoscope of colors across their faces. Ivy gazed up at a Christmas tree with twinkling lights and a star at the top. It was firmly secured, and underneath it were boxes trimmed in different color lights.

While this display wasn't as fancy as Tyler's animated workshop, Ivy thought it looked fabulous—sort of like a floating living room on Christmas morning.

"Wow," Ivy exclaimed. The effect was magical, whisking her back to childhood holidays spent on the beach with her parents. Holiday water parades like this had been going on for years off the coast of Southern California.

"Glad you made it." Bennett extended his hands to help Ivy aboard, though Mitch swooped in and swept Shelly off her feet, laughing.

When Ivy went to climb in, Bennett caught her and lifted her inside the swaying craft.

"You made that look easy," she said, giving him a little kiss.

"That's the sweetest part of my job." Bennett glanced around. "Everyone onboard? Mitch, Nick, Kristy?"

They all answered. Mitch had asked Nick to help them decorate, and in turn, Nick asked if Kristy could come along. They'd gone ahead earlier in the day to prepare everything.

Ivy collapsed on a bench seat in the craft to catch her breath.

"How was your day?" Bennett asked.

"We made it," Ivy said, feeling relieved. "Full occupancy."

"Woo-hoo!" Shelly shouted.

Bennett wrapped his arms around her. "I knew you could do it," he said. "Congratulations."

All day, she and Shelly had been busy with check-ins, even before the young Belle debacle. Some local residents had extra guests that they couldn't accommodate. Most people who had checked in were staying through New Year's Day because Shelly, Poppy, and Sunny had planned a party to welcome in the new year.

Bennett rang a bell he had on board. "Merry Christmas, everyone!" Motioning, he gave the signal for everyone to start the parade.

Ivy tipped her head back, catching her breath after their busy day. Yet there was more ahead, with Misty flying in tonight from Boston, and their sister Honey and her husband Gabe from Sydney. While she and Shelly had met their goal, Ivy was still concerned about the remaining winter months. However, they could cover the inn's expenses for a couple of months if they were careful. They'd just have to dream up more ideas to attract guests.

That can wait, Ivy decided, for tonight she wanted to enjoy herself.

After all, it was Christmas Eve.

As owners began to ease their boats from their slips,

sparkling light spilled across the water. When it was his turn, Bennett did the same.

"This is a beautiful Christmas Eve tradition," Ivy said, appreciating the efforts everyone made.

"It was started years ago when the shopkeepers closed after the Christmas Eve rush," Bennett said. "A few of them went to unwind before supper, threw up decorations, and the rest is history. It's funny how traditions take root."

Ivy tucked her gloved hands into the pockets of the winter coat she'd worn in Boston. On the water, the wind was swift. That morning, a frost advisory had been announced for the central valley of California to the southern tip, so the Holiday Boat Parade would be a wintry cruise this year.

"Too cold?" Bennett asked as he eased into the line of watercraft. He steered slowly along the coastline under the glow of lights from other boats.

"Perfectly toasty," Ivy replied.

"Chestnuts roasting…" Mitch sang from the bow, where he and Shelly were cuddled together sipping from their thermoses.

They're a good match, Ivy thought. She hoped Shelly's plan would work out the way she wanted. More than anything, she wanted to see her sister's wishes for a family come true. Shelly had waited a long time for the right man. As Ivy watched them together, she realized how good they were for each other.

"Nick and Kristy," Bennett said, glancing behind him. "How are you two doing?"

"Having fun," they called from the stern of the boat. Kristy's face was wreathed in smiles as she held hands with Nick.

"Looks like it could be love back there, too," Bennett said softly.

"Whether you call it fate or merely a happy coincidence, I'm glad for them." Ivy was pleased that Nick and Kristy had each other this holiday season. They were two lonely souls who'd found each other. Ophelia and Molly Ann had become fast friends, too. Since they were sharing the room next to Ivy, she could hear them chatting softly late into the night, though the sounds of friendship didn't bother her.

Cheers from the shore went up as they passed, and calls of *Merry Christmas* and *Ho, ho, ho* rang out in the crisp evening air.

"Merry Christmas, Summer Beach," Bennett yelled, waving. "The kids love this parade," he added, raising his hand in the breeze. "Kendra and I used to come with our parents. Dad would build a fire on the beach, and we'd all roast marshmallows. It was usually warmer, though. Sometimes we even wore shorts. That's Christmas in California. You never know what kind of weather you'll get."

"What sweet memories." Slipping her hand into the crook of Bennett's elbow, Ivy said, "It's been a long time since I've had such a magical holiday season."

"I'd like to think it's more than the boat and the lights." Bennett kissed the tip of her cold nose.

"It's everything," she said, teasing him. "The hot chocolate, the flaming wreath, the sprinting Santas..." She smiled up at a sweet pair of eyes that reflected the lights of the nearby Christmas tree and felt her heart skip. "And you. Most of all, you."

Bennett slid his arm around her, and she leaned her head onto his shoulder as he spoke. "It's been a very long time since I've felt the magic quite like this." Emotion edged his voice, and he blinked against the breeze. "It's all because of you, Ivy Bay."

She poured more hot chocolate while Bennett cruised along the coastal communities, and the rich aroma of cinnamon and chocolate made her smile. Shelly had made their mother's traditional recipe.

For the next hour or so, they spread cheer among people

watching from the beaches. By the time they returned to the marina, they were famished and ready for supper.

Ivy's phone dinged as they stepped off the boat. "Everyone arrived. Honey, Gabe, and Misty. Elena is meeting them at LAX airport now."

"The Christmas Eve party is on," Shelly said.

Ivy had reserved a room for Honey and Gabe. Misty was sharing Sunny's room, and Elena and Poppy were staying in Shelly's spacious room. They said they were looking forward to a slumber party, although Ivy imagined that Shelly might stay out late with Mitch since Java Beach was closed for Christmas.

"They're not too far away now," Ivy said to Shelly.

Tonight, the Bay family was gathering at the inn for Christmas Eve, and many of them were bringing dishes. Ivy had put a turkey and ham in slow ovens earlier that day before they left.

As soon as Ivy walked inside the house, she could smell the roasted turkey she'd rubbed with sage and rosemary and oregano. She hung her jacket and rolled up her sleeves.

"Who's ready to help in the kitchen?" she asked.

Shelly and Bennett quickly volunteered.

"I left the bread in the butler's pantry earlier," Mitch said. "Sourdough and rye, and a couple of pies. Peach with cranberry and pumpkin."

Carlotta was bringing homemade tamales, another holiday tradition, and their sisters-in-law were bringing stuffing and vegetables and salad. With the work spread among them, it reduced the burden on any one household.

After the Holiday Boat Parade, everyone returned to the inn about the same time, except for guests who were celebrating Christmas Eve with their families or had made other plans. Some guests were having dinner at the big Christmas Eve celebration at the Starfish Café, where carolers serenaded the diners.

This evening, laughter echoed through the halls of the grand old house, and Ivy imagined that this is how it might have been in Amelia's time, too. The sounds of happiness and holiday cheer warmed her heart and made her smile.

"Mitch, your bread and pies smell delicious," Ivy said, stepping into the butler's pantry. The aromas of sourdough, peaches, cinnamon, and nutmeg made her even hungrier. "Tonight, let's use the holiday plates we found."

Ivy pointed out the Christmas dishes on the top shelf. Mitch brought a ladder and began passing plates down to Shelly and Poppy, while Ivy brought out platters of sliced vegetables, olive tapenade, and hummus that she'd prepared earlier. As she was arranging the appetizer trays, Nick and Kristy joined them.

"We brought a special bottle of wine for you," Kristy said. "To thank you for all you've done. Nick thought you and Bennett might like to enjoy this by the fireplace."

"I appreciate that, but it's been our pleasure to welcome you." She admired the label, then put the bottle on the counter in the butler's pantry. "You two are welcome to join us for supper tonight. We have a large family, so we always make plenty. A few of the cousins are about your age, too."

"Already invited them," Shelly said, ducking into the conversation.

"Kristy and I are pleased to accept your gracious offer," Nick replied. "This reminds me of how the farming community I grew up in came together for the holidays."

"And do you ever go back?" Ivy asked.

"Not since—" Nick stopped and shook his head. "Not in a long time."

Ivy didn't press him. Instead, she said, "I know you'd planned to stay only until Christmas, but you can stay on if you'd like. We'd love to have you."

Shelly nodded with enthusiasm. "You've been a huge help, and I can always find more to do. I hope you'll stay."

"I truly wish I could." Nick put his arm around Kristy. "But I've committed to driving to Phoenix with Kristy. Her children are returning soon, and I don't want her to make that drive alone."

"I drove fine by myself on the way out here," Kristy protested mildly. "Still, I appreciate it."

Nick took Ivy's hand in his. "I want you to know that I will never forget your hospitality and generosity this holiday season." His voice caught in his throat. "I hope to return to Summer Beach again soon. Very soon."

"You're always welcome here," Ivy said, and she meant it. Nick might have fallen on hard times, but with his talent and intelligence, she knew he would find his path soon. She was happy to help him. "And please, have some appetizers. I've probably made too much again." She handed him two plates.

"I can always help you with that," Nick said as Kristy laughed and joined him.

Though Nick and Kristy were guests, even they were beginning to feel more like family. And the spark between them was easily discernible.

Ivy put out more appetizers, and soon the rest of the Bay family began to arrive. Siblings and cousins came with armloads of gifts and immediately stashed them under the towering tree. Ivy had something special for Bennett, though she planned to wait to give it to him.

As Ivy was arranging silverware and napkins, Elena arrived with her parents and Misty. Ivy hurried to greet them.

"Mom," Misty cried out, wrapping her arms around Ivy. "Merry Christmas! I have so much to tell you about the show."

"I can't wait to hear everything," Ivy said, admiring her oldest daughter. Misty was wearing a puffy black jacket and leopard leggings—and looking more and more like the budding Broadway actress Ivy was sure she would be some-day. "It's so good to see you again." Ivy hugged her, and then they turned to embrace her sister Honey with her husband, Gabe.

"Look at this great big hug fest," Shelly said. "Come on, boys. Honey's back."

Flint and Forrest swooped in, and the five Bay family siblings were all together again, welcoming each other and their respective spouses and children.

This was the family that Ivy cherished more than all the jeweled-eggs in the world. She reached out to Bennett and brought him into the group. Flint greeted his old friend like a brother. As Ivy watched everyone, she noticed that Sunny had joined them. On her daughter's face, she saw flickers of raw emotion despite her attempts at concealment. Would this evening be a re-enactment of Thanksgiving for Sunny?

Ivy went to her and put her arm around her. "I'm here for you, Sunny. Whenever you want to talk or just hang out. Tonight will be different from Thanksgiving, I promise."

"It's not easy, Mom. And I know it won't be okay for a long time." She shot a glance at Bennett. "But I'm seeing things differently now."

Misty turned around and hugged her sister. "We're cool now, Mom. Sunny told me all about it."

Sunny's face flushed a little. "I'll fill you in later, Mom."

Ivy had the impression that something had transpired, but she was happy to wait as long as her daughters were fine.

"We've been through a lot, the three of us." Ivy put an arm around each daughter and pulled them close, kissing their cheeks as she had when they were her sweet little girls. They might be older now, but they would always be her girls. No one could ever take their place in her heart.

The heart has room for many types of love, she thought. *Children, family, friends, partners.* Watching Honey and her brothers with their spouses, she wondered if she would have another life partner in her future. Glancing at Bennett, Ivy's heartbeat quickened.

Perhaps, but on her terms this time.

After a while, everyone flowed into the kitchen, and soon they were pitching in and carrying dishes into the dining room. Ivy and Shelly had set up extra tables for additional guests. Flint and Forrest carved the turkey and ham this time, and before long, everyone was enjoying the Christmas Eve supper. Nick and Kristy had joined them, along with Jamir and Imani. Ophelia, Molly Ann, and Rosamie sat together at the end of the table.

"Here's to one big family," Ivy said, raising her glass in a toast. Last year, she never could have imagined this scene filled with the happy faces of family and new friends. "It's been quite a year," she added, and Shelly rose to hug her.

"This was all your idea," Shelly said. "To Ivy."

As everyone clapped, Ivy pressed her hand to her heart. She wanted to remember this beautiful moment forever.

After supper, Carlotta brought out her *Ponche Navideño* in one of Amelia's large crystal punch bowls, and everyone gathered around.

Ivy ladled the warm punch into cups and passed them around. A few people added a little brandy that Sterling had brought, and then they all moved into the ballroom by the tree.

Bennett sipped the punch. "Delicious. Do you mind if I ask how you make this?"

Carlotta beamed at his request. "It's a blend of spices and fruit and brown sugar. I add cinnamon, cloves, and tamarind to a large pot of water with dark brown sugar and heat it on the stove. Then I float sliced apple, guava, pear, orange, and raisins in the mixture. It's wonderful on a cool evening. We've always served it on Christmas Eve."

Soon, wrapping paper and ribbons were flying, followed by squeals of delight and appreciation. Ivy had also painted personalized ornaments for each of their guests, and each one received a gift bag.

When Ivy's parents unwrapped her oil color painting of their five children, Carlotta pressed a hand to her heart. "How lovely. I must say, now that you're painting more, your talent is soaring."

"It's small enough to hang in the cabin of your boat," Ivy said, feeling her face blush at her mother's words. "This way, we can sail the world with you." Although it was the smallest of the paintings she'd done for her family members, the facial details had taken the most time.

The group fell quiet until Shelly spoke up. "I think it's just starting to hit us how much we're going to miss you."

"We're not going away forever," Sterling said. "And if we hear one more peep about our age, or someone starts a sentence with, *at your age*, then we might never return."

Honey draped her arm across Carlotta's shoulder. "Is it okay if we meet you in port from time to time? You know how much your children enjoy traveling, too."

"What a good idea," Sterling agreed.

Between Ivy and Shelly, they could cover for each other during quiet periods. Ivy had been separated from her parents for so many years on the east coast that she really enjoyed living close to them now. However, they had their dreams, and Ivy was glad that they were healthy enough to continue pursuing them.

After they'd all opened gifts, everyone lounged around the fireplace, chatting. Nick brought out his flute and performed a few songs for them. Bennett got his guitar, and the two men played together while others joined in singing favorite holiday tunes.

However, it wasn't long until Misty yawned and stretched. "I'm three hours ahead of you, so I think I'll turn in."

Sunny pulled her sister to her feet. "I'll come with you."

Ivy smiled. The two girls would probably stay up talking as they often had.

"We had a long journey, too," Honey said, rising.

After cleaning the kitchen and tidying the ballroom, the Bay family turned in. Ivy walked through the quiet house. By the fireplace, she saw Bennett.

"Hey, you," she said, smoothing her hand across Bennett's shoulder. "You look deep in thought."

"I'm feeling grateful for everything that has happened between us," he said. "When the fire damaged my house, that was the luckiest day of my life because it brought me here. To be closer to you. We've come to know each other much better, much faster."

"It's been wonderful, but it's not a race."

Drawing her toward him, Bennett smiled and brought her hand to his heart, then kissed her fingertips. "Being with family over the holidays is such a blessing," he said. "This was a special day. Thank you for including me in your family."

"They enjoy having you. And I'm looking forward to seeing your sister and her family here tomorrow."

In the flickering firelight, Bennett gazed into her eyes with gravity, as if a momentous question loomed in his mind. He reached behind him and brought out a small box. "I saw this and thought of you," he said, his voice thick with emotion.

Ivy's heart tightened as she unwrapped the small box to reveal a lovely, dainty necklace. "It's beautiful and exactly my style. I'll wear it next to my heart." Touched by the thoughtfulness of his gift, she placed her hand against his cheek. His skin was warm from the crackling fire.

"It's an emerald cabochon on a platinum chain. I thought it would match your eyes. May I help you put it on?"

"I'd like that." She turned and lifted her hair, arching her neck to him. His fingers shook as he fastened the clasp.

When she turned around, Bennett straightened the pendant and cradled her face in his hands. "Just as I thought. Stunning."

Sinking into his arms, Ivy brushed her lips across his,

feeling a connection that had only deepened over the past months.

"And I have something for you." Ivy hadn't wanted to share this painting with her family. Not that it was inappropriate, but the emotional intensity she'd felt as she painted it came across on the canvas. She handed him a wrapped package.

As Bennett unwrapped it, a smile grew on his face, and he leaned in to kiss her. "This is amazing. It's just the way I remember that night."

Ivy put her head on his shoulder and they gazed at it together. She'd painted the two of them on the beach dancing barefoot in the sand. Bennett holding her in his arms, her hair and her dress flaring out on the ocean breeze. It was one of her favorite memories of them.

"I call it *Seabreeze Dance*," she said.

"That was the first of many, I hope." Bennett's voice was husky, and he drew a breath as if to speak. He held it for a long moment before letting it out.

"Were you going to ask me something?" As soon as the words left her mouth, Ivy felt her face warm. Or was it only the heat from the fireplace?

Before he could answer, the antique clock that was perched on the mantle above them chimed the hour, and they waited until the twelve bells marking the new day had ceased.

Bennett threaded his fingers with hers. "Merry Christmas, my love."

CHAPTER 23

*C*hristmas morning dawned clear and cold, with sunshine streaming through the tall windows that looked out to the ocean. Ivy moved among guests in the dining room, wishing everyone a Merry Christmas and Happy Holidays. This morning, she'd put on Bennett's new necklace, which paired beautifully with her forest-green, crushed velvet dress.

"Good morning," Ivy said, pausing by the long table where Ophelia, Molly Ann, and Rosamie were sitting together and chatting like old friends. Next to them sat Gilda, who had come downstairs early and was holding a wriggly Pixie in her new doggie sweater.

As they chatted, Imani joined them. She was sporting a festive snowman sweater with matching dangly earrings.

"What a fun outfit," Ivy said.

"I've had this sweater since Jamir was a little boy," Imani said, laughing. "It survived the fire only because I'd been doing spring cleaning, and I'd taken a bunch of clothing to be dry cleaned before storing it."

"I thought you'd be with your sister in Los Angeles today," Ivy said. "Though I'm always glad to see you here."

"My sister and her husband flew to Vancouver to be with his family this year," Imani said.

From the corner of her eye, Ivy saw Jamir sneak into the ballroom and stash a gift with a bright red bow under the tree.

"For Mom," Jamir whispered as he hurried into the dining room past Ivy to join his mother and the other guests.

The croissants and biscuits were going quickly, as were the smoked salmon and bagels. Ivy surveyed the breakfast bar, where other guests were congregating. "Enjoy, and I'll bring more juice," she said, starting for the kitchen.

This morning, Ivy had risen early to make a lavish breakfast, starting with coffee for the adults and hot chocolate for the little ones. After turning on classic Christmas music, Shelly had made mounds of scrambled eggs, while their sister Honey fried sausages and bacon. Misty and Sunny rolled out biscuits, and Elena sliced fruit. Ivy loved having her family around her.

Bennett was up early, too. Before his run on the beach, he'd laid fires in the ballroom and the dining room to knock the chill out of the drafty rooms. The entire house was cozy with crackling fires and happy conversations.

All morning, guests had been wandering in at different times. Many were exchanging gifts by the tree, while others were hurrying off to morning services at local churches. Ivy was glad that guests were comfortable treating the inn as their home, especially the long-term ones.

People were laughing and taking photos, posing by the tree and fireplace, and sharing images on social media. A few days ago, Poppy had put out a framed sign on a table that read, *Please hashtag us #SeabreezeInnChristmas!* Ivy had laughed at the time, but they were already getting more reservations as a result.

In the kitchen, Shelly was mixing more Christmas punch, which she had set up in the ballroom on a table in a warming pot. The scent of sliced lemons and oranges permeated the air.

"Is everyone happy out there?" Shelly asked.

"It's all good," Ivy said as she took containers of orange and cranberry juice from a refrigerator. "I'm so grateful that Leilani and Roy gave us such a beautiful tree. It makes guests feel like they're part of a big family holiday."

"And it's only going to get bigger," Shelly said. "I think we're going to have a lot of people rolling in this afternoon for the open house."

"We'll have to do this every year."

Shelly gazed at her thoughtfully. "I'm glad to finally hear you say it like there's going to be a next year here."

Ivy looked through the open door, where people were laughing and having a good time. "I'm feeling pretty confident. It's been a challenging year, but what we managed to do on short notice gives me hope. I know we can put together more special events this winter. And once spring break rolls around, people will be ready to return to the beach. We're going to make it here."

Shelly threw her arms around her. "You bet we are. And for the record, turning this old house into an inn was the best crazy idea you've ever had. We never would've met Mitch and Bennett."

Ivy gazed around the kitchen. "Las Brisas del Mar has been pretty good to us. "

Just then, the fixture that held hanging pots above the center island swayed.

"Was that an earthquake?" Ivy asked. "I didn't feel anything, but something stirred that piece."

Reaching up to stop the swaying fixture, Shelly chuckled. "That was no earthquake. I think that was Amelia's way of thanking us for taking care of her home."

"Well, I'll be," Ivy said softly. "Maybe I believe, after all."

Just then, Poppy came into the kitchen. "Merry Christmas, Aunties," she sang out. Poppy had spread the word around town about their Potluck Open House. Even Darla was excited to bring a special dish.

"Come on into the dining room with me, Poppy. And bring more croissants with you." Ivy picked up the juice cartons.

When Ivy returned to the dining room, she spotted Nick and Kristy, who looked like they were preparing to leave. Nick dropped his backpack beside a chair, and Kristy parked her rolling suitcase near the door.

"Ready to travel?" Ivy asked as she greeted them.

"We wanted to get an early start," Kristy said. "I can hardly wait to see my children, and Nick wants to meet them, too." She linked arms with Nick and smiled up at him. "This trip has been a wish come true for both of us. Who knew what a difference a couple of weeks could make?"

Clearly, Nick was just as besotted with Kristy. When the younger woman excused herself to speak to Ophelia and the other women, Nick stayed behind.

"I owe you a great debt," Nick said, turning to Ivy. "Greater than you know."

"Not at all," Ivy said, taking his hand. "You and Shelly did wonders with the yardwork. You're welcome back any time, and I mean it. Don't worry; you'll find your place in the world soon."

He gazed at Kristy. "Amazingly enough, I think I have. And I have a new group of friends to cherish."

"You're not alone. You have a lot going for you, Nick. You have unique gifts, young man."

Nick chuckled. "My grandmother used to say that, too. Just like that." He ran a hand over his hair, smoothing it back from his forehead. "I have to confess that last month I was feeling pretty low. I didn't know who my real friends were, and I hated where I found myself in the world."

"I'm sorry to hear that," Ivy said, touching his shoulder.

"See, I've always liked to tinker around," Nick said. "I

invented something that a lot of people need, and use, but greedy, unscrupulous people got in the way. They made promises they had no intention of keeping and tried to cheat a lot of people."

The anguish on Nick's usually smooth face was evident. "That's unfortunate, but I'm glad you came here," Ivy said. She wondered if his invention had been stolen. That would explain a lot.

"So am I," Nick said, breathing out a sigh of relief. "When I struck out on the road, I had no more than a vague idea of where I was headed. I just wanted to find a peaceful place where the magic of the holidays still existed, and where people would accept me for who I was, rather than what I had or didn't have."

"I've had people try to cheat me out of things, too," Ivy said. "This house, for example."

Nick looked around the dining room, and his gaze rested on the burning embers. As if mesmerized, he went on. "I'd heard my grandparents talk about a grand house on the beach in a small village in Southern California for years. But I was a child then, so I didn't ask all the questions I should have."

"This house?" Ivy asked, her interest piqued.

Nick swallowed hard before continuing. "My grandparents escaped the war in Germany with nothing more than their clothes. They traveled halfway across the world to come here, a place where they could feel safe and start over." With reverence, he raised his eyes toward the attic. "I'm convinced they lived up there for a while. My grandmother was an artist, so maybe she'd met the Ericksons before in Germany. My grandfather was an electrical engineer and inventor, although he couldn't get a job doing that after they arrived here. So they farmed."

"And you take after him."

"He taught me a lot." Nick paused. "If not for Amelia Erickson, I don't think I would be here today. I remember hearing about how a wealthy woman paid for their transport, helped them find dignity in meaningful work, and arranged their papers so they could stay in this country."

Ivy caught her breath. She'd often wondered about who might have sought shelter in the rooms they'd discovered. A knot formed in her throat.

This wasn't just history; this was personal.

From his pocket, Nick fished out a small carved object and held it up. "This is part of the evidence they left behind."

Ivy peered at the curious object with fascination. It was a tiny monkey curled up. Its tail curved around, and its paws tucked toward a hollow center. "Did you find this in the drawer?"

"It was rolling around with the pencils." Nick nodded thoughtfully. "My grandfather used to carve these from peach pits to relax, and he'd give them out to children. He always had one or two dangling from his key chain. He said it was a hobby he learned as a young man working in Hong Kong on an engineering job."

Feeling a little overwhelmed, Ivy touched a table for balance. "What were your grandparents' names?"

"Sadie and Herschel. They raised me after my parents died in a freak snowstorm accident." Nick clasped Ivy's hands. "So you see, not only did my grandparents discover their path in this home, but now I have, too."

Ivy smiled, amazed that Nick had found his way here. "I've always thought that as long as we commit to searching, we'll find what we need."

Nick drew a square red envelope from his jacket pocket. "You can open this later. And I plan to see you all again very soon." Nick kissed her on each cheek before leaving.

Ivy stood by the fireplace holding Nick's Christmas card for a few moments, taking in everything he had said. Poppy was passing out biscuits and croissants, and Shelly had returned with more fruit and yogurt.

Shelly joined her by the fireplace. "I just said goodbye to Nick and Kristy as they were getting into her car. Are you okay? You look like you just saw a ghost." Shelly glanced around. "Was Amelia in here, too?"

Ivy had to laugh. "I don't think so, but Nick just shared an interesting story. He thinks his grandparents were guests in our attic rooms back in the day." She tapped her fingers on Nick's card. "And I seem to recall some sketches we found. Weren't some of those signed, *Sadie?*"

"Now that you mention it, I think so."

"Well, he'll be back," Ivy said. She made a mental note to look for those.

Just then, Imani bustled toward them, her eyes wide. "I need to talk to you two. My sister just sent me some photos, and as I was looking at them, I noticed an email that I must have overlooked yesterday morning. I know it's Christmas, but I thought you'd want to know. It's about the Fabergé egg."

Looking at Shelly, Ivy said. "Let's go where we can talk."

The three women made their way toward the library, shut the door, and sat at the library table. Ivy laid Nick's Christmas card to one side.

Imani pulled her phone from her pocket and opened her messages. "The attorney for Amelia Erickson's estate said he has received a very generous pre-emptive offer for the Fabergé piece," she said, reading. "After a conference call with the beneficiary charities, the offer has been accepted— partly because of the generous offer, and partly to avoid media attention. An escrow officer and security guards will pick up the Fabergé egg when the bank opens after the holiday."

Imani put her phone on the table and looked up. "Are you two prepared to part with it?"

"That happened so fast," Ivy said. She clutched Shelly's hand. "But we're ready. It's the right thing to do. The Christmas egg was a thing of beauty we had a chance to enjoy. But now, the good that will flow from it for others will be a blessing."

Imani nodded. "That money will be a much-needed windfall for those organizations, especially this time of year."

"I feel good about that," Shelly said. "Maybe my sister's outlook is rubbing off on me. I wonder who bought it?"

Imani consulted the message. "It says we're not supposed to disseminate this information because the foundation will make a formal announcement, but if you promise not to share with the media or post it on social media…"

"We won't," Ivy said quickly, darting a look at Shelly, who nodded.

"It's a technology founder," Imani said. "Nicholas Schneu of Schneu Medical Technologies. He wants to put it in a museum."

Ivy felt a strange sensation on her neck. She rubbed it thoughtfully.

"Anyway, I thought you'd want that news." Imani stood from the table.

"Technology, cool." Shelly pulled out her phone and tapped the screen. "Wonder if it's anything we've ever heard of. Let's see what they do."

Imani paused by the door.

As Shelly studied the screen, her lips parted. "Wow, look at this invention. Surgery robotics." She tapped the screen again. "Let's see what Nicholas looks like. Must be an old rich guy." Peering at the screen, she frowned. "This can't be right."

"What?" Ivy leaned toward her sister.

Shelly spun her phone around. "It's *our Nick*."

Ivy gasped. Sure enough, an image of Nick stared back at them on the phone. His hair was shorter, but the white streak was unmistakable.

"How can that be?" Ivy said. "He couldn't even afford to pay for his room." As she stared at the name, vocabulary from her high school German class came back to her. "Wait a minute. *Schneu* means *snow* in German. So Nick Snow *is* Nicholas Schneu. Why would he use an assumed name?"

Shelly turned up her palms. "Who knows? I've never been a zillionaire."

The red envelope Nick had given Ivy caught her eye, and she picked it up again. "Nick gave me this just before he left." She slid open the envelope.

Shelly peered over Ivy's shoulder. "He gave you a Christmas card?"

Ivy opened the card and pulled a check from inside. "With a cashier's check, it appears." Ivy scanned his note. "He thanked us for our patience while he made arrangements for his room payment." Ivy slid a hand across her eyes, recalling their initial conversation. "He did say that when he first arrived." She looked at the check. The amount was more than the cost of the room.

Shelly leaned back in her chair and laughed. "So I had a gazillionaire out there weeding and trimming branches. Way to go, Ives. Put all the guests to work."

"Says she who had everyone making wreaths."

Shelly opened her mouth. "They loved that class."

"Well, I honestly thought I was helping Nick." Ivy read on. "He says how much he enjoyed the work and that it made him feel like he was back on his grandparents' farm. Happy and fulfilled. And he plans to return to Summer Beach. With Kristy, he hopes." She passed the card to Shelly and Imani.

Shelly turned the note over. "Oh, my gosh! Listen to this on the back. 'P.S. I'm adding a generous finder's fee for the Fabergé egg to the contract for you. Thank you, and keep uplifting others.' Then he added a smiley face." Shelly let out a yelp. "Maybe we can fix the roof."

Ivy thought about the conversation she and Nick shared after the Gingerbread Bake-Off, and what he'd said. *Because you uplift others.* Ivy smiled to herself. "Or we could buy you a newer Jeep."

Shelly grinned and shrugged a shoulder. "Actually, I'm kind of attached to that one, but I wouldn't mind repairing the heater."

Recalling Nick's last words before he left, Ivy added, "He wanted to find a peaceful place where the magic of the holidays still existed, and where people would accept him for who he was, rather than what he had. I guess he found that here."

Imani nodded. "It must be hard to know who your friends are when you have that kind of money. Sounds like Nick learned the hard way."

"This doesn't change how we felt about him," Ivy said. "We met the real Nick. The smart, sensitive young man with a good heart. And remember, this news goes no farther than this room until that announcement is made."

Shelly beamed. "That will be tough, but I promise." She hugged Ivy and linked arms with Imani. "Let's go celebrate Christmas, Imani. By the way, I think I saw a handsome young man put a special gift under the tree for you."

A LITTLE AFTER NOON, FAMILY AND FRIENDS BEGAN ARRIVING at the Seabreeze Inn. Bennett tended the fireplace, Shelly managed the music, and Ivy opened the coat closet off the foyer they rarely used.

"Merry Christmas," Ivy said as each party bustled through the door with coats and mufflers and potluck dishes.

Bennett's sister Kendra and her husband Dave appeared with their ten-year-old son, Logan.

"This is for you, Miss Ivy," Logan said, holding up a flowering, potted amaryllis with velvety red petals.

"It's beautiful," Ivy said. "Let's put it by the buffet where everyone can see it."

While she placed the plant, she watched Bennett with his nephew. Bennett listened while Logan described in detail everything he'd found under the tree that morning. The little boy eagerly asked his uncle to help him learn to play his new guitar, which Bennett immediately agreed to do. *He would have made a good father,* Ivy mused. Logan was fortunate to have such a devoted uncle.

"Where shall I put this?" Kendra asked. She held an insulated dish in her gloved hands. "It's a vegan lasagna. Bennett mentioned that Sunny is a vegetarian, so I thought she might like this."

"Quite a few people will appreciate that," Ivy said. "Right over there on the buffet table. I have special cards to place next to the vegetarian dishes, and I'll sort out the hot plates for the warm dishes."

Her daughters had arranged long folding tables in the ballroom, where there would be plenty of room for people to mingle and eat. Ivy used the old linens from the butler's pantry to cover the tables. After washing and ironing, the tablecloths looked fresh again. She was thankful Poppy had pitched in to help.

"*Joyeux Noël,*" Jen called out from the foyer. She and George, Ivy's friends from the hardware shop, arrived carrying a pot of steamed crab and a Bûche de Noël, a delicious-looking yule log. Chocolate icing and decorative holiday motifs covered the rolled cake.

"My mother's family is from the south of France," Jen said. "We always had seafood at Christmas. It was such a treat that I wanted to share our tradition with others."

Standing next to her, Arthur chuckled. "In England, we had sausage stuffing and mincemeat pie." He lifted an edge of tin foil covering a dish he carried, and a savory aroma wafted out. "So we had to bring that."

"And our traditional holiday tamales are already on the buffet table," Carlotta added. "I feel like we're celebrating Christmas around the world. What fun!"

Ivy led the new guests to the buffet table, where she and Shelly arranged the dishes people brought. All around her were laughter and hugs. She felt warmly included in this group of people who had welcomed her and Shelly into the Summer Beach family.

"This is working out even better than we thought," Ivy said to Shelly as they put out more serving utensils and napkins.

"No one will leave hungry," Shelly said, adding another stack of plates. She paused and caught Ivy's gaze. "It's been quite a year, hasn't it?"

"I think we found our home—in many ways."

Another familiar voice rang out. "Hello, everyone," Leilani said. "*Mele Kalikimaka.*" Leilani and Roy waved from the door, and Ivy made her way toward them.

"Welcome to the party," Ivy said. She nodded toward the large glass containers that Leilani and Roy carried. "Thank you for bringing a dish. Looks delicious."

"I made lomi-lomi salmon with tomatoes and sweet Maui onions," Leilani said. "And Roy has a Hawaiian pork dish. We always have a lot of requests for that."

As Ivy arranged the buffet table, Bennett went outside to turn on the heat lamps. People began to spill outside onto the terrace in the winter sunshine, plates piled high with a delicious variety of holiday flavors.

Ivy stepped outside to thank Bennett. "I'm amazed that so many people are here."

"And there's a lot more to come," Bennett said, putting his arm around her. "I think you've just started a new holiday tradition here in Summer Beach."

"Maybe we have," she said. "I like drawing on the past of Las Brisas del Mar…to create a new future for the inn."

Next to them, one of the heat lamps flamed and flickered. Ivy laughed. "Maybe that's Amelia showing her approval."

"You certainly have my approval," Bennett said, putting his arm around her. "Come on, stand under this heat lamp with me."

"That feels great," Ivy said, smiling up at him. Spending Christmas with friends and loved ones was more than she could have imagined last year. Feeling deeply happy, she leaned her head on Bennett's shoulder and looked out over the crowd. Mitch and Shelly had their arms around each other, and they were talking to Flint and Forrest. Ivy wondered when and how Shelly would propose to Mitch.

Near the pool, Misty and Sunny were hanging out with their cousins on the chaise lounges. The kids were all laughing and eating, and Ivy was glad they were enjoying themselves.

Everyone seemed to be having a good time. Ivy nodded toward the crowd. "There's Tyler and Celia, and Chief Clarkson with Imani. And I see Axe Woodson towering above everyone except Jamir."

Bennett nodded and waved at several more people. "Boz is here from City Hall with the city attorney, Maeve Green. There's Darla, with what I'll bet is her famous layered pumpkin pie. You have to have a slice of that. And look, Megan and Josh Calloway are here. You should see how well the renovations are coming along on their house."

"I'm so glad they moved here," Ivy said. "I have some interesting news to share with Megan for her documentary on Amelia Erickson." She thought about Nick's story of his grandparents.

"Can't wait to hear that."

"You will. Want to have lunch tomorrow? I have a lot to fill you in on." She was looking forward to telling Bennett the news about the Fabergé egg, too. But today, she wanted to celebrate the day and enjoy being with him and her family—and all their good friends in Summer Beach.

LATER THAT EVENING, AFTER MANY PEOPLE HAD HELPED CLEAN up, the guests went home, and the family retired. Ivy sat next to the fireplace and watched as Bennett stoked the last embers. That evening, her family had sat laughing and talking in front of the Christmas tree by the fireplace for hours. Seeing how easily Bennett and Mitch got along with their parents made Ivy happy. She hoped her sister's plan would go without a hitch. Shelly's heart had been broken too many times.

Bennett rested the poker and turned to Ivy. "It's been a long, happy day. Tired?"

"Not really." She thought about the painting she'd created for him and the dance they'd shared on the beach last summer. "Shall we close out Christmas Day on the beach?"

"I'd like that," he said, taking her hand. "The fire pit is still on."

"And I know where we can find a great bottle of wine."

They picked up Nick's gift of wine and two glasses from the butler's pantry, put on their jackets, and hurried outside toward the beach, laughing like the teenagers they had been when they'd met so long ago. Clouds had gathered in the late afternoon, and tonight was the chilliest night of the year. But with the warmth of the fire and Bennett's arms around her, Ivy was perfectly happy.

After opening the bottle, Bennett poured wine into two glasses. Ivy watched the rich, burgundy color liquid swirl into gleaming crystal goblets against the flickering fire.

Ivy touched her glass to his. "To all that brought us here, and to all that lies ahead."

As they tasted the wine, Bennett began humming *White Christmas*, and Ivy threaded her arms around his neck. His rich baritone reverberated through her.

Bennett took her hand and smiled. "How about another Seabreeze dance?"

"I'd love that," she said.

Leaving their glasses by the fire pit, they rose, and Bennett tucked his arms around her. With waves lapping the shore behind them, they swayed across the winter beach. In the distance, festive holiday lights in the village glimmered in the cold night air.

And then, slowly at first, feathery snowflakes drifted around them, soft as a whisper.

"It's snowing!" They cried out together, hugging each other in delight.

"It's a Christmas miracle," Ivy added, kissing Bennett's snow-speckled cheeks. With lacy snowflakes catching in their hair, they continued dancing, swirling amidst the dusting of snow.

"Merry Christmas," Ivy said, gazing into Bennett's hazel eyes that reflected her happy smile.

"And a merry Christmas to you, the woman I love."

Ivy hesitated, but this time, the words came easily to her. The time was right. "I love you, too," she said, giving her words the fullest expression of her love.

Bennett pressed her to his chest, nuzzling his face in her hair. "You've made me the happiest man alive, Ivy Bay." Bennett swung her around and paused before dropping to one knee before her. "Would you consider...allowing me the honor of returning that happiness for the rest of our lives?"

Ivy's heart pounded. Between the chill in the air, the dancing, and the surprise of his words, she could hardly force out her own. "Are you...?"

"Yes, my love." Bennett clasped her hands. "I'm asking... will you marry me? I've been thinking about this for a long time."

Time seemed frozen, suspended in space, and the world around them muted until it was only the two of them, framed against the vast ocean beyond, teetering on the precipice of a promise so great it had the power to change their lives.

Ivy pressed her lips together and gazed at Bennett's hope-filled face. She tried to speak, but she couldn't summon words from a heart so full of love for him. This was not a decision she would make lightly.

"If you're not ready, I will wait for you," Bennett said huskily. "For as long as you need."

"That's an enormous promise," she said softly.

"I've already made that promise in my heart." Bennett blinked against the snow and rose. "A long engagement could be quite romantic."

To her, Bennett didn't have to try to be romantic. With just a look, he could awaken feelings she'd thought long dormant. But she would not be rushed. Not even by Bennett. Ivy wanted a chance to prove that she could take care of herself. She needed to know that she could do that, no matter what happened.

In the last year, she'd discovered that she liked making decisions and being in charge of her life and her destiny. Never again would her finances be obscure. Fate had lobbed almost insurmountable challenges at her, but she had survived and emerged stronger and more resilient. And in the process, she'd discovered new skills and talents, new friends, and even new love.

She wasn't quite ready to abdicate her hard-won throne. In fact, she never would be. She could imagine a partner beside her but never above her.

Could Bennett be that?

Ivy flicked a snowflake from Bennett's lashes. "I think maybe...but only as equal partners. Think you could live with that?"

Enveloping Ivy in his arms, Bennett lifted her again and swung her around. "What I love about you is that you have a fine mind of your own."

Ivy threw back her head and laughed. She hadn't officially committed, but the offer was there when she was ready.

As her feet touched the ground, Ivy gazed at Bennett's happy face. Snowflakes drifted around them, cocooning them in a wintry white wonderland that seemed theirs alone. Ivy brushed her lips against his. On a night such as this, anything and everything seemed possible between them as long as they were committed to each other.

At once, this certainty illuminated her path, and she realized all she had to do was step forward with confidence.

She laced her fingers with Bennett's and smiled. "On second thought, I'm more ready than I realized."

The End

AUTHOR'S NOTE:

Thank you for reading *Seabreeze Christmas*, and I hope you enjoyed spending the holidays with Ivy, Bennett, and the entire Bay family. To find out what happens next with Ivy and Shelly, continue the story in *Seabreeze Wedding*.

If this is your first book in the Summer Beach series, be sure to meet Ivy and Shelly when they first arrive in Summer Beach in *Seabreeze Inn*.

Keep up with my new releases at JanMoran.com. Please join my Reader's Club there to receive news about special deals and other books, including my standalone historical novels, including *The Chocolatier* and *Hepburn's Necklace*. And as always, I wish you happy reading!

MEXICAN HOT CHOCOLATE RECIPES

One of my favorite holiday treats is hot chocolate, especially the cinnamon-laced, slightly spicy Mexican Hot Chocolate. In *Seabreeze Christmas*, Ivy and Shelly prepared their mother's traditional hot chocolate recipe. Sweet cinnamon and the subtle spice of chili powder set this recipe apart from others, so I wanted to share two versions with you.

Many authentic recipes call for rustic Mexican chocolate, or *chocolate de mesa*, from popular brands such as Abuelita or Ibarra. These brands of chocolate also contain sugar and cinnamon. However, if you prefer smooth, dark chocolate, you can substitute 70% dark chocolate, such as Lindt or another brand. Or try artisan chocolates with different flavor profiles. If you're using bittersweet chocolate, you might wish to use a little more sugar to taste (or not).

As to the addition of chili powder, a pinch of ancho chili powder adds flavor with only a hint of heat. Cayenne is much hotter on the heat scale, so if that's what you have in your cupboard, use it more sparingly than ancho. Start light—you can always add more as you like. Guests might prefer to flavor their hot chocolate to their taste.

Another key to Mexican hot chocolate is a frothy foam. Traditionally, a handcrafted wooden *molinillo* is spun to achieve a bubbly froth. You can also use a whisk, immersion blender, or handheld blender to create the foam.

While these recipes make four cups, they are easy to divide for one or two people. These traditional recipes call for whole milk and cream, but you can also substitute low-fat milk. The texture might not be quite as creamy, but it will be just as delicious. And for vegan and lactose-free versions, substitute almond, soy, or other types of milk alternatives.

Don't feel like cooking? Look for spiced hot chocolate mixes, such as Spicy Maya Drinking Chocolate from Chuao Chocolatier. Or, start with an instant hot chocolate packet, add a pinch of chili powder, substitute hot milk for water, and serve with a cinnamon stick. You'll have a sweet hot chocolate treat in no time.

Serve this soothing, rich dessert-in-a-cup by itself or with a slice of your favorite gingerbread.

Gourmet Mexican Hot Chocolate
Courtesy of Ivy Bay's mother, Carlotta Reina Bay

Make 4 cups

8 oz. of dark chocolate, such as 70% Lindt or other
2 cups of whole milk
2 cup heavy cream
1/2 cup light or dark brown sugar (Piloncillo is traditional, or Turbinado)
1 tsp vanilla extract
4-inch Ceylon cinnamon sticks

Optional:
1/4 to 1/2 tsp chili powder (ancho, cayenne, or guajillo chili powder to taste)
Dash of nutmeg
1 cup whipped cream (recipe below)

In a medium saucepan, combine milk, sugar, and vanilla. Heat over medium until the mixture steams, stirring occasionally, about 5 minutes.

While the mixture heats, cut or break up the chocolate into small pieces so it melts evenly. Once the milk is steaming, add the chocolate and whisk until it's melted and incorporated.

Heat over medium, stirring occasionally. Watch closely, and do not boil. When chocolate is melted, and milk begins to steam, whisk with a wire whisk or a molinillo for 3-4 minutes or until a frothy consistency is achieved.

Serve with a cinnamon stick in a mug. If desired, garnish with whipped cream and a dash of nutmeg on top. Enjoy!

Whipped Cream

1 cup heavy cream
1 tsp vanilla extract
1 Tbsp powdered sugar (confectioner's sugar)
1/2 tsp cinnamon

Combine ingredients in a large bowl and whip until stiff peaks form. Hint: Electric mixers or blenders accomplish this task in less time. Do not over beat or mixture will become lumpy.

Simple Traditional Mexican Hot Chocolate

Makes 4 cups

4 cups of whole milk
4 cinnamon sticks
1 1/2 round tablets of Mexican chocolate, also known as
rustic *chocolate de mesa* (such as Abuelita or Ibarra brand, or
others)

Optional:
1/4 to 1/2 tsp chili powder (ancho, cayenne, or guajillo chili
powder to taste)

Break up chocolate in a saucepan and add milk. Add chili
powder if desired. Heat on medium, stirring occasionally. Do
not boil. When chocolate is melted, and milk begins to steam,
whisk with a wire whisk or a molinillo for 3-4 minutes or until
a frothy consistency is achieved. Serve with a cinnamon stick
in a mug, and enjoy!

ABOUT THE AUTHOR

JAN MORAN is a *USA Today* bestselling author of romantic women's fiction. A few of her favorite things include a fine cup of coffee, dark chocolate, fresh flowers, laughter, and music that touches her soul. She loves to travel, and her favorite places for inspiration are those rich with history and mystery and set against snowy mountains, palm-treed beaches, or sparkly city lights. Jan is originally from Austin, Texas, and a trace of a drawl still survives, although she has lived in southern California for years.

Most of her books are available as audiobooks, and her historical fiction is translated into German, Italian, Polish, Dutch, Turkish, Russian, Bulgarian, Portuguese, and Lithuanian, and other languages.

Visit Jan at JanMoran.com. If you enjoyed this book, please consider leaving a brief review online for your fellow readers where you purchased this book, or on Goodreads or Bookbub.